MW00527252

In Dreams, We Fly

In Dreams, We Fly

Erin! Congrats!

Juliet Rose

Above the Rain
2023

Above the Rain Collective
abovetheraincollective@gmail.com
North Georgia, USA

Contributing Editors:
J.A. Sexton
ZaBrina Houston

Publisher's note:

This is a work of fiction. All characters and incidents are the product of the author's imagination, places are used fictitiously and any resemblance to an actual person, living or dead, is entirely coincidental.

ISBN: 978-1-7377970-7-4

First Printing August 2023
Copyright © Juliet Rose, 2023. All rights reserved.

No part of this book may be copied, used, transmitted, or stored in any means without prior written permission of the author or publisher.

julietrose.author@gmail.com
authorjulietrose.com

Cover graphics and interior/exterior formatting by J.A. Sexton
Original cover photograph by Alexas Fotos
Above the Rain logo artwork by Bee Freitag

To the family we find along the way. The ones who protect and love us, in whatever form they come.

"Time travel offends our sense of cause and effect but maybe the universe doesn't insist on cause and effect."

Edward M. Lerner

What happens at the end...

∞

*H*er mother's last breath came hundreds of times. Or so it seemed. Just when they'd think it was over, she'd gasp as her body struggled in its haphazard rhythm again and again, refusing to give up the fight. The young girl sat in the corner, wishing it to be over. Feeling guilty for having such a thought.

When her mother came home the month before and told Sitka she had untreatable cancer and was dying, Sitka ran. She bolted from the house to the nearby playground. She told her friends what her mother said, without emotion... without belief. Then she climbed to the top of the slide and slid down. Her friends thought she was making it up. Another story Sitka liked to tell.

She was famous on the playground for her stories.

When the ambulance pulled up outside her house a few weeks later, the children all congregated across the street and watched, their eyes wide with the truth. A truth they could turn and walk away from at a moment's notice. Something that would become a story of their own in the years to come. A memory of one no longer there.

However, for Sitka, the girl in the corner, the nightmare was just beginning. One she couldn't find her way out of. One she couldn't wake up from. Life as she knew it was over. She was on the precipice of disaster. The nightmare was creeping into her waking hours and would soon consume every breath she took.

Without the safety of her mother's arms, she needed to fend for herself. Vulnerable, like the baby bunny the mother rabbit leaves behind in a thatch of grass to flee from predators. Demons were waiting just beyond the door to drag her under, to steal her innocence and take the very essence of her being.

When her mother took her last, last breath, the girl waited, her own breath caught in her chest. Her aunt moved to her mother's side, also waiting to see if the end had come. After a few minutes of silence, the stillness permanently caught in the young woman's chest, the girl and the aunt both breathed out, knowing there was nothing left to hold onto. There were no happy endings. There would be no miracle.

Her mother lay lifeless with her mouth slack. Her soul had been released from the space which it inhabited for a few decades. Sitka no longer knew the body on the bed. The hands which had once stroked her head, made her supper, now splayed out awkwardly by the body's side. The light which had once been her beacon of safety, extinguished. Death had come, leaving the girl alone and unguarded. The shadows, no longer prevented from their dark intent, descended upon her.

Sitka was now out of time and running for her life.

Chapter One

Sitka picked at the scab on her knee, peering around the almost empty parking lot of the skating rink. The black tar she was sitting on was scorching, so she stood up, wiping sweat from her brow. North Carolina was a lot hotter than New York. She spent her days roller skating at Sports World; cheaper than a babysitter, which she was too old for anyhow. Tommy was late again. She didn't mind much. He was always late and she planned on it most times to be safe. The scab let loose, revealing soft pink skin underneath. She discarded the dried scab and rubbed her finger against the delicate, smooth skin, liking the way it felt under her rough fingertips. At least it'd scabbed over this time. Aunt Leigh was always admonishing her about scratching open her healing wounds too soon, causing blood to run.

A group of teens passed by her, laughing as they threw their skates over their shoulders. She knew they weren't laughing at her, as she was invisible. Never really there, unless she spoke. She watched them walk across the parking lot to a beat-up, yellow Chevette at the far end. One of the girls shook her Dorothy Hamill haircut as she batted her eyes at the boy next to her. A dark blue Ford Pinto skidded into the parking lot, just missing the group of teens, who screeched and hustled out of the way. One of the girls tipped her back, her hand on her hip, and yelled.

"Tommy Halston! You'd better watch out!" she screamed at the car, tossing her long, black ponytail over her shoulder.

Tommy grinned and gave her thumbs up. She paused and watched him, dropping her eyes to show she was fooling around. He blew her a kiss as he slowed the car down. He eased the car to a stop and looked out the window at the eleven-year-old girl sitting on the curb. Sitka crossed her arms and stared at him. He glanced at the group of teens, now cramming themselves into the small Chevette, and shrugged.

"I know, I'm late. They give you any trouble, Sitty?"

Sitka stared at the group and shook her head. "They didn't even see me, I don't think."

Tommy pushed the passenger side open. "Come on, then. We can grab some ice cream from Baskin Robbins on the way home. I know you like that bubble gum shit."

"Strawberry cheesecake," she murmured.

"What?"

"I like the strawberry cheesecake ice cream. The gum balls in the bubble gum ice cream hurt my teeth."

"That so? Well, strawberry cheesecake it is! Don't tell Glenn I was late picking you up. He's been up my ass about everything lately. I don't want it to turn into a fight."

Sitka, who everyone that knew her well called Sitty, didn't want a fight, either. She'd been living with Tommy and her Aunt Leigh for around nine months since her mother passed from cancer. Glenn was Aunt Leigh's live-in boyfriend and Tommy was right, he'd been up his ass about everything. Sitka placed her hand on the hot vinyl of the seat and pulled her shorts down so her legs wouldn't stick to it. She glanced at Tommy, who was watching the car full of kids pull out of the parking lot, the dark-haired girl waving at him as they turned. Tommy grinned and met Sitka's eyes. They were cousins but looked nothing alike. He had light brown hair and blue eyes, freckles across his nose. Sitty had curly, dark brown hair, hazel eyes, and deep golden skin. Their mothers were sisters, but their fathers had been very different.

Not that Sitka knew her father. The story was her mother and father met at a party in New York City, then hooked up for a bit. Not wanting the traditional expectations, he agreed he didn't want to be a father when they found out about the pregnancy, but her mother wanted to be a mother. No stress about it.

Her mother had shown her a picture of her father, a light-skinned, black man with a broad smile, wearing a poncho and smoking a joint. Her mother always said Sitka was his parting gift to her before we went on with a group traveling to Canada. She didn't want a man, she wanted a child, and so Sitka came to be.

She and her mother had lived in New York City in an apartment with a slew of rotating other like-minded folks. *Sitty in the city*, her mother would say. And Sitka was just that. She was taking public buses by the time she was seven and her mother made sure she always had passes for the museums to spend the day visiting.

Her mother was so beautiful. Long, golden-blond hair to her waist and eyes like Tommy's. Tiny but with a big voice. She commanded a room whenever she stepped into it. Men fell all over her and sometimes made Sitka feel like she was in the way, but her mother set them straight. Sitka came first, she was everything. Her mother always had a boyfriend, however, never let it interfere with being a mother. That was her dream in life. To be Sitka's mom.

She told Sitka she picked her name after the Sitka Spruce, a tree she'd seen on her travels to Alaska. Her mother said when she stood under those trees, they spoke to her and she understood everything that happened and was to come. When she first held Sitka in her arms, she understood what the trees were telling her. Sitka was everything that happened and was to come.

For ten years, they lived together in their chaotic but beautiful life. Sitka had many aunties and uncles around, but the day her mother came home and told her she was dying, that all ended. They moved into a one-room apartment and Sitka watched her mother slip away from her. It wasn't beautiful but it wasn't ugly. It just was. Every day, her mother was just there a little less until one day her Aunt Leigh showed up and took care of her over the last few days as Sitka's mother faded away.

"My baby Marie," she'd whisper to Sitka's mother. "I'm here. I'll take care of Sitty. It's okay to go if you need to. You can become part of me, I'll carry you from here."

Sitka watched from a corner, the tears wouldn't come. Maybe she didn't believe it, maybe she couldn't understand.

She'd never seen a television show, so she couldn't say it was like that. She had nothing to compare it to.

It was like nothing.

When her mother finally let go and the rattling in her chest stopped, Sitka waited. She didn't know what to do. Aunt Leigh helped her pack a bag, though she didn't have much. Her mother didn't believe in stuff. Just what they needed. They carried her small case out to Aunt Leigh's car and set it in the back seat.

Aunt Leigh turned to face her. "You're coming home with me, hon. I promised your mom. I live in North Carolina, where we're from. You came once when you were a little, but since your mom didn't have a car, you never came back. I have a son, your cousin Tommy. He's fifteen, so you won't have much in common but he's excited to see you again. You were only two when he last saw you but he remembers you. I'm sorry, Sitty. No child should lose their mother. It's just horrible. She loved you so much."

Sitka nodded and stared back up at the apartment. It didn't mean anything to her. Nothing did without her mother. That had been her only constant in her short life. She climbed into the passenger seat and gazed out the window. Her mother's body was still in there with the coroner. Sitka half expected it to evaporate into mist when her mother took her last breath. Instead, it became a mannequin of her mother, waiting to be hauled away.

Aunt Leigh tried to make conversation on the long drive to Wilmington, where she and Tommy lived, but Sitka didn't know what to say. She didn't know this weirdly similar version of her mother. Aunt Leigh was more matter-of-fact than Sitka's mother. She stated things and pointed out realities. Sitka's mother had always spoken about things in a possibility kind of way. Where they could go, what they could do, how things could change. Nothing was ever nailed down, anything could happen.

By the time they got to Aunt Leigh's house, silence had become the normal between them. Aunt Leigh quit trying to make conversation and Sitka focused on the passing world outside the car window. It was simply easier that way. When they pulled up, Tommy was mowing the front lawn shirtless and cut the mower to come over. He grinned at Sitka and she immediately liked him, even though she didn't remember him. He scooped her up and swung her around, much to Aunt Leigh's shock.

"Hey, Tommy, she's shy. Give her a minute."

Tommy shook his head and continued to swing Sitka, who began to laugh. Aunt Leigh's mouth dropped open as she cocked her head in astonishment.

"I stand corrected. Twelve hours in the car with me and she barely made a peep. Two seconds with you, and she comes alive. Alright, let's show Sitty where her room is and introduce her to Glenn."

Tommy winced at the last part and set Sitka down. "Why ruin her day so soon?"

"Tommy! Don't start in on Glenn, right now. Let's try to give Sitty a good first impression."

Tommy rolled his eyes and glanced down at Sitka. "Glenn's an ass."

She giggled and followed him in. Aunt Leigh showed Sitka her room, a bright, yellow space with a pink and yellow bedspread. Sitka walked over to a small desk stocked with crayons, colored pencils, and markers. They were attempting to make her feel at home. Home was her mother. She glanced out the window to see the neighborhood kids playing in the street. She turned back and faced Aunt Leigh. It all felt like a strange dream.

"Why don't you come meet Glenn? He's my boyfriend who lives here. Don't mind Tommy, he and Glenn like to butt heads about everything."

They walked to the kitchen where a large, sweaty man was sitting, smoking cigarettes at the table. He had a broad face with deep lines, showing he frowned a lot. He smiled at Sitka and stubbed out his cigarette.

"So, this is the guest of honor, huh?" he asked, but in a way that made Sitka feel like an intruder. He rubbed his hand through his unkempt hair. "Welcome to *our* home."

Tommy caught her eye and shook his head, mouthing the word *ass*. "Hey, Sitty, you want to come help me out front in the yard?"

Glenn jerked, staring at him. "You're not done mowing the lawn yet?"

"No. I stopped because Mom drove up and I wanted to welcome my cousin into *her* new home."

Glenn huffed and looked at Aunt Leigh. "See how your boy speaks to me?"

"Glenn," she whispered, "not now. Let's allow Sitty to settle in. Tommy was helping me out. Just drop it."

Glenn glared at Tommy who smirked back at him and motioned for Sitka to follow him. Tommy stopped her once they were outside, placing his hands on her shoulders. He met her eyes, his own turning serious. He gestured with his head back toward the house.

"Me and my mom are your family, we'll keep you safe. Glenn is nothing to us. A mistake my mother made and won't admit to or undo. Steer clear of him if you can. I got your back."

From that day on, Sitka knew who she could rely on. Tommy became her big brother, her protector. She avoided Glenn when she could and found ways to stay away from the house during the day. She roller skated every day she wasn't in school and sometimes Tommy would take her to Water Rapids, the water park near their home. He made sure he was the one to pick her up and take her places, never letting her be alone at home during the day.

Glenn wasn't mean to her, however, he always said things in a way that meant something different. Tommy picked fights with him regularly and Glenn reminded Tommy who was in charge. It was a battle of wills which never seemed to end. Sitka did her best to stay away from their battles and didn't understand why Aunt Leigh didn't side with Tommy, like her own mother did with her. Her aunt seemed to want to keep the peace but never took a stand either way. Tommy held his own, making Sitka admire him even more.

Tommy was her favorite person since her mother died. She liked Aunt Leigh, too, but Glenn was always around, so Sitka never felt she got to know her. Aunt Leigh was funny though, and always made Sitka feel like she mattered.

However, from day one Tommy was her person, the first sibling she'd ever had. Growing up with her mom, she was often the only child around a bunch of adults. Sometimes they'd visit or have people over with children, but most times it was Sitka, her mother, and her mother's friends when she wasn't at school. Being with Tommy, she understood what it was like to have someone around her age to depend on, to share secrets with. As the days passed with them, she began to feel more at home and like she had a family.

It was the nights she couldn't quite remember.

Chapter Two

Sitka was woken up by arguing and a door slamming. She crept up on her knees and peered out the window to see Tommy getting in Aunt Leigh's car and leaving. He backed out of the driveway, flipping off the house, then saw Sitka at the window and grinned. Well, his mouth was smiling, the rest of his face was not. She could hear Glenn yelling at Aunt Leigh about Tommy. How he was shiftless and lazy. Sitka sat back and pulled her knees up to her chest. She hated all the fighting. Besides, all Glenn did was sit at the table, smoking cigarettes with his shirt off. It seemed like he made an issue out of Tommy, so no one noticed he wasn't doing anything.

Sitka waited until it was quiet and crept out of her room toward the bathroom. She couldn't wait until summer was over because at least then, she and Tommy were in school and Glenn had less to bitch about for most of the day. She could see Aunt Leigh leaning with her head in her hands on the counter. She wasn't crying, but she wasn't happy. Not wanting to be spied, Sitka quickly used the bathroom and darted back to her room.

It'd never been like this with her mother. If anyone came around who yelled and caused issues, Sitka's mother showed them the door. She wished Aunt Leigh would do the same thing. Instead, her aunt seemed defeated, like she'd given up on life. Sitka dressed and slipped down the hall, heading for the back door. She took the corner too soon and accidentally kicked the wall, making a thump.

"That you, little girl?" Glenn called out. For some reason, he seemed to want her around as much as he didn't want Tommy around.

Sitka held her breath and waited, hoping he would move on. She heard him push his chair back and panic took hold. She could see the door from where she was standing and bolted for it, getting outside just as he rounded the corner. She ran across the backyard and scrambled over the tall, wooden fence. She knew the way from there to the skating rink. Once she was on the other side, she allowed herself to breathe. Glenn wouldn't follow her there. He rarely left the confines of the house.

Her feet hit the soft pine needles and she made her way through the trees. Behind their fence was an old cemetery. Almost no one ever went there, so Sitka found it comforting. A place of her own. She wandered through the rows, letting her hand run along the worn headstones. Sometimes the other kids in the neighborhood liked to sneak back there and tell ghost stories, but she found it a place of peace. She made her way to a far corner, overgrown from years of neglect. These were the oldest stones. Ones time and history forgot. Sometimes she'd pull weeds to tidy the area up, but today she just wanted to sit in the shade.

To be invisible.

After about an hour of sitting, she watched a weathered, gold Buick drive in, moving slowly down one of the rows. An old lady got out, clutching a bunch of flowers. Sitka liked to watch people when they didn't know she was around. Not that it mattered, she felt like sometimes people couldn't see her at all. If she didn't speak, she was transparent. In order for people to be able to see her, she needed to use her voice.

The hunched woman hobbled over the grave and placed her hand on it, her face contorted in pain. She placed the flowers in a holder beside the headstone and stared for too long at the etched letters. Finally, she straightened herself up and went back to her car. Once the car had made the last turn out, Sitka slipped out of her hiding place and walked over to the grave. The flowers were fresh and Sitka knelt to smell them. She glanced at the words on the headstone and considered where her mother might be now. The words read:

Ellen Anne Monroe
Beloved Daughter
Gone but not forgotten...
4/17/45-12/14/67

Sitka did the math. The woman buried there died when she was twenty-two years old. Dead for twelve years. So she would've been around Sitka's mother's age had they both lived. She wondered if the aged lady was the woman's mother. This made Sitka sad and she ran her fingers against the letters.

Most of the graves were old in the cemetery, but not this one. Again, her thoughts went to her mother. Aunt Leigh said she'd been cremated, and kids at school asked if they burned her body in the backyard, laughing at their cleverness. Sitka hadn't been part of putting her mother to rest. No ceremony, no saying goodbye. Just whisked off to a new life... as if the time with her mother was merely a fleeting memory.

She made her way to a part of the cemetery she never understood. Where they buried children who died. She didn't understand why children were hidden away as if their deaths were shameful. In the shaded area, she took time to read each headstone, the ones which weren't faded from the years of weather. Some of them had moss-covered, carved angels on top while others had stone lambs, especially the ones for the babies who'd died. Sitka placed her hands on one of the lambs, warm from the sun. It was worn from time and smooth like soap, making it feel almost alive. This is where she felt the most close to her mom. The baby's name was John Nichols. The nickname "Johnny" under the full name.

"Hey, Johnny," Sitka whispered, imagining he was there with her. A breeze rustled through the trees and she let go of the lamb, taking a step back. Its hollow eyes stared back at her, expressionless. She glanced around, however, the cemetery was empty and she smiled. She liked when the space was just hers. At least with the living.

Her stomach began to grumble and she headed for the skating rink. Once she was out of the cemetery, she cut behind some warehouses through a field where wild strawberries grew. She picked a few but had her mind on hot dogs and cotton candy at the skating rink. She came up from behind the rink and saw there was already a line waiting outside the door. She checked her pockets to make sure she had her money. Tommy always gave her enough to skate and eat. A wad of sticky bills was stuffed in her shorts pocket and she clutched it, afraid it would disappear.

When her time came to pay, Sitka stepped in and the gust of air-conditioned wind hit her face. She took a deep breath and smiled. This was her other home. Here and the cemetery. She needed to rent skates as she didn't have her own, but one day she would. One day, she'd have a pair like the older kids did, in some bright color with brand-new wheels. She paid for entry and skate rental, following a loud group of boys in. Sometimes she didn't get her skates right away, liking how the geometric patterned carpet felt under her sneakers as she wandered around the arcade area.

A mirrored ball hung in the center of the rink, casting prisms of light all over the carpeted walls. Sitka paused and watched as it spun, taking her out of the world outside and into this one. Disco music blared from the speakers and skaters whizzed by her, both on the floor and the carpeted area. She could smell popcorn and cotton candy coming from the snack area and decided to eat first. She'd skipped breakfast to avoid Glenn and was feeling it. She wandered in, counting her money. She had enough for a hot dog, drink, and cotton candy, thanks to Tommy. She put the money on the counter and ordered from a boy about Tommy's age, who seemed like he wanted to be anywhere but there. He pointed for her to move to the end of the counter and handed her her change. Enough for a couple of arcade games.

She liked pinball best.

Once her order was up, she slid into the orange, smooth plastic booth and watched the skaters while she ate. Here she was happy. Here she was free. She couldn't finish the hot dog and threw it away with her trash. She hated to throw away food, but one time she tried to save it in her pocket and forgot, causing Aunt Leigh to gasp with disgust when she went to do the laundry. Days old, pocket hotdog didn't age well.

Sitka went to the skate rental and handed them her ticket. They came back with a pair of tan skates with orange wheels which looked like they'd been worn no less than a thousand times. She wrinkled her nose, trying to avoid touching the bottom of the fabric which was stained a dark brown from so many sweaty feet. As she went to find a bench to put them on, she passed the counter where they sold roller skates, wheels, socks, jackets, and everything she wanted to have. She stared for a second, wishes filling her head. One day.

As soon as her wheels hit the wooden floor, Sitka began to fly. Here there was no Glenn, no dead mothers, no bigger kids, no school, no worries. Just the forced air and crisp sound of her wheels keeping up with the motion of her legs. She darted around the oval, cutting in and out of slower skaters. It was as if she should've skipped walking and just jumped right into skating as a baby. This is where her body felt the most hers. After a couple of hours, she skipped off the floor for water and to use the bathroom.

When she came back out, the announcer was calling for the speed skate races. Sitka had done the ones for her age and easily won. She was too scared to go up against the older kids, however, when the announcer said the winner would be added to a raffle to win a pair of new skates on the Fourth of

July, she knew she needed to try. As the kids fourteen and up were called out, Sitka slid in next to a boy who towered over her. No one saw her because she didn't speak. One of the staff went around giving each competitor a number. When she got to Sitka, she paused, staring at the clearly younger child.

"What's your name?"

"Sitty."

"Sitty, this is for kids fourteen to eighteen. Your group already went," the girl explained.

"I want to skate. I'm too fast for my age group," Sitka replied, not willing to back down.

The group she was in started to laugh, causing a titter to run through the crowd. Sitka swallowed the burning in her throat and stuck her chin up. She'd spoken, so now everyone could see her. The girl shrugged at the announcer, who waved his hand with disinterest. They'd let her compete. The girl handed Sitka a number to pin on her shirt and went on.

As the skaters lined up for the race, an older girl rudely shoved Sitka aside. This only made her more determined. She lined up next to them and crouched down, ready to shoot like a bullet once the race started. The announcer counted down and once he yelled, "Go!", Sitka became one with the rink.

The older kids kicked off faster, leaving her behind. When her legs began pumping, she flew through them, weaving in and out of their bodies like they didn't exist. As the music blared, she found herself slipping into a tunnel where only she and the floorboards existed. She rounded the corner, putting distance between her and the other racers. However, she didn't notice.

This was a race against herself.

By the time she got to the second round, she was so far ahead some of the other skaters dropped out. When she crossed the finish line, a roar went up in the crowd. She spun around, skating backward, and stared at the bystanders. Some of the other racers were shooting her the evil eye, but most of the watchers were cheering her on. The girl handing out numbers from before waved her to the center of the rink and put Sitka's hand in the air when she skated up. Sitka didn't care, she only wanted to win those skates.

Once all the hubbub died down, the girl had Sitka fill out a raffle form and added it to a clear, square container on the counter where they sold skates. Sitka mentally counted and there were already about ten forms in there. She needed to keep winning. She skated to the arcade area and spent her last two quarters on pinball.

She watched the smooth, silver ball knock around the inside of the machine. As she deftly directed it with the flippers, she felt a sense of kismet. Since her mother died, she felt like that metal sphere, getting sent all different directions. *Sitty live here. Sitty go there. Sitty wait for this. Sitty wait for that. Sitty bang. Sitty boom. Sitty whack. Sitty spin. Sitty stop.*

Her life was no longer her own. Aunt Leigh was nice, however, her life wasn't her own, either. Tommy took care of her, but his life was still controlled by the adults around him. They were all stuck inside the pinball machine, getting smacked around. Once the last ball slipped in the hole, she glanced at the clock. Tommy would be there soon to pick her up. She scooted over to turn her skates in, again pausing at the sale skate counter. This time she could see her name peeking out from the window in the raffle box and smiled. This was something that was hers. This was something she *could* control.

Tommy was outside, leaning against his car. He was flirting with a tan girl in very short, shiny, teal shorts. The girl had her hand on Tommy's shoulder and was giggling. When Tommy saw Sitka come out, he waved the girl off.

"Gotta go. Duty calls."

The girl pouted and eyed Sitka, then forced a plastic smile, shaking her ass as she walked away. Sitka wandered to the passenger side and frowned.

"I don't want to be a *duty*," she said as she slid in.

Tommy climbed in next to her, reading the hurt on her face. He rubbed her head and laughed. "Sorry kiddo. I didn't mean it. You're the one person I look forward to seeing all day. How was skating?"

Sitka grinned as she looked out the window. "Magical."

Chapter Three

I t was dark when Sitka placed her hand down under her covers. It was cold and damp. *Not again*, she thought.

She climbed out of bed and began to strip the sheets, embarrassment washing over her. She took off her wet pajamas and shoved them in the pile. She didn't know why she'd started wetting the bed and was too ashamed to tell Aunt Leigh about it. She never had until she'd moved to North Carolina. A check of the hallway showed all was quiet. Everyone was asleep.

She carried the load out to the washer in the garage. Stuffing it in, she poured what she hoped was the correct amount of soap into the barrel, then started the washer. She'd done this many times before, never having been caught. She took off her fresh pajamas and rinsed in the hose outside the garage door, luckily hidden behind a bush.

Afterward, she slipped back on her clean pajamas and made her way down the hall to her room. There were extra sheets and blankets for her bed in her closet, so she remade her bed and sat on the edge. Wetting the bed worried her, but what concerned Sitka more was the gap in her memory.

She remembered having dinner the night before, and Aunt Leigh coming to say goodnight after Sitka read for a bit. She guessed she'd fallen asleep right after, but there was always this missing piece. Like awake to just waking up. As if part of her disappeared for a period of time. It hadn't been like that before her mother died. Then, she'd stare at the ceiling and dream about things. Listen to her mother talking with the others long into the night. Sitka could remember actually getting drowsy before she dozed off. Now, it was just bedtime wide awake to morning wide awake with nothing in between. That scared her.

She climbed back into bed and waited. She wouldn't fall asleep again. She was too afraid to turn on a light and stir the rest of the house, so she stared at the window, willing the sun to rise. Eventually, it did and she began to hear the sounds of the rest of the family getting up. Aunt Leigh was always first. She once told Sitka it was because it was the only time during the day she could just be herself.

"Time to breathe," she'd say.

Sitka sat up, waiting until she heard Aunt Leigh get in the shower, so she could move the sheets to the dryer. However, she didn't hear the shower start. She strained to hear where Aunt Leigh was when her aunt appeared at the door, a frown lining her face.

"Hey, honey. Is everything okay?" Aunt Leigh asked.

Sitka shrugged, waiting to see why her aunt was asking. Aunt Leigh came and sat down on the edge of the bed. She watched Sitka for a minute before speaking.

"I went to get a towel from the dryer and noticed your sheets in the washer. They weren't there last night when I threw the load in the dryer. Did you get up and put your sheets in there?"

The revelation brought all the shame to the surface and Sitka began to cry. Aunt Leigh must think she was a big baby, wetting the bed and trying to hide it. Her aunt moved in and put her arms around Sitka.

"Shh, shh, honey. You didn't do anything wrong. Has this happened before?"

Sitka nodded, then peered up at her aunt's face. Aunt Leigh looked teary herself and pushed the hair from Sitka's cheek. She took a deep breath and gazed out the window.

"I think we need a girls' day out. Does that sound like fun?" Aunt Leigh offered.

Sitka never had time alone with her aunt, but she was worried about Tommy being alone at the house with Glenn. "Can Tommy come?"

Aunt Leigh chuckled. "I doubt he'd want to, but we can ask him."

She got up and went to the door, pausing in the doorway. "Sitty, please talk to me about these things. You lost your mom, and that's hard. You don't have to do this all alone. She was my sister, so maybe a small part of me can understand. You never have to feel embarrassed about things you can't control. Go ahead and get dressed and we can leave in a bit. Why don't you see if Tommy is awake and wants to go? Alright?"

Sitka bobbed her head and slid out of bed. She dressed, hoping Glenn would stay asleep until they left. She went to

Tommy's room and climbed into his bed, watching him sleep. He was on his back with his arm over his eyes. Sitka poked him and giggled. He moved his arm, staring at her.

"What's up micro-muffin?" His voice was barely above a whisper and he looked like he'd been up all night.

"Aunt Leigh wants to have a girls' day and I want you to go, too."

"Cause I'm a girl?" Tommy asked, sitting up in his bed.

That seemed like the funniest thing to Sitka and she cracked up, almost falling off the bed. Tommy grabbed her right before she toppled over and shook his head.

"Yeah, could be fun. As long as you don't mind if I dip if things get a little too mom-like."

Sitka didn't know what that meant but would've agreed to anything to have Tommy go along. She nodded and motioned for him to hurry, her ears attuned to the possible sounds of Glenn getting up to move to his daily spot at the table. Tommy sighed and climbed out of bed, rooting around his drawers for clean clothes. He stopped and looked at Sitka.

"You gotta get out, so I can change. Unless you want to make this weird for both of us," he said dryly.

Sitka giggled again and darted out of the room. Aunt Leigh was just finishing the shower when Sitka heard the sound she was hoping she wouldn't. Glenn groaned from the bedroom where he was sleeping and grumbled about something or another. He constantly woke up in a bad mood, finding things to pick at. Sitka didn't want to end up alone with him, so she went to her room.

Aunt Leigh slipped into her own room and shut the door. Immediately, she and Glenn started arguing. He went out, slamming the door, and stomped into the bathroom, again slamming the door. Sitka wished they could just leave.

Glenn came out, glancing into her room as he passed. It sent shivers down her spine. He went on, then took up where they'd left off, arguing about nothing with Aunt Leigh.

"What do you mean you are taking the kids for a day out? What have they done to deserve that? They should stay home and get chores done. That boy is hardly a child and needs to be doing man's work, not hanging out with his mommy and her sister's kid."

"Cousin," Aunt Leigh corrected him. "Sitty is my niece and his cousin. We are family."

Glenn snorted. "Whatever you say, Leigh. You coddle them too much. You need to make them grow up and face the real world."

Silence fell as it often did when Glenn lashed out. Aunt Leigh wasn't mean and didn't know how to respond to his cruelty. Tommy came to Sitka's room, gesturing for her to follow him. Glenn and Aunt Leigh were at the end of the hall, facing off, so Tommy and Sitka were able to slip outside. Tommy lit a cigarette and leaned against the car.

"I fucking hate him," he said, staring back at the house, his eyes locked on the front door.

"Why doesn't Aunt Leigh not be with him?" Sitka asked.

Tommy laughed, shaking his head. "That's the million-dollar question, right? I don't know. He wasn't like that when they met. I was about your age and he was Mr. Nice Guy. Always coming around and bringing presents. Then as soon as he moved in, everything changed. He changed. Mr.

Nice Guy became Mr. Raging Dickhead. Sorry, I shouldn't use that language around you."

"I don't mind," Sitka said and rubbed the toe of her shoe against the ground. She liked that Tommy didn't treat her like a baby. "I wish he'd leave."

"Ha. You and me both, sister," Tommy replied, stubbing out his cigarette. Then he muttered, "Fucking come on, Mom."

The longer they waited, the worse they knew it'd be between Glenn and Aunt Leigh. Finally, she came running out, her face splotchy from crying, and motioned for them to get in the car. Glenn came out right behind her in only his boxer shorts. Sitka and Tommy got in, locking the doors. Glenn was all talk, but neither of them wanted him to open their doors. Aunt Leigh gunned the car in reverse as Glenn threw his hands in the air, his eyes fixed on Tommy with hatred.

"He'll grow up to be nothing just like his father, Leigh!"

Tommy's face turned red and his mouth set in a straight line. "Why the fuck do you let him rule everything, Mom? Or speak to us like that?"

"Tommy, I'm sorry. Your father was a good man."

"No shit. Better than that tub of crap you have sharing your bed," Tommy spat.

"Tommy!" Aunt Leigh yelled.

"Whatever, Mom. Different day, same bullshit."

Sitka sat frozen in the backseat. She'd never heard Aunt Leigh and Tommy fight that way. Aunt Leigh reached out to touch Tommy's face and he shoved her hand away, glaring out the window.

"Don't. Just let me out up here, I don't feel like pretending happy family today." Tommy already had the door partially open when they pulled up to the light.

"Tommy, don't go," Sitka pleaded.

He turned back and watched her for a second, his face softening. "Sorry sprite, I can't do this. One day, you and I can go have some fun, okay?"

He didn't wait for her reply before he shut the door and sauntered off. Sitka stared at Aunt Leigh, who was watching her son's retreating form. Her aunt lit a cigarette with shaking hands and turned to face Sitka, her eyes full of apology.

"Move up here, honey. It would be weird me driving you around back there like a chauffeur."

Sitka climbed over the seat to the front as the car behind them laid on its horn. Aunt Leigh rolled down her window and flipped them off while Sitka fastened her seatbelt. Once she was buckled, her aunt put the car in gear, pulling off as slowly as she could to piss off the other driver. She smiled at Sitka, her hands still shaking.

"Did you know your mom and I were twins?"

Sitka stared at her, wrinkling her nose. Aunt Leigh and her mother appeared alike in some ways, but not exactly. Aunt Leigh saw her looking, then laughed.

"Not that kind. We are fraternal twins, so we were born at the same time but aren't identical. Well, I was born first, like seven minutes before she was, so I called her my baby to tease her. Not sure I should get into the whole egg and sperm explanation of the difference between identical and fraternal twins, but suffice it to say we were born on the same day. We were inseparable growing up until I met Tommy's father."

"Was he nice?" Sitka asked, trying to imagine Tommy's dad. If he was anything like Tommy, Sitka was sad she never got to meet him.

Aunt Leigh's face became soft and distant. "Oh, he was the nicest. We met in high school. I was so in love with him from the moment we met. Tommy looks a lot like his dad. He was also Tommy, well, Thomas... Tommy was named after him. We dated for a couple of years when I ended up pregnant with Tommy, so we got married right after high school graduation. Thomas tried to find work after graduation and did this and that for a few years. Then came the war..." Aunt Leigh didn't speak for some time and Sitka didn't know if the story was over. She turned away, focusing out the window.

"I don't know if you really know about the Vietnam War, honey. Tommy, uh, Thomas got drafted when Tommy was little. If he'd just stayed home after the first tour, maybe we could've had a life. He didn't and we didn't. He went back, by choice. He wasn't the same. He promised he'd come back after that tour and we could continue our life together." Aunt Leigh paused, lighting another cigarette as she stared off. "He never came home."

Sitka listened, her heart feeling heavy and confused. So, Tommy didn't have a father, either. They drove past the USS North Carolina, a battleship anchored in the water, now a place people could walk around and go inside. Sitty had seen it from afar a few times, but this time it made her uncomfortable. Aunt Leigh saw her looking at it and touched her hand.

"Did you want to go see the ship?"

Sitka shook her head, still staring at the large, gray vessel looming in the water. "No, I don't like it."

Aunt Leigh snickered without humor, her eyes locked on the metal monstrosity. "Me either, hon. Elaborate, expensive machines men make to kill other men.... I have a better idea. Why don't we go to Chandler's Wharf to visit the shops and grab lunch along Riverwalk, instead? The weather is beautiful and we can sit outside to eat."

To Sitka that sounded like a much better idea.

Chapter Four

∞

T hey spent the morning popping into gift shops on the waterfront and strolling along Riverwalk, a wooden walkway between the water, shops and restaurants. Sitka only wished Tommy had joined them. Aunt Leigh was right though, he would've been bored. As they sat down for lunch, Sitka stared out at the water moving slowly by. She wondered why her life had been separated into two segments. The one with her mother, and the one now.

Why had her mother never come back to North Carolina for so many years?

As if Aunt Leigh read her thoughts, she reached out, placing her hand over Sitka's. "I know it's hard to be here without your mother. I miss her, too. She always wanted to come back to visit, but life got in the way." As if it was a secret, she cleared her throat, whispering, "She didn't like Glenn."

"Do you like Glenn?" Sitka asked point blank, as only a child could.

Aunt Leigh gazed out across the water, then shrugged. "I did. When I met Glenn, I'd been alone for so long..."

Glancing back at Sitka, she turned red as she realized she was probably telling her niece more than she should. The waitress came and dropped off the menus, smiling at Sitka.

"Would you like something to drink, darling?"

Sitka glanced at her aunt for approval, kicking her feet back and forth. Leigh nodded. Sitka grinned and blurted out. "Rootbeer float, please!"

The waitress winked and turned to Aunt Leigh. "What about you, hon?"

"Sweet tea, thanks."

After the waitress left to get their drinks, Sitka looked at her aunt. "I don't like Glenn."

Aunt Leigh visibly recoiled and shook her head. "Sitka, don't say that. He seems to have taken a shine to you. Is this Tommy putting thoughts in your head?"

Sitka thought about Tommy for a moment, then her mind went to Glenn. When she thought about Glenn, her stomach tightened. "No. He just makes me feel funny."

Aunt Leigh didn't respond, but some notion flashed across her face, making her frown. The waitress came back with their drinks, then took their order. Sitka stabbed her straw through the ice cream on top, creating a hole for the rootbeer to seep up. This gave her great satisfaction.

Once lunch was done, they walked back to the car, Sitka clutching a bag with a small, marionette-type toy she'd gotten at one of the shops. It was a lady with green hair and an orange outfit. When the string hanging down from her body was pulled, her arms and legs jerked up into the air, causing

Sitka to laugh. She felt like she had something worth having. As if the toy had been waiting for her to find it.

On the drive home, Aunt Leigh swung down Oleander Drive, pointing to a large structure in the middle of a field. Sitka peered at it, not sure what she was looking at.

"That's the mall they're building. Independence Mall. It's going to be something special," Aunt Leigh said, almost dream-like.

Sitka stared at the looming shape, not seeing what was so special about it. It made her feel very small. "What's a mall?"

"Oh, honey! There will be all kinds of shops and things to do in there. It'll be all inside. So if the weather's bad, we can still shop and eat. I can't wait. They're saying it should be open in the next couple of months."

Sitka had never seen Aunt Leigh so excited about anything. She couldn't see what all the fuss was about and tried to picture what a mall looked like inside. Unsuccessful, she diverted her attention to the toy on her lap, tugging the string over and over. Once they got to the light near her school, Winter Park Elementary, she stared back out the window, recognizing a familiar shape.

"Aunt Leigh! It's Tommy," she exclaimed, pointing at the figure crossing the road.

Aunt Leigh sighed and began cranking down her window. "It sure is. Hey, Tommy!"

Tommy turned and grinned, wandering over to the car. "You have a nice *girls'* day?"

"It would've been more fun with you," Sitka replied, slightly pouting. She held up the dancing lady she got. "Look, if you pull her string, her legs and arms go everywhere."

"So, they do," Tommy said, leaning in the open window to get a better look.

"Come on, get in, you can ride home with us," his mother offered.

Tommy shook his head. "Naw, I'd rather stay away. Why doesn't Sitty come with me and I'll take her to Long Leaf Park for a bit? Maybe you can go home and make sure Glenn has cooled down and it's safe to bring Sitty home."

Aunt Leigh and Tommy were at a standoff as the light turned green. Not wanting a repeat of earlier with the car honking behind them, she shook her head and gestured she was pulling over.

"Fine, but have her home by dinner. I'm making fried chicken tonight."

Aunt Leigh drove into the park entrance and Sitka bounded out, excited for some alone time with Tommy. She hugged her aunt through the window opening and thanked her for her toy and lunch. Aunt Leigh looked tired, smiling a worried smile.

"Should I come back for you? You'd have to walk all the way past the golf course."

Tommy shrugged. "I think we're okay. You up for some serious walking, munchkin?"

He never ran out of small-themed nicknames for Sitka. She nodded too vigorously, making him laugh. Aunt Leigh shook her head and gripped the steering wheel.

"Alright, then. I'll see you by dinner time."

After she left, they made their way into the park. Tommy wandered over to a grove of pine trees, motioning to Sitka. "Sitka, come here. I want to show you something."

He never called her Sitka. She followed him and peered at what he was pointing at. A very large bug was braced on the side of the tree and she jerked back, her heart racing. He laughed and gently pried it off the bark.

"It's okay. It's just a shell left behind. The bug is long gone. Do you know what a cicada is?"

Sitka shook her head and tentatively came closer. Tommy balanced the cicada shell in his hand, holding it out to her. Sitka poked it with her finger, surprised about how light it was. It appeared like a bug, but only the outside. It even looked like it had eyes.

"Do you want to hold it? There are a bunch. When I was your age, I collected them." Tommy waved at the trees.

Sitka took the delicate shell, both horrified and mesmerized by the creature, or what it once was. She gazed around and could see other shells balanced on the bark of the trees around them. There were so many. She tried to carry the shell without crushing it. However, if she held it too gently, the wind blew it out of her hand. If she held too tightly, she could feel the shell begin to crumple in her grasp. Tommy chuckled and took it, placing it on a few strands of her hair. Sitka touched it, the feet of the shell clinging to her hair. She shook her head and it stayed in place.

They crossed the street toward the elementary school, winding around the side to the playground. Sitka had never been there when school wasn't open. It seemed so much bigger. She wondered if they'd get in trouble for being there, however, Tommy didn't seem to care. He took her back to the swings and she giggled when he got on one and began pumping his legs back and forth.

"Are you going to swing or stand there grinning, you looney?" Tommy asked as he worked his way into the air.

Sitka ran and took the swing next to him. Soon she was flying through the air with him, in a race to nowhere. Once their legs were tired, they slowed down and went to the merry-go-round. Sitka never went on it when other kids were there because the boys made it their goal to spin it so hard, other kids would go flying off. Tommy climbed on next to her and began to gently turn it with his feet as he reclined back. Sitka lay next to him, staring up at the trees. He sounded sad when he spoke.

"I'm glad you came. I mean, I'm sorry about your mom. She was nice from what I can remember. I guess, what I'm saying is, until you came along it was just me. When I was little, my dad would take me to the park. He showed me the cicada shells. I remember. My mom thinks I don't remember much, but I do. He used to take me to the kiddie train at Greenfield Park. That's not there anymore, but they have paddle boats. I'll take you one day, okay?"

Sitka glanced at Tommy who had tears on his cheek. This made her dislike Glenn even more. Why was he so mean to Tommy? Tommy needed a father. She never knew her father, so there was no one to miss. Tommy obviously missed his. They spun in silence for a while when Tommy sat up.

"I suppose we'd better start walking home. It will take us a bit and fried chicken sounds pretty good."

Sitka sat up, disoriented from going around in circles. She pointed to the edge of the playground at bushes with tiny yellow and white flowers. "Can we have some honeysuckle flowers, first?"

Tommy grinned and jumped up. "Hell, yeah! You may not know it, but I went to school here, as well. The boys were always too cool to mess with the honeysuckle, but the girls would spend recess picking and sucking on the flowers, near the end of the school year when the bushes bloomed. To be honest, I was always a little jealous."

They headed for the bushes, Sitka running ahead. Once she got there, she turned and waited for Tommy. "Now, you can have as much as you want!"

Tommy took her up on that and they spent about thirty minutes picking the flowers, biting off the tips at the bottom, and sucking out the nectar. By the time they were done, they each had a pile of slightly wilted flowers at their feet. Tommy rubbed his stomach dramatically.

"Filling. We'd better head back. We don't want to piss anyone off."

The mood shifted when he said that and Sitka shivered. Glenn. She nodded and followed Tommy out along the fenceline to the sidewalk. They wandered down the road, talking about not much, Sitka just happy to be close to Tommy. Maybe when they got home, Glenn would be gone. *Maybe even dead,* Sitka thought. She wanted to feel bad for thinking that, but she didn't. It was unfair he was still alive and her mother wasn't. That Tommy's father wasn't.

They cut across the golf course, checking the golf ball washers for forgotten golf balls. Tommy found one in the last washer they checked and tossed it to Sitka. They cut through the backyards of the houses which lined the golf course into the subdivision. As they got to the house, they were disappointed to see Glenn's car there.

Aunt Leigh was in the kitchen cooking. Glenn was in his usual spot, sitting a the table smoking cigarettes. He smirked at them and rolled his eyes.

"Made it home? Just in time to eat a free dinner after a day of no work. Sounds about right."

Sitka could see Tommy biting his tongue and tried to distract Glenn. "We went to the park and the playground at the school. It was so much fun."

Glenn glanced at her, his face shifting out of its frown. "That so? Well, that's good. Oh! You have something gross in your hair," he said with disgust.

Before she could stop him, he snatched the cicada shell out of her hair and crushed it into flakes on the table with his meaty fist. She bit back tears as Tommy walked out, slamming the door behind him.

∞

Chapter Five

∞

*O*n a particularly hot Saturday morning, Sitka heard the neighborhood kids in the road, making a ruckus. She stepped outside to see a boy named Dean from down the street, pedaling his bike as fast as he could toward a set of ramps with other kids lying down between them. The ramps seemed too far apart and Sitka held her breath as he raised a fist in the air and ascended the ramp. One of the boys on the ground sat up slightly to see as Dean flew over the top of them, his back wheel grazing the boy on the forehead. The boy slammed himself back on the ground as Dean's front wheel caught the ramp on the other side, barely dragging the body of the bike clumsily onto the thin wood. As Dean skidded to stop at the bottom, the group of kids on the pavement jumped up, cheering wildly. Sitka let out the breath she'd been holding as she watched the stunt.

Dean spied her and winked with the confidence of Evel Knievel. Sitka blushed and stared down at her sneakers. She felt like an outsider with most of the neighborhood kids because they'd all grown up together, but Dean was always nice to her. She glanced back up and his attention was focused on the loose chain on his bike. She wandered over to him and stood awkwardly, watching him fiddle with the links.

Right about the time she summoned the courage to speak, so he knew she was there, a boy with a heavily freckled face came behind Dean and hit him with a water balloon. It burst, splattering both Dean and Sitka in the process. Sitka stepped back, wiping the water off her arms. It was cool but smelled like powder and latex. The boys seemed to always have a backstock of them ready for attack.

"Damnit, Roddy, you got my chain wet, you turd!" Dean yelled at the retreating redhead. Roddy looked back, laughing as he flipped Dean the bird.

"Can I help?" Sitka asked, not sure what she was even offering to do to assist.

Dean peered up, noticing her standing there. "Naw, it's fine. He's a dick, but it's so hot out here the water will evaporate in a few minutes. You have a bike?"

Tommy had gifted her his old bike, so she shrugged. "I guess so. Why?"

"We're going to ride down to the pond and look for tadpoles. You want to come?"

She really did. She never got invited to go anywhere with the neighborhood kids. She ran to the garage to pull out Tommy's old bike. It was dusty and the chain was hanging loose. She tugged it free from all the junk shoved into the garage. As she pulled, a shelf fell over, making a loud thud on the concrete floor.

Aunt Leigh opened the garage door, frowning. "Goodness day, Sitty, you startled me with that noise. What are you doing?"

"Dean asked me to ride bikes to the pond. Can I go with him?"

Her aunt snickered at the state of the bike. "I'd say you mean 'may I' but from the looks of that bike you may have been right with 'can'. Why don't you let Tommy fix it and come inside for some Tang while he does?"

Sitka saw Dean was on his bike and ready to go, afraid he'd leave her behind. She shook her head and ran, pushing the bike toward Dean as Aunt Leigh stood shaking her head. Dean glanced down at the bike, then took off a backpack he was wearing. His white-blond hair fell over his eyes and he tucked it behind his ears.

"I have some chain oil and a tool. Let's get that chain on right, so you don't get all caught up in it." He climbed off his bike and quickly got the chain tightened up, shining with a fresh coat of oil. He checked the pedals and squirted some oil on them as well. He eyed her, his light brown eyes glinting in the sun behind his glasses, then nodded. "You ready?"

Sitka slid on the banana seat and placed her feet on the pedals. She hadn't been on a bike since New York and was afraid she'd forgotten how to ride. She pushed down and the bike glided forward easily. Dean took off and she pedaled as hard as she could to keep up. He almost left her behind when he glanced back and laughed. He circled back and came up behind her, matching her pace until they got to the pond.

A large group of kids was already there and a couple of boys were smacking each other with pussy willows, sending tufts of fluff into the air. A group of girls was gathered on the other side of the pond, crouched down with their hands in the water. Sitka watched them, not feeling like she belonged, too shy to approach them.

"Come on, I'll show you where the best spot is to find tadpoles and minnows," Dean said, dragging her by the arm along the path.

They wound around the far side of the pond through the tall grass. Sitka plucked a pussy willow, liking the density in her hand. She squeezed it, drawing up the sense of memory she couldn't quite place. Like she'd been there before. Déjà vu of sorts. Dean was at the edge of the water, staring down past his reflection. Sitka joined him and peered into the murky water. A black dash slipped in and out of the pond vegetation and Dean reached in, cupping it in his hand. A minnow.

"Oh! It's so tiny," Sitka whispered in awe at the little fish moving around his hands. "Can I hold it?"

Dean nodded as she put her hands together and he poured the water with the fish into her hands. Sitka lifted it close to her face, seeing the dark wiggle moving around. She knelt down, placing her hands back in the water as the minnow swam out of her hands and out of sight. It made her feel big and small all the same time.

She could disappear just like the little fish.

Dean made his way to a pool of water off the main pond. The ground was muck and Sitka felt her sneakers sink in as water crept into the canvas. She plucked her feet out of the mud, setting them on a patch of grass. Every step she took squished and water oozed out. Dean had a plastic bucket he'd taken from his backpack and was scooping up water.

He waved her over, grinning. "Hey, come over here and check this out."

Sitka looked in the bucket and gasped. The creature inside had a smooth brown head and a tail, but two tiny legs were sticking out on either side of the tail. "What *is* that?"

"A tadpole. Some people call it a pollywog. It's a baby frog. It's forming its legs so it can be on land."

Looking at it made Sitka feel weird. It was like a creature from another world. She glanced away to settle herself, then peered back in. She was mesmerized by its little eyes. Frogs started out like that? Dean put it back in the water and used the bucket to gather more. He poked his fingers around and drew out another one. This one didn't have legs.

"See, this one is younger. They start out with just a head and tail, then legs grow. Eventually, the tail goes away and you have a frog!" he explained. "Have you never seen a tadpole before? They don't have them where you come from?"

Sitka thought about it. She'd grown up in the city and they had parks, but everything had been so controlled and manicured there. Not like here, where it seemed wild.

She shook her head. "We had frogs in New York, so I guess there were tadpoles, too, but I don't remember ever seeing them there."

"That where you're from? New York?"

"Yeah."

"What's it like? My dad says it's dirty and people from there aren't nice."

That hurt Sitka's feelings. Everyone she grew up with was nice. She stuck the toe of her sneaker in the water and hoped he didn't notice the heat rising in her face. "I liked it. It was me and my mama. Everyone was like family to us. We knew all our neighbors and they looked out for me when my mother had to work. I miss it. Sometimes we'd go to museums and get ice cream in the park."

Dean listened, taking in what she told him. "Oh, I always imagined, like, cops and robbers. Trash everywhere. People yelling."

"It's not like that!" Sitka felt tears rise up and was angry at Dean for being so mean, for making fun of her home. She turned and stormed off, her sneaker coming off in the muck. She reached down, yanking it out. She lost her balance and fell on her knees in the mud. Hot tears stung her cheeks and she wanted to get as far away from Dean as she could. She was wrong about him. He wasn't nice.

A hand reached down in front of her face. Dean was there, offering to get her out of the mud. "I'm sorry. I was only going off what my dad told me about it. He doesn't like people from up north. You're really nice, so that proves he's wrong. Let me help you up."

Sitka took his hand and glared at him. "Your dad is wrong. He sounds mean."

Dean laughed, then shrugged. "Sometimes he is. He doesn't like black people, either. So, you've proved him wrong on both counts."

"What do you mean?" Sitka asked, confused.

Dean's face turned red. "I mean, you're black, right? You don't look like the other black kids at school, but you're not white."

Sitka didn't know how to respond. Her father was black, but her mother was white. As she thought about it, since she'd moved in with Aunt Leigh, she hadn't met another kid like her. They were either black or white, not both. "I'm both."

Dean frowned, his brain struggling with a concept he wasn't familiar with. "You can you be both? How?"

Sitka almost laughed. He totally didn't understand. "My mother was white, but my father was black."

"Oh. Man, that'd make my father's head explode."

Sitka thought about her grandparents, her mother's parents, who refused to have anything to do with her because she was both. Why did it make a difference? She sighed and chewed her lip. "Does it matter to you?"

"Why would it? You're fun to hang out with. You aren't like other girls."

"How am I not like other girls?" Sitka stared over the group of girls, giggling and playing together on the other side of the pond.

"I don't know. You aren't like the boys, either. I guess you're one of a kind, Sitka." Dean smiled and tucked his bucket back into his backpack. "You want something to eat? My mom packed fried bologna sandwiches, chips, and Kool-Aid."

They made their way to a grassy spot and he pulled the food out, handing Sitka a sandwich as they sat down. They shared the bottle of Kool-Aid back and forth, talking about the upcoming school year. It was their last year in elementary school before junior high school. They were going into sixth grade, which seemed so much older than fifth grade.

The other kids began to filter out, going on to the next adventure. Sitka stood up and brushed grass off her legs. Dean gathered the trash and shoved it back in his backpack. He stood up and stretched, then tugged his jeans up. How he wore jeans in the middle of summer, Sitka couldn't understand. She was hot in her tank top and shorts.

"I have to go home and do my chores before my dad comes home from work. He flips his shit if they aren't done by then. This was fun," he said and flung his backpack onto his shoulders. "We can ride together until I get to my road. I want to hang out with you again. Maybe tomorrow we can check out the old warehouses. I find some cool stuff back there. I'd invite you over but..."

He paused and Sitka knew. He met her eyes apologetically, letting her know he didn't feel the same as his father.

She nodded. "But I'm black."

Chapter Six

The next few weeks of summer fell into a routine leading up to the Fourth of July. Sitka went to roller skate almost every day and saw her name piling up in the raffle box. They were drawing the winner on the Fourth and she just knew she'd win. No one laughed when she came out to participate in the speed skates anymore. She won the races almost every time, so they pushed her into the next age group up. The adults. Still, she won at least half the time and had a small crowd who cheered her on.

When the Fourth came, she woke up early, ready to go when Glenn stopped her at the door, shaking his head.

"Not today, kiddo. Today is family day. We're going to cook out, then go see the fireworks. You'll have to give the wheels a rest for the day."

Sitka's heart fell. She wouldn't be at Sports World when they drew the winner. She tried to think of an excuse to leave, but Glenn was blocking the door. Tommy came around the corner, then spying Glenn tried to duck back behind the wall. Glenn turned and stared at him.

"I need you to scrub down the grill and clean up the backyard. We have some friends coming over and it needs to be shipshape before they arrive," he instructed, seeming to enjoy Tommy's discomfort.

Tommy glanced at Sitka, then shrugged. "Whatever you say, Glenn. You want to help me, Sitty?"

Sitka knew Tommy was trying to put space between Glenn and her and was happy to spend the time with Tommy. Even if it meant scrubbing things down. Glenn started to protest when Sitka replied, "Yes! I want to help with the grill."

Tommy grinned and put his arm over Sitka's shoulders. "Well, we'd better get to it before the mystery guests show up." He guided her away from Glenn, who was fuming by the door.

Aunt Leigh came through and smiled at them. "Where are you two off to?"

"Glenn told us to clean the grill and pick up the backyard," Tommy replied shortly.

"Oh? I thought you were doing that, Glenn?" Leigh asked, it being clear she'd asked him to do those chores. "Okay, since the kids will do that and I'm prepping food, why don't you run to the store for this list of things? Throw in ice cream for the kids. What kind do you like, Tommy?"

"Rocky Road," Tommy answered with satisfaction. Glenn had gotten caught in his own game, trying to pawn his work off on Tommy.

"How about you, Sitty?" her aunt inquired.

"Strawberry cheesecake!"

"Hmm... not sure they have that, except at Baskin Robbins. What's your second choice in case they don't?"

"Rocky Road!" Sitka liked all ice cream but knew if she also said Rocky Road, Glenn couldn't pretend to forget.

"Rocky Road it is! Glenn, grab a couple of tubs. Margie and Dan are bringing their two kids, that way we have enough to go around."

Glenn snatched the list and stomped out the door, revving the car as he pulled out. Aunt Leigh sighed, then turned to them. "You can do the yard in a bit. Would you mind taking this bucket of flags to the cemetery and put them on as many graves as you can? My father used to have Marie and I do that on the Fourth of July, it only seems fitting to carry on the tradition."

Tommy took the bucket and headed for the back door. They could walk through the streets to get to the cemetery, but climbing the back fence was quickest. Sitka followed him, hoping she could keep one of the small, fabric flags for herself. They scaled the fence and Tommy extended his hand to assist her jumping down. She did it all the time by herself but liked having a big brother around to help. He handed her a stack of flags and they began wandering down the rows, placing flags at graves that seemed left behind. Some graves had flowers, toys, or mementos. Others seemed like they hadn't been visited in a very long time.

Tommy paused at a headstone that read *veteran* and ran his fingers across the top. Sitka could tell he was thinking of his father.

"Is he buried here at this cemetery?" she asked, peering down at the engraved name.

"No. This place was already full when he died. He's buried across town near his parents' house."

"His parents? Your grandparents?"

"Well, his father passed away a couple of years ago. His mother lives over there, still. I don't see her much. I think I reminded them of losing him. They kinda blamed my mom. That if she hadn't gotten pregnant with me, he could've gone to school and avoided the draft."

"They said that to you?"

"No, not to me. Once when I was little, I heard my mom saying that on the phone to your mom."

"Oh." Sitka didn't know what else to say. Aunt Leigh and Tommy's father had loved each other. It was sad his parents didn't see that. "I don't even know who my father is."

"Maybe it's on your birth certificate... his name. Did you ever meet our moms' parents? They moved to Florida. I didn't know if you'd ever visited them?" Tommy asked.

Sitka hadn't. She shook her head and glanced around the cemetery. She cleared her throat. "My mother told me they were racist. That they didn't like that she was with my father because he was black."

Tommy raised his brows, surprised her mother had been so open. "Yeah, they are racist, among other things. They moved away after the Wilmington Ten incident."

"What's that?"

"Oh, man, that's a lot to cover. Long story short, before 1969 whites and blacks went to different schools. When they started integrating the schools, they did a shit job and it caused issues between the black and white communities. White supremacists came out of the woodwork and a group of ten, mostly black, students were accused and arrested for arson. There were riots and all kinds of shit going on. That's barely scratching the surface. Point is, our grandparents decided Wilmington was 'going to the blacks' and moved away. Be glad you don't know them. They were miserable, hateful people."

Sitka chewed her fingernails, feeling shame rise in her. "They didn't want me because I'm half black."

Tommy could see she was struggling with the information and knelt down to her. "You are, and that makes you perfect in every way. Some people just have shriveled hearts. Your mother knew that and that's why she left. My mom asked her to move back the time she brought you down here when you were little, but your mom didn't want you raised here. Things have changed a lot though, there are more open-minded people here than there used to be. But still..." his voice trailed off.

"Before they put the kids together in school, what happened with kids like me?"

"What do you mean?"

"Kids that are both black and white?" Sitka asked.

"Oh, shoot, I don't really know. Knowing the bigots around here, I guess if you were any black, you went to the black schools. Your mother would've been in danger having you here. Some of these people wouldn't have been satisfied with name-calling and dirty looks. The South has a bad reputation for doing some heinous things," Tommy explained.

"Heinous?"

"Cruel. Horrible, unspeakable. I'm sorry, Sitty, I didn't mean for this conversation to come up. I'm glad you're here. My mother and I love you more than anything. Times are changing, at least I hope so. Do you ever feel unsafe around here? In Wilmington?"

Sitka thought about it. Sometimes she got weird stares and certain white kids at school avoided her, but she'd chalked that up to her being different on the inside, not different on the outside. She shook her head. "I don't think so."

"Okay, good. If you ever do, you tell me and I'll kick some ass," Tommy promised.

That made Sitka giggle. He handed her more flags and they wandered to the part of the cemetery where the children's graves were. Sitka went to Johnny's, placing a flag on it and whispering, "Hey, Johnny."

Tommy didn't seem to notice and went around adding flags to the rest of the children's graves. He ran his hand along one of the carved lambs and sighed. "I wonder if these kids ever felt abandoned, being shoved in the corner like this."

Sitka knew the feeling. She'd wondered the same. "Well, now they have us."

Aunt Leigh was calling for them, which probably meant Glenn was back and bitching about the yard and grill. Tommy took Sitka's hand and they headed back to the fence. They paused before climbing over and Tommy turned to Sitka, watching her for a moment.

"Just remember, us kids have to stick together. The adults around us like to act like they have their shit together, but they don't. They're a fucking mess."

Sitka nodded and climbed the fence. Tommy was right behind her and they began cleaning the yard, avoiding Glenn at all costs. About the time the grill was sparkling, guests began to arrive. Aunt Leigh introduced Sitka to a girl about her age. A delicate, red-haired child with large green eyes. She sized Sitka up, her face expressionless. Sitka thought about what Tommy told her about how not too long ago girls like that and girls like her were kept separate. The girl broke out with a shy smile.

"I'm Annie."

"I'm Sitty."

"Do you want to play?"

Sitka grinned and took the girl's hand as they ran to grab hula hoops off the back patio. Within minutes, they were giggling and swaying their hips, trying to keep the rings from falling to the ground. Sitka rotated her hips quickly, sending the colorful hoop in circles around her. Annie's kept dropping and she shook her head.

"I wish I could move mine like yours. My hula hoop won't stay up."

"Keep trying, you just need to move your legs like this," Sitka explained, bending her knees slightly and using them to shift her hips.

The girls kept at it until it was time to eat. They set the hoops down and made their way to the table on the patio where the food was being spread out. Annie grabbed a plate and went to find her mother. Sitka picked up a plate and selected a hamburger, potato salad, baked beans, green beans, and a roll.

When she turned to look for a place to sit, she saw Glenn watching her. He waved her over and patted the seat next to him. Sitka didn't want to sit with him but didn't see Tommy or Aunt Leigh around to divert to. She walked slowly toward him, wishing Annie would come back.

"Hey, girl, come sit here," Glenn said, his eyes fixed intently on her.

Sitka sat, balancing the plate in her lap. She sat on the edge away from Glenn, but he put his arm around her, pulling her right next to him. His hairy leg brushed hers and her stomach clenched. He stared down at her.

"Saw you over there swinging your hips around. You're a natural. You've got something those little white girls sure don't have."

Little white girls? Glenn was white, so that seemed a strange thing for him to say. She stared at her food, not sure how to reply. She tried to move on with the conversation.

"Annie was doing good, she just needs to practice some more."

Glenn laughed in a way that didn't make sense. Almost like he was angry. "No, not like you. You got something they weren't born with. Girls like you have something extra, something which begs for attention."

Sitka froze, a hint of a memory flashing across her brain. It was gone as soon as it came, but her hands began to sweat. *Little white girls... girls like her?* Black girls? What was he saying? She searched for Aunt Leigh and stood up when she saw her across the yard. As she stepped away, Glenn grabbed her wrist, his mouth twisted in a odd smile.

"Don't worry, Sitty. We have an understanding, you and me. I'll keep your secret and you'll keep mine."

∞

Chapter Seven

∞

*W*hen Sitka began waking up in the cemetery, she knew she was in trouble. First, she'd started wetting the bed. However, when she woke up curled in next to a headstone, she thought she was only dreaming. After shaking herself awake and stretching her sore legs, it was clear it was no dream. The first time she woke up there, it was next to Ellen's grave. The next night, it was Johnny's. She had no recollection of getting over the fence, but her legs were scratched up, and she needed to pick sandburs out of her feet. She didn't tell anyone.

She tried locking her door before sleep, but it always ended up unlocked. She left toys by the door in the hopes she'd trip over them and wake up, but somehow they always ended up pushed aside. She'd tuck her sheets tightly around her legs to try and keep them in place.

They didn't stay.

No matter what she did, her mind and body found a way to get to the cemetery. She wanted to tell Tommy but was afraid it would somehow get him in trouble. By the fourth night she woke up there, she was out of ideas.

She hadn't been to the roller skate rink since before the Fourth of July, mostly because she was so tired. She wanted to know if she'd won the skates and planned on going the morning after the fourth night. That morning, she heard Glenn get up and go out for cigarettes, so she crept out of her room. She'd been avoiding Glenn as much as possible since the Fourth of July. He didn't say anything else to her that day or since, but she had a feeling he'd corner her and say more weird things to her.

Aunt Leigh was in the kitchen washing dishes and Tommy had picked up some mowing jobs, which took him out early in the morning. She snuck into Aunt Leigh and Glenn's room and climbed up to view the top of their dresser. She'd noticed a bowl with change in it and scooped out a handful. Tommy had been so busy, he'd forgotten to give her money for skating. She shoved her pockets full of the coins and jumped down, scooting back to her room before Aunt Leigh spied her. She thought she should feel guilty, but getting out of the house and away from Glenn was more important.

She heard Glenn's car drive back in, so she made for the back door. Aunt Leigh saw her as she passed through and put her hand up. "Hold on."

Sitka's heart started to beat in her chest. Did Aunt Leigh know she'd stolen the money? She stopped and eyed her aunt. "I'm just going skating."

Aunt Leigh came around the corner and handled her two dollars. "Here, honey, Tommy asked me to make sure you got this to get in. He said you might not have enough."

Now, the coins in her pockets felt like lead bricks. She took the two dollars and gulped, forcing a smile. "Thanks, Aunt Leigh. Can you tell Tommy I'll be done at four, so we can make it back for dinner?"

"Sure thing, hon. Have fun!"

Glenn came in and set a paper bag on the table, watching Sitka. "I'll give you a ride over there."

Sitka began to panic and met her aunt's eyes. Aunt Leigh smiled. "She's okay, Glenn. She goes almost every day. I think she knows the way."

Glenn looked like he was about to say something, then muttered under his breath and sat down at the table. Sitka took that as her chance to leave, scurrying out the back door and over the fence before anyone changed their mind. She hurried through the cemetery, not feeling the need to visit today. Especially after her nightly stays there. She paid at the rink and rushed in, straight to the skate counter. The girl behind the glass display looked at her.

"Can I help you?"

Sitka took a deep breath. The raffle box was gone. "Who won the skates?"

The girl frowned, then peered around. "Oh, that was a few days ago. I'm not sure. Let me ask Jim."

She ducked into a back room and was gone for a while when Sitka began to think she'd forgotten about her. A tall, skinny guy came out holding a slip of paper. He eyed Sitka.

"What's your name?"

"Sitka Ellison."

The guy looked at her and squinted an eye at her. "You have any ID on you?"

64

Sitka didn't know what he meant and stared, confused. The announcer slid open a window between his booth and the skate shop. "Trust me, that is Sitka Ellison. That girl has won just about every race in the last month."

He winked at Sitka and closed the window. The guy holding the paper smiled. "Alright, then, what size skate do you wear?"

As he handed her the box of skates in her size and color of her choosing, Sitka wanted to pinch herself to make sure she wasn't dreaming. Her hands shook as she took the box and found a place to put on the skates. They were mint green with sparkly laces. The wheels were a pinkish white and spun like only wheels never used and not filled with gunk could. Sitka tied them and stood up, feeling like all eyes were on her. She took a few steps forward, amazed at how the skates glided like they were on ice.

She took a couple of turns around the rink, mesmerized by the ease with which she moved. There was no clunkiness or stickiness. Her legs barely had to move and they rolled forward. All of a sudden, she was very aware of her presence and decided to step off to get a snack. The next time she went out, she felt more confident and let the skates and her legs work together to fly her around the rink.

Somehow the hours flew by, then it was time for Tommy to pick her up for dinner. She switched into her sneakers and slung the skates over her shoulders like she'd seen the big kids do. She felt older now. She waved at the announcer, who grinned with a thumbs up, and walked out to the parking lot without a care in the world. She couldn't wait to show Tommy her new skates. He'd be so proud of her.

Except it wasn't Tommy waiting for her in the parking lot. It was Glenn. Sitka ducked behind a post and scanned to see if Tommy was there. He wasn't. Glenn glanced up and was watching the door for her. He must have heard her tell Aunt Leigh what time she needed to be picked up. She skirted around the side of the building, clutching the skates to her chest. She couldn't go with him. Why hadn't Tommy come? Hadn't Aunt Leigh told him?

Sitka bit her lip, deciding what to do. She'd just pretend like she thought she was supposed to walk home. That she didn't see Tommy when she left and began walking. She made her way around the back of the building and waited. If Glenn saw her on foot, he'd make her get in the car. She cut through the woods in the opposite direction, knowing he wouldn't look for her that way.

She wandered for a while, realizing she wasn't sure exactly where she was. She'd gone into the woods, thinking she was skirting along the back of the neighborhood, but now nothing seemed familiar to her. She stopped and looked around. She thought she recognized a dirt road as being the one behind the cul-de-sac she passed in the neighborhood on the way to the bus stop and cut down the road. After about fifteen minutes, she doubted herself. She could see the brick back wall of a store and headed through the woods toward it. It was a convenience store called Zip Mart.

A gust of cool air hit her face as she scooted in and a heavyset man behind the counter eyed her. She placed her hand on her pocket, feeling the remaining change against her leg. She went down the candy aisle and grabbed Bottle Cap candy and a Charleston Chew. She looked at the candy cigarettes but remembered they tasted like sweet chalk. She counted her money and had enough for a soda, the candy, and still had a little left. Placing the items on the counter, she handed the man the change.

Sitka sat behind the store, eating the candy and drinking the soda. She was pretty sure if she cut back through the woods, she'd come to the far end of the neighborhood. Then, she could walk the rest of the way on the streets. Setting her resolve, she finished the soda and put the rest of the candy in her pocket as she headed back into the woods. Once in the trees, she was cooled by the shade and went toward the back end of the neighborhood, or so she thought. She crossed the dirt road again and wandered into the woods on the other side.

Within twenty minutes, she realized she was wrong. She turned back to the road, figuring if she followed it, it should take her to a main road. From there, she could find her way home. She headed down the road for a bit and heard a vehicle coming her way. Afraid it was Glenn, she ran into the forest and ducked behind a log. A large, dark blue van drove slowly down the road as if the driver was searching for something. Sitka crouched even lower and watched as it came to a stop close to her. She couldn't see the driver through the trees but heard doors open and feet hit the ground. She squinted to see what was going on and saw the back doors of the van swing open.

There was rustling and grunting but Sitka couldn't make out what was happening. She could hear movement through the woods and held her breath. They were coming her way. Something heavy was dropped in the leaves, then she heard the people retreating. She peered through the trees and saw the van pull away. Following them out, she stood on the edge as the van rumbled down the road away from her.

"Phew," Sitka mumbled to herself in relief, as the van kicked up dust in its departure.

At that moment, the brake lights came on and the van began to wind in reverse back down the road. Sitka froze as it drew closer. She'd been spotted.

A voice yelled out from the window at her. "Hey! Don't run!"

Sitka didn't wait and ran into the woods. She stumbled, running blindly to get away from the person in the van. She could hear them behind her, crashing through the branches. She was smaller and quicker, so she made it deep into the forest long before they could reach her. She thought she heard someone calling her name, but couldn't be sure. After a while, it fell silent and she knew they'd left. She stayed in place, afraid to move for what felt like a long time, then finally followed the way she'd come back to the road. The van was gone. It was beginning to get dark and she was scared. There was no way she'd be able to find her way home, now.

Sitka thought if she could get back to the Zip Mart, she could have someone call Aunt Leigh. She'd be in serious trouble at that point, but she didn't care. She just wanted to get home. Back to her room, back to Tommy. She turned and trudged through the woods, tripping over something large and smooth in the leaves. She sat up and stared to see what she'd stumbled over.

It was very big, wrapped in a thick, plastic sheet of some sort. She moved closer and tugged on the cover. That must've been what the people in the van left. She pulled harder and the cover gave way slightly, causing Sitka to scream and scramble away from the sight. Horrified, she covered her eyes, wanting what she saw to go away.

Released from its plastic sheath, a bloody hand, still attached to its owner, fell with a thud against the wet ground.

Chapter Eight

"*H*ello?" Sitka whispered to the body in the plastic roll. It didn't respond. She stepped a little closer, her heart thumping in her chest. She picked up a branch and poked the outside of the covering. Nothing inside moved. Whatever, or whoever, was inside was most definitely dead. The hand was a man's, that much she could tell. Attached to an arm. Thick and rough. Hairy. The skin looked white but tan in spots and freckled. Or dirty and splotchy, she couldn't quite tell from her viewpoint. Definitely a grown man's arm.

Sitka was too afraid to look any farther into the plastic and convinced herself if she went back to the road, whoever dumped the body would find her. They'd seen her. Seen that she'd seen them.

Dump a body.

It was getting dark. Aunt Leigh would know she was missing by now. All the neighborhood kids knew to go home once it began to get dark. They were probably all out searching for her. If she could just get back to the Zip Mart, she could call for help.

No, they were probably closed by now. It was late.

Maybe find a house. No, not a house. How would she know if the people who did this, didn't live in one of the homes around there? Or if they were waiting around until she emerged from the woods. She'd need to go to the Zip Mart in the morning once it was open, so she could keep her eyes out for the van.

Not wanting to be near the body, she peered around and made her way back into the safety of the deep woods. She'd need to hide there until daylight. She was beginning to lose the ability to see anything in front of her, tripping over roots and sticks. She fell flat on her face, scratching her cheek. Sitting up, she could feel wetness on her face and realized she was bleeding. It was time to stop moving before she ended up seriously hurt, so she crept through the brush until she felt a fallen tree. She inched along the rough bark and found a place she could tuck in where the trunk met the lower branches. She climbed into the space, imagining it was her mother's arms wrapped tightly around her to keep her safe.

Sleep didn't come easy and Sitka jerked awake repeatedly with the sounds the forest makes at night. Owls, cicadas, things large and small shuffling through. She thought she heard the trees saying her name which was oddly comforting, yet terrifying at the same time. She did exist and they knew it. At one point, she thought she saw lights flashing through the trees, sure the van people were coming for her. She tucked her head to her knees and held her breath. When she glanced back up, the lights were gone.

In the morning, Sitka was feeling delirious with sleep deprivation and stumbled out of her hiding place. She realized in the events of the previous evening, she'd lost her bag with her skates and any change she had left. Her mouth was dry and her body shaky with hunger. All she'd eaten since she left the skating rink was candy and soda and she was suffering the effects of it. She needed to get to Zip Mart and call Aunt Leigh. She headed in the direction she thought was right, but after an hour, knew she'd gotten turned around.

By lunchtime, Sitka became aware she was walking in a circle and stopped. Things all looked the same, so she was having a hard time finding markers to guide her way. She came across an old washing machine and later the body of a rusted truck. She wondered how those things ended up so deep in the forest. When she stumbled upon an old shack, she realized people had once lived in those woods. The shack was abandoned, but from the outside she could see the windows were lined with bottles of all shapes and colors. Not like any bottles she'd ever seen. She made her way to the door and pushed. After some effort, it opened enough for her to peek her face through.

"Anyone in here?" she asked, knowing there wasn't. When silence greeted her, she shoved her body through the door crack and went in.

It was a small shack and appeared like it had maybe been someone's workshop at one time. Counters ran on two sides along with the windows holding the bottles. Dried plants littered the counters but turned to dust when Sitka tried to pick them up. She ran her fingers along the bottles, some with raised lettering as part of the glass. Most were empty, but a few on the counters contained what looked like some sort of concoctions in them. Herbs and plants suspended in liquid. From the layer of dust on everything, no one had been there in a very long time. Until she could figure out how to get home, Sitka could at least stay there and hide.

Hoping to find something to eat, Sitka searched the small cabin but came up empty-handed. From the shack window, she spied a blackberry bush outside and looked around for something to gather them in. On one of the counters was a glass bowl. It was dirty, but a quick swipe with her shirt made it usable. She slipped back through the door and went to the bushes she saw from the window. They were brimming with ripe blackberries and Sitka ate as many as she could as she gathered them into the bowl.

If she wasn't hiding for her safety, it would almost be fun. Once the bowl was full, she set it down and peered around. There was no sign of civilization and she felt like she'd not only stepped away from her neighborhood, she'd gone back in time. Out here there was nothing but the chirping of birds and gurgling of water.

Water.

Sitka realized she was hearing water running over rocks and followed the source, making sure to not lose sight of the shack. She wandered through the woods until she came upon a small creek. The water danced over the stones underneath, reflecting sparkles in the sunlight. Sitka bent and cupped her hands to catch the cool liquid. Once she was full, she knew she needed to come back with some sort of container to fill. She made her way back to the shack, clearing a thin path by breaking branches and pulling up weeds as she went.

By evening, she had a belly full of blackberries, a bottle of water, and a bowl of the berries on the counter. *This isn't so bad*, she told herself. She could almost live out there. When it began to downpour late in the evening, she missed Aunt Leigh and Tommy. She shivered as the rain cooled everything down, wishing for a blanket or something to cover her.

She'd been gone for now going on two nights. She imagined Aunt Leigh beside herself with worry. Tommy was probably out looking for her. Glenn was still sitting at the table reading his paper, grumbling about one thing or another. Sitka missed her bed, but she didn't miss waking up in the cemetery or wetting the bed. Maybe it was because she wasn't really sleeping, but she hadn't woken up wet the past night.

The next day, her stomach began to cramp from eating only blackberries and she felt nauseous. She found a sunny spot to lie down in and dozed off, sleeping better than she had either night. When she woke up, Sitka considered her options. She could try to find the road or the store again, but if she left the shack, she might get even more lost. Here, she had water and berries. Once in the woods, she might not have anything. However, here, she might never get home. She listened, straining to hear any sounds of civilization but only heard the trees around her moving in the breeze.

How could she be so far from home?

She wandered around the area, searching for other food but wasn't familiar with what she was looking at for vegetation. She found a small blueberry bush, but the birds had already eaten most of it. The remaining berries were old and tasteless, but still, she ate them. She saw mushrooms, however, remembered her mother telling her a story of a pioneer family who ate the wrong kind of mushrooms and died. So, she avoided those. Berries it was.

By the fourth day, she was convinced no one would ever find her. Not the bad people. Not the good people. Fear kept her in place, but hunger was starting to make her wander farther and farther from the shack. Plants began to seem more appealing and she wondered if she should risk it. She nibbled a few here and there, most were bitter. How did people survive before grocery stores?

On one of her outings a few days later, she contemplated if she needed to catch and eat a lizard or small animal. The thought turned her stomach, so she figured she wasn't hungry enough yet. Her mother had been a vegetarian but Aunt Leigh wasn't. Sitka wasn't opposed to eating something she could catch, but the idea of having to kill and then cook it was too monumental. As she walked and considered that, she made a critical mistake. She pulled herself out of her thoughts and glanced around.

Where was the shack?

She stopped as her heart began to race. Where was she? She couldn't have gone too far, however, she'd been buried in her own thoughts and wasn't tracking where she went. She turned around but the forest had closed around her, absorbing any trail she'd left. She listened but didn't hear the creek anymore. What direction had she gone in?

All of a sudden, the stress of the past days washed over her... how many days was it? A few days? A week? More? Sitka began to bawl. The fantasy of living in the woods was beaten by the reality of her situation and Sitka came to grips with her own mortality. She could die out there. Just another body, rotting in the leaves. She stumbled to where a tree had fallen a long time ago, its wood becoming one with the soil. An area where the tree had once arched out toward the sky was now a small cavern, being reclaimed by the earth. Sitka crawled in and rested her head on her knees.

What if no one ever found her? What if she couldn't get out of the woods? How could her mother have left her, all alone and vulnerable? Why had no one come? Maybe they never even looked for her. After all, she was forced on them when her mother died. They didn't want her to begin with. She sobbed until she felt like dry twigs and closed her eyes.

She didn't know how long she was asleep but when she awoke, the sun was in a completely different place in the sky. It was going to set soon and she was lost again with no food and no water. She rubbed her nose and stretched her legs out of the tiny cave. A rustling caught her attention and Sitka gasped when a large, female deer came out of the trees into her line of sight. It stopped in a wide-open area between the trees.

It was beautiful, its expressive brown eyes watching Sitka, her lashes like feathers extending out. It flicked its ear, the only motion it made. Sitka stared, afraid to move and scare it away. The deer bent and took a mouthful of leaves in her mouth, chewing slowly. Sitka took note of the type of leaves, figuring if the deer could eat it, she could, too. The deer stopped chewing and rested her eyes on Sitka. It was as if it was telling her something. For some reason, it reminded Sitka of her mother in the way it observed her.

Sitka climbed out and brushed the dirt off her legs. The doe didn't move. Sitka moved a little closer, not wanting to scare her only companion off. The deer was cautious but didn't bolt. Sitka was able to get close enough to pick a leaf of what the deer was eating. She nibbled the leaf, surprised by the savory flavor. She stared at the leaf and reached down, pulling the plant from the ground. She recognized the tall, red stalks in her hand. One of her mother's friends had made pies from it when she was little on a trip upstate to their farm. Root-barbie, Sitka thought the woman said, much to everyone's delight. Rhubarb. The pie was sweet and earthy.

The deer continued nibbling, then in a moment, bolted toward the trees. Sitka dropped the Rhubarb, startled. She gathered the strewn stalks off the ground and stared back at the deer, now perched at the edge of the forest. The deer gazed back at Sitka, unwavering.

Beckoning her to follow.

∞

Chapter Nine

∞

The doe moved as if she didn't need eyes to see. Sitka followed along, watching the white tufts of the deer's behind disappear into the woods. As she walked, she realized she wasn't tripping and falling. She glanced down and noticed a thin trail had been worn. It dawned on her, the deer knew exactly where it was going. There was a system of hidden trails all around the forest, made by animals and followed by instinct. While the deer knew where it was going, Sitka didn't, and she began to worry she was being taken farther into the forest. Just as doubt made her want to stop and turn around, she saw the corner of the shack roof in the distance. As they drew closer, the doe paused and glanced back at Sitka, her eyes sending a secret message, "This is the way."

Sitka silently thanked the deer, who then in a flash, darted into the woods and was gone. Sitka made her way to the small cabin, clutching the rhubarb in her fist. She pushed into the shack, grabbing the bottle of water off the counter and chugged it all at once. She set the rhubarb down and considered what just happened.

Did the deer find her and lead her back, or was it a series of coincidences? If the deer *had* led her there, could it show her the way back to the road if Sitka somehow let it know? She was thinking about the shack and not being able to get back there when the deer appeared. Had she been thinking about home, would the deer have taken her there or at least closer? Perhaps though, the deer was just following the trail it made and happened to come close to the cabin. Maybe it didn't even know Sitka was following behind, so when it saw her again was startled and ran off.

Sitka chewed on a stalk of rhubarb, mulling it over in her mind. She liked the tart sweetness of the plant and again thanked the deer for showing it to her. She wondered if her mother had sent the deer her way as a guide to save her. To take her back to the shack. Since her mother's death, Sitka tried to not dwell on her mother being gone. It made her sad and feel like the world was too big. When she went to the cemetery, she was able to feel close to her mother without feeling like it would drag her down endlessly. It was a like a portal. When she went in, she was with her mom. When she left, she was able to shut that door and go back into the world.

"I miss you, Mama," she murmured as she felt her eyes get heavy. She knew she needed to get more water before it got dark, but wanted sleep to take her away.

When she woke up again, it was dark and she'd missed her chance to gather water. She shivered and sat up, peering around the small shack. Moonlight was coming in through the grimy windows, creating a delicate light on the rows of bottles.

She noticed a latch on the floor she hadn't seen before and scooted over to see what it was. The latch was rusted shut. She tried to open it, but it hurt her fingers and wouldn't budge. Slipping out into the night, Sitka found a rock and brought it back into the shack.

After a few whacks with the rock, she was able to get the latch to move slightly. She used the rock on the sliding bar, tapping it to move along. Finally, it came open and she pried up the floorboard it was holding shut. The board creaked as she shoved it wide. At first, she couldn't see anything. As her eyes adjusted to the darkness, she saw there were some items in the space.

A bottle with some sort of brown liquid in it. Sitka pulled the cork out and sniffed it, wrinkling her nose in disgust. It was either alcohol or had been alcohol, now smelling like sour floor cleaner. She set that aside and reached in, hoping there weren't spiders in there. Her fingers brushed a box and something soft. She yanked her hand out, convinced it was a large rat or creature of some sort. She waited a minute, then placed her hand back in gingerly. The soft thing was still there, not moving.

Drawing up courage, she grabbed the item and took it out. A baby blanket. A baby blanket? That seemed off, especially considering the bottle of liquid. Sitka sat back, holding the blanket. Had someone lived there? They couldn't have, the space was so small. Smaller than a bedroom. Besides, there was no furniture, no bed. It was too dark to see what else was in the floor space, so she closed the board, deciding to wait until morning. She didn't want to open the box and have bugs come crawling out into her space.

The baby blanket was dusty but warm, so Sitka spread it over her chest. Even though it was summer in the south, she still got cool at night and this brought her some comfort. She thought back to when she was little. Her earliest memories. She thought she could remember being an infant, lying on a flat, elevated surface and feeling uncomfortable in her diaper. Next, was maybe a year old, standing in her crib and holding onto the side. She was jumping and the crib bottom fell out. She clung to the side crying, when her mother came rushing in to save her.

Four and skinning her knee when one of the neighbor boys was play-chasing her on his bike. Six, riding a pony at her "Aunt" Betsy's farm upstate. Her eighth birthday party, where her mother had done so much to include the other children, Sitka felt like it wasn't even her party. Ten. Sitka tried to push the memory away but it came anyway. It always did. Coming home from school and her mother waiting at the kitchen table, her face twisted in worry...

"No!" Sitka yelled and pounded her fist against the floor. She wouldn't let it in. Not now. "Leave me alone."

The moon watched her through the window, its presence reminding her she couldn't hide forever. Truth and memory come out. She squeezed her eyes shut and tried to think of something else. Anything else. She thought about Tommy, how he never let her fall. The day she arrived in North Carolina, he became her best friend. They were alike, her and Tommy. She thought back to the first night in her new room. Aunt Leigh had said goodnight, but Tommy came in a little while later and sat her on her bed.

"Hey kiddo, you alright?"

"Yes."

"You don't have to be," he whispered.

"Have to be what?" Sitka asked.

"Alright."

Sitka knew in his words then, he understood her suffering. That nighttime was the hardest and the loneliness was smothering. She'd wanted to ask if she could move to Tommy's room to sleep but was afraid to. Afraid to ask too much, to make herself too big. Because then she might not fit in the house and they'd send her away. Tommy got up and paused at the door.

"We're family, Sitty. You and I. Never forget that. I'm sorry about Aunt Marie. I'm not sorry you're here."

Sitka still felt warmed by those words. She didn't know what she'd do if Tommy left. *When* Tommy left. Glenn would surely drive him away. That first night after Tommy went back to his room, Sitka huddled under her covers and cried. Every inch of her insides felt raw and she wanted the pain to end. She'd cried until nothing was left and pushed the memories down. As she drifted off to sleep, a shadow in her doorway caught her eyes. Then it disappeared.

Little did she know, that shadow would haunt her nights over the following months. The pain of losing her mother would pale to the horrors it carried with it. Her child mind would become very accustomed to running and hiding, and there was no one to protect her. Her mother's death had brought something much worse in its wake.

A monster who preyed on her vulnerability. Who devoured her innocence and delighted in her pain. A monster who couldn't be seen in the daylight by her eyes.

Sitka jerked awake, covered in sweat. Sunlight poured through the windows, casting yellow beams with dust particles dancing in them across the shack. She ran her hand through the light, causing the particles to swim and swirl. Water. She needed to get water as soon as possible. Her throat ached and her stomach hurt. She folded the baby blanket and stood up, feeling woozy. Eating rhubarb and berries was taking its toll and she dreamed of Dean's fried bologna sandwiches and cherry Koolaid.

She gathered bottles and hiked to the creek. Once there, she gulped down handfuls before filling them. She took her time getting back to the shack, searching around for anything that could constitute food. She came across a patch of mushrooms and considered them. They looked like normal mushrooms, but how would she know the difference? Hunger swayed her thinking and she plucked a handful to take back. She'd only eat them if she had nothing else.

Later that day, Sitka decided she needed to start venturing out to see if she could get back to the road. Any road. No one had found her so far, so she figured they'd stopped looking. Her eyes began to recognize the deer trails and she remembered the story of Hansel and Gretel. How they marked their trail with things to find their way back. Not bread crumbs, those had gotten eaten. Sitka laughed to herself. If she had any bread crumbs to begin with, *she'd* be the one eating them.

She thought about what would be obvious if she left a trail and what she could carry. The bottles would be too much. Rocks would become part of the land. Leaves could blow away. She searched the shack, finally deciding on the corks from the bottles. She gathered all the ones she could find into a pile. It wasn't much, but she'd break branches as she went along, as well, to let her know the way back. The corks would mark the path periodically to let her know she was going the right way. They were heavy enough to stay in place and wouldn't blend into the landscape.

Before she left, Sitka considered the box in the floor. She decided she'd wait until she returned to open it. It gave her something to look forward to and she knew if she was going to leave the shack, she needed to go as early as possible to get back before she lost daylight. Hopefully, she found civilization and wouldn't need to come back at all.

She drank water before she headed out and packed a bottle to drink along the way. She'd go the opposite way of the trail the deer brought her back on because she'd been that way and gotten lost. Stepping outside the shack, she peered around the area. Her eyes traced the ground, looking for telltale signs of a deer trail.

There it was. Almost unnoticeable, but the dirt was packed down and the vegetation ever so slightly parted. Sitka checked her water and had a few stalks of rhubarb. She'd shoved corks in both her pockets and began on the trail, breaking branches and pulling up plants as she went. Every once in a while, she'd put a cork in the middle of the trail as a marker.

She almost didn't see it until she saw it. She'd been walking for some time, intent on making the trail more clear. When she stepped out into the opening, she didn't even realize where she was. The sun glinting off glass drew her attention and she glanced up, her mouth dropping open.

Zip Mart.

There she was on the far side of the Zip Mart. Her heart began to race and she was about to run full speed through the doors when something on the other side of the store caught her eye. It couldn't be. She ducked back into the trees and squinted toward the store. Parked on the far side of the store was a large, dark blue van. She shook her head. A lot of people had vans.

Sitka could be steps away from going home, yet she was frozen in place. She racked her brain, trying to remember other details about the van that dumped the body. Dark blue. What else? Older. Kinda beat up. What else? Sitka replayed the memory of that day and what she saw. There was something about the van. What was it? Something that struck her memory, something that stood out. She let her mind put her back on the side of the road. She remembered something as the van backed up toward her. A sign? No, a sticker. The van had a sticker in the back window. A symbol of some kind. A triangle or something like that.

Sitka wasn't close enough to see, so she crept around the perimeter of the woods until she was on the other side of the store. She went as close as she could to the van to see the back window as her heart thumped in her chest. There it was. The sticker. Whoever dumped the body was at the store. She heard the doorbell chime as it swung open and a man's voice call out from inside. The man she'd bought the candy and soda from before.

"I remember that little girl, alright. She was in here at least a week back. If I see her again, I'll sure enough give you a call and let you know."

Chapter Ten

∞

Sitka wasn't sure exactly how she found her way back to the shack so quickly, but when she busted through the door and collapsed on the floor, she let the shakes take over her. The kind that comes when someone has a brush with death, like a near-miss car accident or a potential fall from deadly heights. She was doused in sweat but felt like ice coursed through her veins. Scratches covered her arms and legs, blood running down her shins.

They were searching for her. The bad people. The people who killed a man and dumped his body in the woods without a care. She could only imagine what they'd do if they got a hold of her. She was small enough to bury or stuff almost anywhere out there. Maybe it was just one person, she only heard the one voice yell at her. Even so, she was no match for a murderer.

She'd been so frantic, she hadn't bothered to collect the corks on her way back and hoped no one could use them to find her hiding spot. Once the shakes passed, she sat up and rubbed her arms. She picked out the little barbs from plants that had embedded in her skin and sighed. Those people, the bad ones, wouldn't stop until she was found. So, she couldn't be found. Which meant she needed a different plan.

Later that evening, her stomach felt like it was turning in on itself. Sitka tried to ignore the nauseating twisting but knew she wouldn't be able to sleep if she didn't find something to quell it. She nibbled rhubarb and almost immediately felt her bowels cramp. She pushed it away and fought back tears. If she went to where people were, she risked the bad people finding her. If she stayed hidden, she risked starvation.

The mushrooms teased her quietly from across the shack but she shook away the call. What if they were poisonous? Instead, she focused her attention on the latch on the floor and slid over to it. She pried open the hatch and peered in. It was dark, however, she could make out the corner of something down in there. She reached in, hoping nothing jumped on her hands from the darkness, then withdrew a box. It was old and wooden, looking like someone had put it together by hand. Not intricate or ornate. Simple. Like someone had found random pieces of wood and hammered them together into a makeshift box.

Sitka sat back and ran her fingers through the years of dirt and grime on the container. She considered it might be someone's pet's final resting place and set it down. Lifting the lid slowly, she closed one eye as if that could lessen the horror of what might be inside. Both eyes opened as she saw it was trinkets and pictures. A baby shoe, an old iron key, and some documents so ancient that when Sitka tried to unfold them, they began to crumble. The photos were what caught her attention the most. They were old, black and white. One was of a newborn baby, its face wrinkled in an unaware state. There was one of a couple standing beside an old car. A really old car. Nothing like what was on the road nowadays. There were a few others of random people in different places, smiling at the person behind the camera.

The one that made Sitka stop and stare was of an old man, sitting on a stoop. His face was worn and leathered, one of his eyes cloudy and unseeing. He wasn't smiling, but the lines on his face said he'd spent a lifetime laughing. In the photo, he appeared like he was simply waiting on death. Maybe even wishing for it. He stared at the camera with a sense of irritation, impatience. Get it over with, already. Sitka felt connected to this old man.

She peered closely at the photo and recognized the step he was sitting on. She placed the other photos back in the box and stood up, holding the photo of the man. She went out of the shack and walked a few yards, turning back. There it was. The old man was sitting on the steps of the shack. There wasn't much visible in the photo but Sitka could make out the door frame and the vertical wood slats that made up the walls of the structure. He'd been there. Why this was a surprise to Sitka, she wasn't sure. However, it made her feel closer to him. Less alone. Once, he was out there, too. Hidden in the woods just like her.

Was the baby his? Was he the younger man with the lady in the photo in front of the car? Was the shack his home? Sitka clutched the photo and went back inside. She glanced around, trying to imagine someone living there. It was small, but it was possible if they didn't have much. In that corner could've fit a cot, over there a small dresser. The counters made her think it was a workshop. Even so, one person could've lived *and* worked in the space. What about the lady and the baby?

Hunger drew Sitka away from her musings. No matter how busy she attempted to keep her brain, her body said otherwise. She needed to eat if she was going to be able to sleep. She placed the photo back in the box and noticed a painting crammed at the bottom. It was on an old piece of tin, showing a deer watching from the woodline. Sitka ran her fingers over the surface, feeling the places where the paint was laid on thicker. It was beautiful, capturing the delicacy of the moment. It reminded her of the deer which lead her back to the shack that day. She placed it on the counter, so she could see it from where she lay at night. This made the space seem more personal.

She drew out the photos again and sifted through them, realizing for the first time the photos had something in common. In all the photos, the people were black. This was oddly comforting. While she was half black, it was part of her life she never connected to. Her father wasn't around and everyone else was white. She'd been raised around love and never felt like she didn't belong, however, she always wondered. What was her father like? Did he have brothers and sisters? When she'd asked, her mother always told Sitka what she could, but admitted she didn't know much about his life before they met. They hadn't known each other long, he'd moved on before Sitka was born. They hadn't shared a lot of details about their previous lives with each other.

Both seemed happy to stay in the present.

Her mother would always say with a smile and shrug, "He was a rolling stone that gathered no moss."

Sitka didn't know what that meant but her mother seemed so sure, she never asked further. Sometimes she'd lay in bed at night and imagine him showing up at the door one day in his woven poncho, smiling ear to ear. He'd scoop her up and place her high on his shoulders as he took her around town. She'd cling on to his head, trying to not cover his eyes and everyone would smile as they strolled by. It was one of her favorite make-believe scenarios when she was little. As she got older, the scene would still play out but they'd walk hand in hand, instead.

By evening, Sitka could no longer ignore her stomach's cries for food and an attempt at eating the rhubarb or berries sent her straight to the woods with diarrhea. She eyed the mushrooms and said a little prayer. Please let them not be poisonous, or if they were, not the kind that would leave her writhing in pain on the floor until she died.

She nibbled one and waited. It tasted bitter and earthy. After she didn't keel over dead, she ate the rest, figuring if they were going to kill her, a lot would kill her just as much as a little would. As soon as her stomach found peace in the sustenance, she took the baby blanket and bedded down, watching the light disappear from the shack through the window. She dozed off, remembering how sometimes her mother would sing lullabies to her before bed. Sitka smiled as sleep took over.

Sometime in the night, Sitka was woken by a long, shrill wail outside. She sat up straight, straining to hear what it was. The moonlight cast a soft glow around the space and she heard the sound again, this time farther away. Whatever it was, was moving on. She drew the blanket tighter around her arms and shuddered. She heard something shift near her and slowly moved her eyes toward the sound.

The light was playing tricks on her eyes. She thought she saw the outline of a man sitting across the floor from her. She slammed her eyes shut, reminding herself how her toys and coat would sometimes look like creatures in the night, but when the sun rose, they adjusted back to their inanimate selves. She held her breath and opened one eye just a tiny slit, still seeing the shadow man in the corner. When he cleared his throat, she screamed so loud, she was sure the walls shook.

"Now, now. No reason for all that. Was just going to tell you that sound you heard was only a bird."

His voice was raspy and a little phlegmy. A bird? That was now the least of Sitka's concerns. She closed her eyes again, positive she was dreaming. Attempting to drag herself through the gauzy layers of sleep to the surface, she soon knew she wasn't asleep. Or if she was, it was like no sleep she'd ever experienced. The shack fell silent and she kept her eyes closed until she knew for sure the man was gone. She pulled the blanket up to eye level, covering her face as she peered over the top. He wasn't there. She sighed and dropped the blanket.

A match lit across the space, making Sitka jerk toward the sound. The man was now standing in the corner by the counter, gazing out the window in the moonlight.

He turned toward her, a smile playing on his lips. "You about done hollerin' for now?"

Sitka sat frozen. She nodded at her make-believe apparition. He nodded back, then lit a hand-rolled cigarette.

He shook out the match, just his cigarette leaving a glow by the window. He touched the painting of the deer. "You found my painting, I see. That was from this here window."

This couldn't be happening. Sitka knew she wasn't dreaming, but the man talking to her and standing only feet from her was the man from the old photo. She knew she could either sit there, staring at him, or commit to the delusion. Someone needed to make the first move.

"Who are you?" she squeaked out.

He turned to her, his smile catching the light from the moon. He had a few teeth missing, but his face in the window crinkled with the motion. "Well, I suppose you can call me Davis."

Davis. Sitka let the name sink into her brain. Boogeymen didn't have names like Davis. Did they? She tried to make out more of what he looked like but it was too dim. "I'm Sitka. My family calls me Sitty."

"Hi there, Sitty. Nice to meet you. So, why am I here?"

Sitka didn't move or speak. How was she supposed to know why this apparition showed up? A ghost? He had to be, he was an elderly man in the photo and the photo was old. He didn't look any older than the photo, but then again, it was too dark to really make anything out.

Sitka frowned. "I don't understand. Why are you asking me?"

Davis laughed softly and took a long drag of his cigarette, the end burning brightly. "Because, little one, *you* brought me here."

Chapter Eleven

*T*he sun woke Sitka and she sat up, clearing the cobwebs from her brain. She'd dreamed about the old man from the picture. Davis, he'd said his name was. Making sure it was a dream, she stood up and walked over to where he'd been standing, smoking. There was no ash from the cigarette and the dust was untouched. Then again, did ghosts leave behind clues? Sitka put everything back into the hole under the trap door and fastened it tight. She had enough to worry about without conjuring up some old guy. She needed to find food. She wouldn't risk the Zip Mart again, since the van people were searching for her. She'd try to gather berries and whatever else she could find. There were minnows in the creek but she didn't know how she could kill and cook them. She certainly wasn't going to swallow them whole.

Since she'd left the corks for the bottles behind, Sitka had no way to mark her trail and couldn't risk getting lost again. She considered if there'd been anything in the hole which might help. Nothing came to mind and she stared up at the colorful bottles. How many could she carry? If she broke them, she could leave shards of glass. Considering this made her feel bad, maybe they'd meant something to Davis.

"Davis. Davis?" she muttered. "Stop being stupid, Sitty. Ghosts aren't real. Otherwise, your mama would've come by now to see you."

She set her mind to breaking some of the bottles and took the plainest ones, not being able to bring herself to break the blue and green ones. She took them outside and dashed them against stones until she had a pile of small, but sharp, pebble-sized pieces. She carefully placed them in the baby blanket, so she wouldn't cut herself. Heading out, she made sure to drop a piece of glass where the sun might catch it to find them easier later. She followed a deer path and snapped off branches as she went.

Sitka wandered for a bit when she noticed something out of the ordinary. What appeared like weathered headstones, like the ones from the cemetery behind her aunt's house, stuck up out of the weeds. It didn't make sense because there was no marked cemetery. Just some random stones. She set down the baby blanket and made her way toward one of the larger ones, tripping on a line of rocks. She peered down and could make out a border of the rocks. It *had* been a cemetery. Out in the middle of the woods?

As she walked through the area, she stumbled upon more headstones and realized the vegetation had overtaken whatever semblance of organization there'd once been. She cleared a few of the stones and read them. The latest date she could find was from the 1950s. Her eye caught one and she sucked in her breath at the coincidence. Maybe the name was more common than she'd realized. She went over and pulled grass and weeds away.

Davis Butler
B. August 22, 1897
D. August 29, 1959

What were the odds? The age could be right. Sitka rubbed her fingers against the poorly carved stone and stood up. A rustling from behind startled her and she jerked around. To her surprise, Davis was leaning against a tree watching her. A ghost in the middle of the day, hanging around like any living man. How could there be such a thing? It didn't seem right. Sitka glanced back at the headstone, feeling like she'd been caught with her hand in the cookie jar.

"I'm sorry, I didn't mean to," she sputtered.

Davis laughed and shook his head. "Didn't mean to what? Look at my grave? There's no crime in that. We all die one day."

"So, it is you? Buried there? You're Davis Butler?"

"One and the same."

"Oh. Why out here? It seems, I don't know... I guess, bad that you're buried out here in the middle of nowhere in a bunch of weeds and no one cares." Sitka wasn't trying to seem disrespectful but she couldn't understand why this cemetery was in such disarray.

"No one cared when I was alive out in the middle of nowhere, so why would they now that I'm dead?" Davis reasoned, unperturbed that his final resting place was absorbed by the forest. He walked over and touched the top of the stone. "At least someone gave me this to mark my resting place. You know how many people are buried in the ground right under your feet, and you don't even know it?"

Sitka took an involuntary step back away from him. She stared down at her feet and considered the possibility. How many bodies were under there?

She thought about the body she saw dumped in the woods and shuddered. "I saw someone leave a body in the woods about a week, or so, ago."

Davis eyed her and lit a cigarette. "That so? Did you get a look at 'em?"

"The body?" Sitka asked.

"Well, I meant the person leaving the body, but I suppose either could be true."

"No. I ran. I saw their van, though. It's how I ended up at your..." Shack? Home?

"My cabin," Davis finished for her.

"Did you live there?"

"I did."

"Was the lady in the picture your wife? Did you have a baby?" Sitka tried to stop herself from asking so many questions, but if she was going to talk to a ghost, she wanted to know everything.

Davis's face turned somber and he chewed the end of his cigarette. "She was and we did."

"Did you all live in the sh- uh, the cabin together?"

"No, ma'am. That was my solitary confinement after... We had a home. Our daughter was Letty, her mother Ruth. They both died young."

Sitka knew she was being nosy and stopped. They died? Well of course they did, that was a long time ago. He was a ghost, after all. "My mother died, too."

"Did she? I'm sorry to hear that, little one. That why you're all alone out here?"

"I guess. I mean, I live with my aunt and cousin, now," she explained.

Davis watched her for a moment, then turned as if he was going to walk away. "It's hardest on those left behind. My daughter Letty died when she was about your age. Ruptured spleen. The hospital near our home wouldn't take her in. We begged them, but they told us we needed to go to a negro hospital. She died there... sepsis. Ruth was so distraught, she stopped eating. I tried forcing her but she'd throw up anything she choked down. After a few months, she was found floating face down in a pond. She may have stumbled in there and was too weak to get out, or didn't even try. Either way, within four months I lost everyone I loved."

"That's horrible," Sitka mumbled. "My mother had cancer. It was just her and me."

Davis faced her and cocked his head, his face serious. "There's a lot of ways people die, but only one way for the living to keep going on."

"How?"

"Breath by breath."

Here she was in the middle of an unmarked cemetery, talking to a ghost, and for the first time since her mother died, Sitka felt understood.

"I'm sorry, Davis. About your wife and daughter. I really am. That's so sad. I bet they were pretty. I... I need to go.

I have to find some food before it gets too late and I can't find my way back."

Davis motioned for her to follow him. "I may be able to help you there. Come with me."

He wandered into the woods, not marking his way and Sitka was scared she'd get lost again. He could just evaporate, abandoning her in the middle of nowhere. He turned back and waved at her again. "I won't leave you behind."

Sitka grabbed the baby blanket, and they meandered through the woods a ways when they came upon a clearing and a house. Sitka shook her head and backed away, waving her hand in front of her. "I can't go up there. Bad people are looking for me because I saw them dump the body. They'll kill me. They might live there."

Davis shifted his weight and pointed toward the side of the house. "The root cellar. They keep jars of canned food down there. A lot of places still do. Not as many as used to, but some. Sneak on in there and grab a couple of jars, they won't notice a little missing."

Sitka was afraid, but her hunger was stronger. She snuck around the side of the house and pried open the cellar door. A few steps led down into the cool darkness. As Davis said, there were shelves with jars of various-shaped foods. Sitka could make out some words and grabbed one that said peaches and one that read pickled eggs. She couldn't carry anything else and thought those would be the best choices for now.

Davis was sitting on a rock, smoking a cigarette when she came up and smiled. "See, now, there are ways to get food. You can't stay forever at the cabin though, girl. Your aunt must be worried sick. I imagine they're out searching for you."

"I don't know what to do. I don't know who the people were who dumped the body and I know they're looking for me. I saw their van at the store. They were asking about me. They could've told everyone to be on the lookout for me. I don't know who I can trust and I don't know the right way back home."

"That so?" Davis twirled the end of the cigarette with his tongue on his lips and tapped his chin. "Someone good has to be searching for you, too. You just have to find them before the other people find you, I reckon."

He stood up and began walking back into the woods. Sitka followed, trying to balance the two jars and the baby blanket. She didn't suppose Davis could help her carry anything since he was a ghost. The thought made her chuckle, picturing the jar of peaches passing right through his hands, shattering on the ground.

They walked for so long, Sitka was for sure they were lost and panic began to set in. What if Davis wasn't real? Or, well... more real than a ghost could be. What if she was hallucinating and getting herself even more lost? Just as she was about to doubt any of it was happening, the cabin came into view between the trees. Relieved, she practically ran the rest of the way, almost dropping the jars of food on the ground in the process.

"Slow down there, girl. Don't want to lose your supper," Davis chided.

Sitka repositioned the jars, then set them on the steps. She turned to face Davis, tipping her head. "Thank you. For showing me the cellar and telling me about your family. Are you, like, a ghost?"

Davis considered the question as he stared up at the clouds. "I'm Davis. Davis here, Davis there. Not sure what that means, to be honest."

"What about your family? Are they there with you, now? Like, are you a family in-" Sitka stopped herself, not sure what else to say. In what? Heaven? She wasn't sure that was actually even a thing. The sky? The stars?

"No. When I died, there wasn't a group of my loved ones waiting for me at the end of a bright tunnel. Only a place like this, maybe even this place. I don't know. Time is strange. It feels like I just died and yet seems like hundreds of years have passed. However, no Ruth and no Letty. I haven't seen them since *they* died."

Sitka thought she'd cry. If there was no Letty and no Ruth, did that mean when she died, there'd be no Mama waiting on her? The thought was too much to bear. "Davis, where are they?"

Davis sighed, then shrugged. "Sitty, where are any of us? All I know, is they're not here... but I am."

Chapter Twelve

T he next couple of days, it poured like it can only do in the south. The sky lit up angrily and the earth around the cabin shook. Sitka was grateful for the peaches and eggs, finding her stomach settling back into a peaceful state. She didn't see Davis during that time but let her mind wander over their conversation. His life has been disrupted like hers, however, it left him completely alone. That made her sad and she wondered how many years he'd lived in this one-room cabin in solitude. His daughter died when she was around Sitka's age and his wife a few months later. So, he'd been alone for decades, she figured. She hoped to see him again as she had so many questions.

On the morning after two solid days of rain, the skies let up, allowing bits of sun to peak out from behind the clouds. The trees still dripped with the heaviness of too much water, creating a mist and light shower through the intermittent rays of sun. Sitka watched from the window, finding the array absolutely beautiful. As she was peering out of the window, movement in the brush caught her eye. Through the dripping wet leaves, a deer appeared, flicking its tail. It paused and stared at the cabin before moving on. Behind it, followed a row of other deer in all different sizes. A family.

Sitka watched in wonder, imagining what it would be like to follow them. Where would they go, would they accept her? Her mind drifted back to a rainy day in New York. Her mother was feeling cooped up in the apartment and put Stevie Wonder on the record player. She was dancing around the living room, her long blond hair waving behind her like a shimmering curtain.

"Come here, Sitty, and dance with your mother," she encouraged.

Sitka giggled and ran over, clasping her mother's open hands and they swayed to the music. Her mother spun her around and dipped her, causing Sitka to erupt into a fit of snorts. When the song ended, Sitka's mother flopped back on the couch and pulled Sitka down beside her, wrapping her in her arms.

"You're everything I ever wanted," she murmured into Sitka's hair. "I'm glad you're mine."

"I'm glad you're my mama," Sitka agreed. Her mother wasn't like other mothers. She was like a big sister, talking to Sitka about everything and including her in whatever she was doing. Sitka gazed at her arm, resting on top of her mother's. Flesh and blood, yet so different. She peered up into her mother's green eyes and thought about her father. What he was like. Was he like her?

"What was his name?"

"Who, honey?" her mother asked, nibbling the tips of Sitka's fingers.

"My father. Can you tell me a little more about him?" Sitka replied.

"Well, let's see. His name was Dug. Everyone called him Dug the Rug. Not sure if Dug was a nickname, but that's how we all knew him. I never asked otherwise. He was cool as a cucumber. I never saw him angry or heard him raise his voice. He could sing, too, boy could he sing. He used to serenade me." Sitka's mother giggled like a schoolgirl. "I was enamored from the moment we met."

"Why didn't you get married?"

"Oh, honey, neither one of us believed in that. We just wanted to experience each other. We were only together a few months before I found out you were on your way."

Sitka had heard the story many times before but this is where it always left her wanting more answers. "Why didn't he want me?"

Her mother turned to meet her eyes. "Not everyone is ready to be a parent, Sitty. I knew since I was a little girl, I wanted to be a mother. So, I was elated when I found out. My own little doll to carry around. Dug wasn't upset, he just wasn't ready to be a father."

"Do you think he's ready, now?" Sitka asked with the innocence of a child.

"I don't know, hon. Dug was always on the move. Always running. He was dodging the draft, his number had come up."

Sitka had no idea what any of that meant, but she imagined the man in the picture with the poncho, ducking behind trees and peering out. Like in a cartoon. It made her laugh. "Why was he dodging giraffes?"

At this, Sitka's mother laughed so hard, tears came out of her eyes. She squeezed Sitka and touched her cheek. "You little goon. Not giraffes like the animal. The draft. It's where they make young men, boys really, take guns and fight other boys. It's horrible."

It sounded horrible. Sitka saw pictures of boys in her head, pointing guns at each other on the playground. "How old was he?"

"About the same as most of them. When I met him he was nineteen. He was one of the first to be drafted. When he left, he was heading on to Canada, so they couldn't find him. Couldn't make him kill other boys. But he stuck around for me, at least for a bit."

At the time, nineteen didn't mean much to Sitka but now, knowing Tommy wasn't much younger than that, she saw her father differently. He was a teenager. A big brother. Bringing these memories into the current day, made her see things differently. Her mother had always supported Dug's decision to go, but now Sitka understand things more clearly. He was hiding like she was... from something very bad.

Sitka focused back on the disappearing deer and considered where her father was right now. She knew where Canada was on the map and that sometimes her mother's friend, Aunt Betsy, would go there and bring back maple leaf-shaped candies. It was a far-off land. Inaccessible to a child like her.

Sitka turned and faced the inside of the cabin. She imagined Davis living there for years and considered if he felt like he was hiding from something bad, as well. Sitka didn't want to hide anymore. She wanted to go home. Back to Aunt Leigh's. Back to having a room next to Tommy's. She wondered if they were still looking for her. If they thought she'd been kidnapped. If they'd put up flyers with her picture around town, the killer would see them and know where she lived.

Would she ever be safe?

As the day wore on, Sitka began to feel claustrophobic in the space and pushed the door open, letting the muggy air in. A light breeze was moving through the leaves but the air was still dense. She gathered her bottles for water and headed to the creek. The water on the leaves dripped down her legs as she moved down the path and the ground squished beneath her feet. The deer were nowhere to be seen, yet she felt they were still watching her.

She knelt at the creek as she filled the bottles and listened to hear if she could make out any road sounds. It was quiet except for the sound of the water burbling over rocks. It was as if she existed alone in the world. She wondered if her mother was seeing her move around the Earth. She tried to imagine where her mother was but could only picture a huge white room, a void really, with her mother curled up in the fetal position in the middle of it. The thought scared her. Maybe her mother was trapped in nowhere. Other kids in school had talked about Heaven, but her mother always dismissed it with a wave of her hand.

"No one really knows, but I sincerely doubt some big, bearded, white guy is staring down at us," she'd say.

Her take was about the same on Santa Claus. Why lie about some "old white dude" handing out presents while kids were starving? Her beliefs on everything were pretty matter-of-fact, but then sometimes she'd talk about wood sprites and fairies. Sitka was unsure about the world beyond what she could see, but always considered there might be more. She hoped her mother's doubt about Heaven didn't prevent her from being somewhere beautiful.

Sitka moved back toward the cabin when something shifting in the trees stopped her in her tracks. She quickly ducked down behind some brush and watched. A few men, their faces red and sweaty, were carrying guns as they came through. They hunched down like they were sneaking, talking low to one another. They were carrying packs and too much gear. Even though they were whispering and acting like they were stealthy, their movements were clumsy and apparent.

"I think they went this way, we're right on their tail," one said.

"A whole bunch of them it looks like, see the droppings?" asked another.

The men were following the deer along the trail. Sitka held her breath, hoping they wouldn't spot her. They were too focused on the path ahead to notice the young girl crouched just yards away from them. The men paused to take swigs from their canteens and one peered around, his eyes glazing over the spot where Sitka hid. He wiped sweat off his face with a dirty handkerchief.

"You hear about that missing girl?"

"The little black girl they had in the paper? How long has she been gone? A couple of weeks, now?"

"About. What do you suppose happened to her?"

"Who knows? Those people don't watch their kids."

Sitka knew they were talking about her, and wondered what they meant by *those people*. Aunt Leigh? Did they know her aunt? Why would they think Aunt Leigh wouldn't watch her? She crouched lower, trying to make herself invisible.

"Might find her body out in these here woods today, I reckon," one said, then snickered. "Don't even know if I'd tell anyone. Who needs all the fuss? Maybe she ran off with a boy or something."

"She was like eleven or twelve," another replied.

"Yeah, and your point?" came the sarcastic response.

Laughter erupted from the small group and they continued on. Sitka didn't know why, but their conversation made her feel dirty. Like when Glenn stared at her. She shuddered and waited for them to disappear into the denseness of the trees before she headed back to the cabin. Just as she made it to the door, the sound of a gunshot shook the air around her and she could hear the men whooping and hollering in the distance. They'd found the deer.

She hustled inside and closed the door, her heart racing in her chest. To the men, taking a life was just a game, something to do on a day off. Finding her body in the woods wouldn't have even been a minor inconvenience to them. She belonged to *those people*. Not even worth telling anyone about. A sick story they'd share between them.

"Remember that time we found that girl's body when we were hunting? Serves her right." Followed by laughter and nasty comments.

A little while later, she could hear the men moving back through the area. They were talking loudly and boasting about their "kill." Their words were slurred and they were thrashing through the underbrush without a care. Sitka watched from a corner of the window and could see their movement in the distant trees. *Please keep going*, she thought to herself. She couldn't make them out completely but could see they were carrying the body of a dead deer between them. Her stomach recoiled in disgust.

They were just about through the area when one of the men stopped to relieve himself. He stumbled over in the direction of the cabin and spread his legs while he closed his eyes in the process. He was zipping back up his pants when the glint of the cabin window caught his eye. He squinted toward it, trying to make out what he was looking at.

All of a sudden, his eyebrows shot up and he turned to his buddies, grinning. He waved at them to get their attention and pointed to what seemed to Sitka as right at her.

"Look over here, boys. An old, abandoned shack. You want to check it out and have a beer, or two, while we catch our breath?"

Chapter Thirteen

*S*itka panicked, recognizing she was cornered in the shack. If she tried to leave, they'd spot her. There was nowhere to hide in the small space. Tightness squeezed her chest, her instinct telling her she was most definitely in danger. What if they were the ones who dumped the body? What if they found her alone and wanted to harm her? No matter what, she was trapped like the deer they shot.

She could hear them draw closer and saw the handle of the door jiggle as they tried to open it. The moisture from the air was causing it to stick, thankfully, and she thought they might give up and move on. However, drunk men in a group often have other ideas.

"Just kick it in, Jim!" one of the men yelled, followed by raucous, drunken laughter from the group.

"Not like anyone will give a shit!" another replied.

A heavy thud fell against the door and Sitka knew that's precisely what they were going to do. Tears pricked her eyes, waiting for the inevitable. At that moment, another thud sounded from behind her and she glanced to see where it was coming from. It sounded like they were trying to come in through the floor. She caught a scream in her throat and gripped her arms around her.

At that instant, the door in the floor banged open, causing her to jump in her skin. She shifted her eyes toward it, fully expecting the men to pop out of the floor and grab her. Instead, a wrinkled, mocha hand reached out of the space and waved her over.

"Come on, little one, before they tear this place down," Davis's voice beckoned from the opening. Sitka darted over and peered in. What had once been a small space containing only mementos, now contained Davis. From what it looked like, not just him. Seeing past his shadowy form, Sitka could see what looked to be a tunnel of some kind.

She heard the door to the outside begin to crack and she knew one more kick would splinter the door open. She grabbed Davis's hand and felt him tugging her into the opening. She wasn't sure if there was a ladder or if she'd tumble head over heels into the tunnel. However, as she was drawn in, it was as if the earth formed around her, carrying her down. Davis reached up and slammed the trapdoor shut just as the men busted into the shack. Sitka held her breath, waiting for the men to fling open the door and snatch her out.

Even if they had, all they would've found when the door opened was a small space containing a few mementos. No Sitka, no Davis, no tunnel. That didn't exist in their world.

Davis held her hand tightly and pulled her along. What should've been a straight drop down from where Sitka came from, altered into a gradual path. Instead of climbing down, she was walking almost flat. It was too dark to see much, but she felt like she was brushing against tree roots as they moved. Were they under the earth, under the trees? Davis didn't speak but headed on with purpose.

"Davis, where are we?"

He squeezed her hand but didn't speak at first. After a few minutes of traveling, he paused and turned to her. She could hardly make out his shadow but a glint caught his eye. He shook his head, waving his hand around him.

"That's no easy question to answer. Where isn't just a place, you see?"

Sitka didn't. Where *was* a place. She'd been in the cabin, now she was somewhere else. "I don't understand. Was there a secret escape tunnel under the cabin?"

Davis laughed. "I guess you can say that, but not like you're thinking. I didn't make it. No man did. At least as far as I know."

"What do you mean? That doesn't make sense." Sitka was thoroughly confused, now.

"Well, so there *is* a tunnel under the cabin, but that tunnel runs lots of places. It exists everywhere and nowhere."

Sitka was getting frustrated with the riddles and stomped her foot. "Stop talking to me like that, Davis. Where *are* we? I'm scared."

"Now, there's no reason to be worried. You're safe. We're in a tunnel under the earth of sorts. But not, too. This tunnel isn't just under the earth where you were. This tunnel is never and always. Something and nothing. Here and there. It is and it isn't."

Great, more riddles.

"Can it get me home? Back to Aunt Leigh's?"

"I suppose it can, but only if you're meant to go back at this time. Otherwise, you could end up somewhere else. I can't explain it, but let's move on and I'll show you something." Davis gave her hand a tug and she followed, unsure of anything he was saying.

As they walked on, the tunnel widened and became brighter. Sitka could see the walls were turning from dirt to stone and forming into more of a structure. Ahead she could see a small beacon of light that became bigger as they neared it. Once they were in sight of the source of the light, Sitka could make out the shape of a door. Not the cabin door, or any door she recognized. The windows in the door were the source of the light and she squinted to see if she could make out what was beyond it.

A few yards from the opening, Davis stopped and faced her, his eyes lined with concern. Sitka watched him, noticing something was different about him. She couldn't quite put her finger on it, but it made her feel funny in her gut. Not bad, but strange.

He motioned his hand to the door, shaking his head. "I probably shouldn't have brought you here, however, I could tell those men were up to no good. I had no choice. There are some things, Sitka, we only know after we die. Some things we aren't meant to know when we are alive on Earth. Knowing this now can cause a split in our souls."

Sitka frowned, trying to understand what his words meant. Split in their souls? What did that even mean? "What's on the other side?"

Davis glanced at the door, then back at her. "What's beyond this side? Everything. Everywhere. You have to listen to me. What I'm about to show you won't make sense, yet it will in time. Trust me, and stay close. I'll get you home as soon as I can, but for now, we're here. We can't change that. You need to heed everything I say to stay safe, you hear?"

Sitka nodded. What choice did she have? "I understand. But where are we?"

Davis rubbed his face and thought. "We are here. But here isn't there, or at least the there you know. I could say *when* are we but that doesn't sum it up, either. There are many worlds within one world, many planes of existence. When we are alive in our bodies, we only know the one. When we're set free, we can travel beyond that. I guess some people call it Heaven and to a degree that may be right. Not like they yell and sing about in churches, though. Bless my granny, she'd slap me upside the head for that, but it's true. Time and space as we know it does and doesn't exist here."

Here? Sitka took a step away from Davis and gazed at the door. Here, as in the afterlife? Her chest fluttered with fear and she wanted to run back the way they came. Her eyes darted behind them and she realized the tunnel had closed in. There was no back. Only the door.

"Am I dead?" her voice squeaked out.

David eyed her, considering how to answer. "No, not in the way you're thinking. Not like when I died. You're just on a trip to a different place, think of it that way."

"A different place? Can I go home?"

"I think so."

"You think so?" Sitka blurted out. "You don't know?"

Davis chewed his lip and nodded. "Not a hundred percent, but I think so. To be honest, I never brought anyone here before."

Sitka fought the panic forming in her chest and dug her fingers into her arms. "Where is here?"

"Here is when."

"Huh?"

Davis pointed at the door. "In the living world, a door leads to another space and this isn't so different. It's just that the space is not linear."

Linear? Sitka didn't know that word. She shook her head at Davis, confused. Davis tipped his head, furrowing his brow as he considered the best way to explain what he meant in a way she'd understand.

He used his finger to draw an imaginary horizontal line in the air. "Linear, like a straight line. A clear path from here to there. What we're doing is more like this." He moved his finger to point at his chest, then acted like he was pulling it out of his ear. "We go one direction and come out a completely different one."

"So, like magic?" Sitka asked, thinking of one of her mother's friends who showed her a quarter in his hand, before pulling it from behind her ear.

"Like magic... like reality. Things are different than you've ever been shown, Sitka. There are more places and spaces to explore than you can go by plane or car. To best explain, think of yourself as a time traveler."

Sitka couldn't wrap her brain around what he was saying. Time travel wasn't real, it was the stuff of stories and make-believe. She shook her head. "That's not real."

Davis chuckled. "Well, you're right there. Not in the way we're told. See, the world you live in today and the world I lived in before I died, exist in the same time and space. You just can't see it. So, no, you don't hop in a time machine and end up in a different time, because it's happening at the same time. The vehicle is inside you, your body is the prison."

"I don't understand." Sitka didn't. The more she thought about it, the less sense it made.

Davis took her hand and walked toward the door. "The best way to explain it is to show you."

He pushed the door open as if he was walking into a room and drew Sitka with him. The light was blinding and Sitka covered her eyes with her free hand as they adjusted from the dark. The door behind them closed and she found they were standing on a busy street. As her eyes relaxed from the light and she was able to see, she took a step back. It was a street in a town. Wilmington. She recognized some of the buildings.

What she didn't recognize was everything else. There were fewer buildings than she remembered. What struck her most was none of the cars looked the same from what she saw every day. They looked like the cars from the picture of Davis and his wife when he was younger. Like cars she had seen in the old movies her mother loved so much. The people were dressed differently, as well. It looked like a costume party. Nobody was in shorts or t-shirts. The women wore dresses and the men all looked like they were dressed for church. This world was not her world, or at least not her time. That's what Davis had meant about her being a time traveler. It was like she'd stepped into the photos in the wooden box.

Sitka glanced at Davis for an explanation of what she was seeing and gasped. The thing she'd sensed about him in the dark tunnel, the difference in him she couldn't quite place then, became very apparent in the light of day on the street. Davis smiled down at her, his teeth a row of perfect white pearls. His eyes clear and bright. His skin with barely a wrinkle to mark his expressions. His hair was full and smooth, pressed neatly against his head.

Davis was young again.

Chapter Fourteen

*D*avis grinned at her, cocking his head. "Yes, ma'am. This is who I use to be before time and life took it out of me. Quite dapper, wasn't I?"

Dapper didn't even come close. Davis was smooth as silk. From the top of his coiffed head to the tips of his shiny leather shoes, he was a sight. As if he'd stepped off a movie screen. Sitka suddenly felt underdressed and dirty, being surrounded by such fancy cars and everyone dressed to the nines. A woman walked by and scowled at her, then glared at Davis. Sitka took a step back, embarrassed, not knowing why.

"Where are we, Davis? Why is that woman mad at us?" she asked, her voice squeaking in the middle.

Davis ducked his head and grasped her hand. "We better go before we cause any issues. I think her clothes would fit you. Let's get moving."

"Where? Whose clothes? What's happening?"

"Time for that later, honeybee. We need to beat feet."

Davis led her through a series of alleys, knowing exactly where he was going. It seemed like they walked for miles, eventually leaving the city streets and ending up in a residential neighborhood. Davis stopped in front of a small gray house with white shutters and a flower-lined sidewalk. He glanced around, then nodded.

"Alright, no one is home, so we can go in."

"You want to break into someone's home?" Sitka asked, aghast.

"Not someone's. Mine. I'll explain more later. Let's get you inside and cleaned up, so you don't draw any more attention. Right now, you stick out like a sore thumb."

Her draw attention? Sitka glanced down and recognized she probably did, unkempt and unbathed. Not only was she dirty, she wasn't dressed like everyone else. Davis went around the side of the house and checked a door, which was open. He waved her over and they slipped inside. The home smelled like clean. Like fresh soap and flowers. They wandered through the house which was tidy and quiet. Davis checked rooms as they went, making sure they were alone.

"You live here?" Sitka asked, admiring how every item in the home seemed to have a place and was set just so. Whoever decorated the home paid attention to every little detail and took pride in the space.

"I do. Or I did. Part of me still does. As I was saying, all time exists at the same time, just on a different shifting plane. On *multiple* shifting planes."

That made no sense to Sitka, but she couldn't deny she wasn't in her own time. "Are you here, too? Like can you run into yourself?"

Davis rubbed his chin and thought. "No, you can't do that. I am still here in my own time, though. Me and my family. This was before she died... my little girl."

"Oh. So, you can come and see her whenever you want? Can you save her?"

"No, not that either. See, I can be here but I can't cross paths with anyone I knew then... because I'm already here. Say I was to try, or by accident, I'd get spit back out of this time into another time. I have to be very careful," Davis explained.

"Spit back? Like to my time?"

"Your time, any random time. Just not this time. I can't exist when I exist if that makes sense."

It didn't. Sitka frowned. "If your little girl was here, you couldn't be? Why? That's sad."

Davis chuckled. "You have no idea. Yes, if she walked through that door, I'd just disappear and show up somewhere else. Some *time* else. That's why we need to be very aware of our surroundings. I'd hate to have you stuck here, then I get shot off to somewhere else."

"What would happen to me, if you did?" Sitka was scared by the possibility.

"Honeybee, I have no idea. I never brought anyone living with me. I wasn't sure you'd even be able to walk through that door, to be honest."

"Why did you bring me, then?"

Davis's eyes got dark and he shook his head. "One of the 'gifts' I guess you could call it, is that I can see, or sense, things that are about to happen. Those men were up to no good. They were drunk and they don't like people like us. They would've hurt you. I brought you here to get you out of there. I couldn't fight them, you see? I'm not really there when I'm there."

Sitka felt a chill up her back. What would those men have done to her? She didn't want to know. "People like us?"

"Sitty, come on, now. You know white people don't care for black people."

"My mother was white."

"Maybe some white people in your time are different, but it's still out there. The hate. You need to be careful. Just because your mama was white doesn't mean people don't see you as black. 'Cause they do. They don't see you as a little white girl, or even a partially white girl. If you have a drop of black blood, you're black," Davis answered, not hiding the firmness in his words.

"Is that why that woman glared at us on the street?" Sitka asked, the reality dawning on her.

"Partly. We were where we didn't 'belong'. No matter how educated or finely dressed we are, there will always be those who see us as dirty or unwelcome." Davis eyed her, then laughed softly. "Well, in your case... we do need to get you cleaned up. Here, let me get you some clothes and run you a bath. Wait here and I'll get things ready. If you're hungry, there are probably some biscuits in the icebox."

He ducked down the hall and Sitka peered around the kitchen. Some of her mother's farm friends didn't like modern appliances, so they used an icebox and an old stove. She spied those in Davis's home, though they looked brand spanking new, as opposed to the old ones in the farm kitchen. She opened the icebox and there was a plate of biscuits covered with a tea towel. She slipped one out and took a bite, marveling at the delicate buttery layers. If she didn't stop herself, she'd eat the whole plate of them.

Davis called to her from the bathroom, so she finished the biscuit and wandered back toward the sound of his voice. He had a fresh dress and shoes laid out for her and pointed to the tub. "There's soap and a cloth there. Get washed up and put on these clothes. They should fit. Letty was younger than you but thicker. You're a skinny thing. I picked one that ties in the back, so we can fasten it to fit you. Be quick, though. Letty is at school and my wife and I are at work, but you never know who might pop in that I know. They pop in, and I pop out."

Sitka nodded, terrified by the thought. He pops out and who knows what would happen to her. Would she get stuck in...? "Davis where are we? Or when are we?"

"We are in Wilmington. 1929."

1929? Fifty years ago? Sitka began to feel faint and clutched the sink as the room spun around her. Davis grasped her arm and held her up as she regained her senses. She met his eyes. "Why?"

"I don't know how it all works. I don't control it. I can be sent anywhere, more or less, but most times it picks me. I suppose it felt we needed to come to this time."

"So, is there no Heaven? We don't join our family?" Sitka asked, her heart clenching with the thought she'd never see her mother again.

"Honeybee, don't think like that. I think some people do. I believe others have work to do before they can join their family. I think my wife and Letty went on to a different place. Heaven of sorts. I've been bouncing around different timelines for a long time. Since I died."

"Oh. That's terrible. You lost them when you were alive, then you died and you still didn't have them? You can't see them here? That's just not right. Why?"

"As I said, I don't know. I suppose I still had work to do. Now, climb on in and get yourself bathed. I'll keep an eye out on the front door to make sure no one comes around. Holler when you're done and we'll clean everything up. I don't want Ruth coming home seeing the bathroom a mess, thinking we had the strangest burglars. I'll tell you more about this time and place after. I think we'll need to tidy up your hair, as well. Girls here don't wear their hair all wild like that," Davis said, pointing at the mass of hair around Sitka's face. She touched her hair, which her mother always left free.

He shut the door behind him as he left and Sitka climbed in the tub, sighing with pleasure at the warm water. She scrubbed every ounce of herself. By the time she was done washing her hair, the tub water was brown and she pulled the plug, rinsing herself with fresh, clean water. She stepped out and dried off, slipping the dress on over her head. It was loose around the middle, so she fastened the tie with a bow, cinching it around her waist. She bent over and washed her own clothes with soap and water in the tub and rung them out. Davis knocked lightly on the door.

"Sitty, are you done?"

"I am, you can come in."

Davis came in and peered at the tub "Woowhee, you washed about three layers of dirt off of you. Let me get a look at you."

Sitka smiled bashfully and did a little curtsey. Sadness passed over Davis's face as he looked at his daughter's dress.

"I'm happy it fit. My Letty, she always loved to dress up. I hope she doesn't notice that dress has gone missing. It was pushed to the back of the closet, so by the time she does..." he trailed off.

Sitka remembered that Letty died. She didn't know how close to the time they were that would happen, however, she could see how much Davis grieved for his lost daughter. Like she did for her own mother. She had no words and stood quietly. Davis rubbed his nose, then cleared his throat.

"Alright, go on and get something more to eat. Don't take more than a little of anything, so Ruth doesn't notice. Just a bite here and there. I'll clean up everything and make it look like we were never here."

Sitka went to the kitchen and opened the icebox. She took pieces of everything she could find, but not so much it looked like she had. She made sure she didn't move anything and cleaned up any crumbs. By the time Davis was done, she was full for the first time in a long time. Davis came out and scanned the kitchen. Satisfied nothing was amiss, he handed Sitka her damp clothes. He rooted around the closet and found a small paper bag.

"Put those in there. We'll lay them in the sun to dry, once we find a place to be where we won't draw attention. You get enough to eat?" he asked, as he began to wind her hair into braids on either side of her head.

"I did, thank you. Davis, you said you had work to do before you can join your family. Have you thought about what that might be?" Sitka wondered aloud.

Davis was quiet as he quickly made the volume of her hair into two neat rows on either side of her head. He tied them off with ribbon that matched her dress and turned her to face him, checking the braids for continuity. He met her eyes, considering.

"I hadn't understood up until this point. I've been lonely meandering through this side, trying to figure out how to get there to them. There was never anyone to guide me, no great spirit of truth. Time is different, of course, on this side. I can't explain it. Not like hours or years. Like wisps. Until you showed up in my cabin and opened my wooden box, I'd never felt called to a specific place or time. I sensed you there and knew I was supposed to come."

"To me in the cabin? I thought you were there because it had been yours," Sitka said, thinking about the first time he appeared to her.

"I'd never been back there. Of all the times and places I was, it was never there," David explained.

"Why do you think you were supposed to come there to me, then?"

Davis chuckled and touched the ribbon on her braid. "Ever since Letty died, I've been lost. I can't explain it, but being a parent without a child to mind is a soul without purpose. I suppose you were a child who needed a parent to watch out for you, to protect you."

It all made sense. Sitka was a child wandering the world without her parents and Davis was a parent wandering the afterlife without his child. Both were trying to traverse a world while grieving someone they loved. They didn't randomly cross paths.

They needed each other.

Chapter Fifteen

They headed to a nearby park and sat down on a bench, watching people pass by. Davis seemed nervous and kept shifting his eyes around, letting them land on a person's face before moving on to the next. He tapped his foot rapidly and wiped his hands on his pants. At one point, he saw someone and acted as if he was going to stand, grasping Sitka's hand in his. Then he relaxed and smiled down at her.

"I'm going to tell you some things, but first let me explain what's going on. I want to make sure I don't see anyone I know because if I do, it can send me elsewhere. Leaving you here, I think. If you are connected to me, like your hand is in mine, I believe you'll go with me. I don't actually know that though, to be honest."

"Can't we just go back to the door?" Sitka asked, confused. "Like to go home?"

"Mmm... I don't know. Usually, those doors are temporary. We could go back and open it, and it might just be a store. Or not be there at all. I've never paid it too much mind because I was simply passing through, however, I've never been able to travel back through a door. I only learned about not seeing people I know because after I died and traveled, I rushed in to see my family and it kicked me out. I thought it was because I was there, as well as myself here in this time with my family. So, me times two. Then I tried when the me here wasn't around to see my family and it still sent me away. I think I can't exist where I exist in someone else's mind here."

Sitka shifted uncomfortably. "What about me? I'm not a ghost, so can it spit me out?"

"I reckon it can. However, you never existed here that we know of. That could be a problem in itself because you don't belong here in the first place. You're an interloper."

"Interloper?" For some reason the word made Sitka think of antelopes, and she definitely wasn't one of those.

"You don't belong here. The timeline may resist and force you away, send you elsewhere. Hopefully, just to home, but I can't say for sure."

"Can't I just go home, anyway?"

Davis turned and watched her, his eyes unreadable. He shrugged, then gazed around them. "Well, to tell you the truth, I don't know how to do that."

"Can me being here mess up things in my time?" Sitka wondered aloud. "Change things?"

"Like the Butterfly Effect, where one small change in the timeline can change everything from that point forward? No, I don't believe so. In order for the Butterfly Effect to happen, the idea of time is more linear. From here to there. Time isn't like that. Right now, all time exists at the same time.

The time you came from is running parallel to this time. You're a baby with your mother and an old lady at the same moment."

"That doesn't make sense. How can I be both? I was a baby, I will be an old lady. I'm me, now." Sitka couldn't make heads or tails of what he was saying.

Davis was quiet, staring at the sky. He shook his head and glanced around at the ground, bending to pick up a pile of leaves. He moved over and placed them in a row on the bench between them.

"We think of time like this. Beginning-" He placed his finger on the first leaf and drew a line across it to the last leaf. "-to end. However, it's not like that."

Sitka wrinkled her nose and stared at the leaves. That was how she thought of time. Sunup to sundown. Year after year. Davis collected the leaves, stacking them together neatly, then held them up.

"See, time is more like this. Layers. What's going on in the top leaf, is happening at the same time as what is going on in the bottom leaf. You can't change time because it's happening at the same time. Somewhere in the stack, you are a babe in your mother's arms, at the same time you are taking your last breath. So, if you do something different in one of these layers, it doesn't change anything later because it only becomes part of that layer."

Sitka's head hurt trying to understand but she could see if time was like that, how nothing they did would impact the other layers. "What if I did something big? Like killed someone here?"

"Time would've already known that you were going to do that, even if you didn't. I can't explain it, but what happens was always meant to happen. While you think you're doing something different, time always knew what was going to occur," Davis explained as simply as possible.

They sat in silence, pondering the thought. Finally, Davis squeezed her shoulder and sighed. "We'd better get moving and figure out how to get you home. Let's go back to the door and see if it leads anywhere. I need you to stick by me. If anyone asks, you're my daughter. You're really light-skinned so hopefully, with your hair braided, no one questions who your mother is."

"Who my mother is? Why would that matter?"

"If anyone thinks your mother is white here, it could get us in heaps of trouble. I might end up taken from you."

Sitka stared at Davis, her mouth hanging open. She snapped it shut and stared around. "Oh. Because you're black?"

"Indeed."

Sitka knew enough about history from her mother and school to know there was a time when black people and white people weren't allowed to be together. She imagined this was that time. Things were still separated here. She nodded understanding, when a thought crossed her mind.

"Davis, aren't you a ghost? Like, if you died, how can people see you in this time?"

Davis chuckled. "I think I'm only a ghost in the times after I died. Here, I am who I was. Well, sort of. Normally, I can see them, but they can't see me. Not a ghost, but not a person, either. However, I'm still an interloper of sorts."

"Like me."

"Yup, like you. Them layers again. I suppose since I was alive here during this time, part of this me is, as well. I don't know how it all works. I've been wandering around this side for what? Twenty years since I died? I still haven't figured it all out and there's no book on it. I've only learned by trial and error."

Twenty years was a long time to be alone, to be lost. Sitka felt bad for Davis and took his hand. They left the park, being careful to skirt side streets back into the town. He kept his eyes down as they passed white people, and moved over to let them pass without touching him. Most were oblivious and paid him no mind. Some sneered or made derogatory remarks. Sitka, not used to being in that time, watched everyone and more than once made eye contact with someone who glared at her. She quickly averted her eyes and hung her head to not cause Davis any trouble

By the time they made it back to the door, the sun was beginning to drop in the sky and Sitka's feet hurt. The door was still there but a group of people were standing outside it, talking to each other. Davis guided her into an alley and waited, peeking out to see when they left. After the group moved on, he made sure the coast was clear and walked slowly to the door. He put his hand on the knob and yanked, just as a group of patrons were exiting, surprising them with the door flinging open.

"Sorry ma'am," Davis said to a large, pasty woman carrying bags. "Let me hold this door for you."

The woman grunted and heaved her way through, barely giving Davis a second glance. Once the patrons left, Davis peered in, shaking his head. Sitka glanced past him and saw the door now just went to a clothing shop.

Her heart sank. "How will I get home, now?"

Davis shut the door and turned around, staring out at the street. "Don't worry, honeybee. We'll figure it out. It's getting dark soon, so we better find a place to be until we do. Come on, I know where we can go for the night to be safe."

Sitka fought back tears and nodded. Davis led her through the streets to another part of town. The buildings were not as pretty and some were rundown. The people also shifted to mainly black, but Davis still kept his eyes down, furtively glancing up as they walked. Sitka realized he was making sure he didn't see anyone who might recognize him. They ducked down a side street and came to a small shop. He waited a moment, then peered through the window first.

"Alright, looks like I left for the day. We'll go in through the back. I have a key hidden there."

"What is this place?" Sitka asked, noticing the lettering on the glass. *Butler & Sons Timepiece Repair*.

Davis followed her eyes and smiled. "My shop. Well, was my father's at first and he taught my brother DJ and I. He'd passed on years before and my brother wasn't interested in watch and clock repair, so I took it over. Used to be mainly pocket watches and grandfather clocks, but at this time it'd switched over to a lot of wristwatches."

Sitka giggled. Davis raised his brows and looked at her. Sitka pointed at the sign. "Funny that you fixed clocks and watches, then told me how time isn't in a straight line."

Davis chuckled, getting her point. "I suppose that's true. When we're alive, everything is determined by a ticking clock, minutes counting away. Then we die and find out none of it's real. Even so, people sure are in love with their watches. Checking every few minutes to make sure they don't lose track of time. Was a good business for me. People were lost when their watches stopped. Like they didn't know what to do with themselves. Even white people saw past the color of my skin for my skill. I did very well for my family."

Sitka could hear the pride in Davis's voice. He slid a key off a ledge and eased open the back door. He glanced in and knocked lightly, grasping Sitka's hand with this other hand. When it was clear no one was there, he drew them inside. A soft light came from the front of the shop as they made their way through. On one side, was a long wooden counter with a variety of watches. The other, a workstation where he did the repairs. The walls were covered with hanging clocks, their pendulums swinging in unison. Sitka looked at the watches in the case, displayed to catch the light.

"You sold clocks and watches, too?"

"I did. Not at first, but as business picked up, I started carrying a selection. As I said, people loved their watches. Most of the clocks you see came to me after their owners passed and their family wanted a little extra money."

Above the counter was a picture of Davis with his wife and daughter. The daughter was maybe nine in the picture. A pang hit Sitka's heart as she realized how much happier he seemed in the picture.

Like he was always cracking a joke.

His daughter was the spitting image of him, her wide, toothy grin making her face round. His wife, Ruth, smiled gently, almost with a touch of sadness as if she knew it wouldn't last. It was like she sensed what was coming in the future for their family in her soul. Davis caught her gaze and followed it to the picture.

"They were the reason for everything I did, for all of this. After they died, I gave up. Sold the shop, moved out to the woods."

"To the cabin?"

"Yup. Spent the rest of my days out there. DJ asked me to come live with his family, but I just couldn't. I loved them, but seeing him with his wife... being a father to his children, made me miss Letty and Ruth even more. The hurt never went away and it was easier to be alone with my thoughts than to try and make myself fit in."

Sitka understood. Sometimes seeing Tommy and Aunt Leigh together made her miss her mother more than she thought she already could. She loved them and they were her family, but it didn't take away the feeling of loneliness she'd had since her mother died. The feeling of being in one timeline, while wanting to exist in another. Maybe if she'd had her father around when her mother died, she wouldn't have felt so alone. Instead, it was as if she'd gotten trapped inside a television where she could see everyone going on with their lives, while she screamed behind the glass. No one around her could hear her cries.

Until she met Davis.

Chapter Sixteen

S ounds from the street woke Sitka up and she blinked, expecting to see the walls of her bedroom around her, or at worst the cabin. Sunlight reached through the shop windows, catching dust particles in its grasp. Davis was sleeping in a chair, his feet kicked up on the counter. Sitka remembered he'd pulled out a blanket for her and let her curl up on a small couch a the back of the shop. She sat up and glanced around the tiny space. Outside, the world was coming to life and the bustle of people in their own time was somewhat soothing.

Sitka got up and peered out the window, feeling like she was watching a large movie screen show about the past. There were a lot fewer cars, but the ones she saw seemed like a work of art. Fancy and decorative. Even though everyone was dressed like they were going to a wedding or church, not all were matched to the same quality. While some were tailored and fitted from head to toe, others wore ill-fitting and threadbare clothes. Still in the church style, just not as fine or new as some of the others.

Then, there was the difference in skin. Even though, like in her own time, people of different shades were equally on the street, they seemed to stay away from one another here. If they passed one another, it was as if they didn't see the other, each moving in their own bubble. No friendly greetings, no laughter between races. From what Sitka could see, black citizens owned businesses and were well enough off, but it was as if they still didn't exist when the white citizens went by. Davis told her that behind the scenes, both groups were much more interactive with each other, but there was still this expectation of separation in the public eye.

Sitka was considering this when she saw the woman. Her eyes were following people as they made their way to work or running errands when a familiar shape drew her attention. She would've known the pattern of the gait and shift of the hips anywhere. The woman was weaving through the sidewalk in a hurry to wherever her destination was, dressed to the hilt. Sitka caught her breath and watched in total disbelief. The woman bumped into another person and she turned to apologize as the sun hit her perfectly coiffed blond hair. The expensive clothes and the hair were different, but everything else was the same.

Sitka ran to the shop door and yanked as hard as she could to get it open. It was fastened tight, so she fumbled with the locks until she figured them out. When she flung open the door, the woman was disappearing out of sight around a corner.

Sitka yelled at the top of her lungs, "Mama!"

This startled Davis awake and he jumped up as Sitka bolted out the door. He ran after her as she stumbled down the sidewalk, attempting to catch up with the fleeting woman. He caught her just as she was about to disappear into the crowd on the next street and grabbed her arm, pulling her back toward him. People around them frowned and shook their heads.

"Get control of your child," one of them muttered, disgusted by the scene.

Sitka tried to dart away and her eyes fixed on the last place she'd seen her mother on the street. "Davis! My mother. Let me go!"

Davis looked thoroughly confused and glanced at where Sitka was staring. "Come on, Sitty, we need to go back to the shop before anyone else takes note of us out here."

Sitka yanked free and screamed, "No!"

Davis was truly taken aback by her reaction and gazed apologetically at a passerby, who'd paused in their path to stare at the petulant child.

"Sitka, you're going to get us in some real trouble, here. We can't have this kind of attention and if someone recognizes me, I'll be gone, leaving you to fend for yourself," he whispered firmly.

Sitka, realizing the danger she'd put them both in, nodded and followed him back to the shop, stopping to glance back at where her mother went. Once in the shop, Davis locked the door and sat her down on the couch, pulling a chair over to sit in front of her.

"Now, tell me what that was all about. What just happened? Why did you run out of here like you were chasing after something or someone?"

Sitka couldn't help but feel the tears stinging her eyes. She pointed out the window. "I saw my mother out there. She was walking down the street."

Davis sat back in his chair and rubbed his face. "You think you saw your mother? Here?"

Sitka glared at him through her tears. "I *did* see her. She was dressed differently, but it was her, Davis. I'd know my mother anywhere."

"Of course, you would, honeybee. I don't doubt that you saw a woman who looked like your mother. However, no matter what, we need to stick together. If we get separated here, you may never be able to go home. You can't run off from me like that."

"I don't want to go home if my mother is here." Sitka pouted. She knew she was being unreasonable, but all she wanted was her mother back. To wrap her arms around her again. To smell her perfume.

Davis leaned forward and took her hands in his. "That wasn't your mother. Even if she looked exactly like her, even if she was in her skin, she isn't your mother. This is a different time and place, Sitka. If a black child ran up to a white woman, calling her 'Mama', people would be horrified. Not to say it don't happen ever, but that is kept behind closed doors or gotten rid of. You would've scared that woman doing that."

Sitka shook her head. "My mother would know me."

"No, Sitka, that lady wouldn't know she was your mother, even if on some plane she is. You haven't happened yet in her existence."

"But you said all time happens at the same time. In layers. So, she's my mother on some layer," Sitka reasoned.

"She might be, but not on this one. While all time happens in layers, the bottom layer doesn't know the top layers exist, if you get my meaning. To the bottom layer, they are the top layer in their timeline. To them, that time above hasn't happened yet. It doesn't exist."

Sitka let a few tears slip out and angrily brushed them away. "That isn't fair. How can I know about her and she doesn't know about me?"

Davis sighed. "Why do I know my daughter is streets away, yet I can't go see her? It's just the way it is. I know it hurts, honeybee, but we have to play by the rules."

"Who makes the rules?" Sitka asked, frustrated.

"That, I don't know. I just know there is the way things work and if we try to go around it, it'll set us straight. What if I get sent away and can't get back? Are you ready to be stuck here alone? A half-black child out of her time and place?"

The thought terrified Sitka when she considered it. She supposed she could find the Davis there to help her, but he'd have no idea who she was or how to help some strange child. Besides, what would happen to future her? Would she never be born? Or would she, and she'd be stuck in two places?

As if reading her thoughts, Davis tipped his head. "You'd simply become part of this time. You'd still be born then, but you'd have no recollection of being here, now. This would all repeat. In your time, you'd become another missing child, never to be seen again. However, you might still show up here like you did and who's to say what could happen, then? One of you couldn't be here. So, you see how serious this is, Sitty. I'm trying to get you home as soon as I can, but you can't do things that might jeopardize that."

The thought wrenched her heart, knowing how scared Aunt Leigh and Tommy must be, thinking she may never come home. She met Davis's eyes and nodded. "I need to get home."

"That you do. So, don't go chasing ghosts, you hear?" Davis said firmly but with tenderness.

"Yes," Sitka agreed.

"Alright, let's get something to eat and figure out how to get you back."

"Davis, do you think that was my mother, though? Like her soul? Do people live over and over? Like, could I be here already, just as a different me?"

"I suppose. I can't say as I've been stuck in this loop since I died. I don't see why we can't die and come back in another body and another time. Sort of as ourselves again."

"I mean, if the other you lives here in this time and since you came back with me this time, you're a real person as both Davis's. Wouldn't that go against time?"

Davis shrugged. "As I said before, I never have been previously, so it must have something to do with you. Maybe being here with you, makes me have to be. Some part of your existence here is making me flesh and blood."

Sitka considered this and a warning went off in her head. Not about Davis, but something else was causing bells to go off in her mind. She was in danger and needed to get home. She watched Davis and could see he couldn't sense it. The danger. He turned and peered out the window.

"I know somewhere we can get some food. We need to be leaving here, anyway. I'm about due to show up for work." He folded the blanket and put it away, looking around to make sure nothing else was out of place.

"Why do you have blankets here?" Sitka asked curiously. The space in the back of the shop was set like a small apartment.

"Well, some nights I'd end up working late into the evening. Too late and would stay here til morning for safety."

"Saftey?"

"Different time, different place. It wasn't wise for black folk to go out after dark alone. Sometimes they'd end up missing. End up dead," Davis explained, his voice showing he knew from experience.

Sitka shuddered. "Oh."

Davis took money out of a locked box under the register, counting it out. "I keep a little extra money under the shelf. Let's get some food. Then we can see about how to get you home."

They walked the back alleys until they came to a worn door that looked like it didn't go anywhere in particular. Like the back door to an apartment by the garbage bins. Davis pulled Sitka aside.

"I need you to knock on the door and ask for two ham, grits, and egg breakfasts on toast. Give them this money and tell them to keep the change."

"You want me to?"

"They can't see me. They know me. I'm going to go stand around the corner. I know them well, they're real nice. They'll get you taken care of."

Sitka took the money and stared at it. "What if you disappear?"

Davis stroked his chin. "Let's set up a meetup place, in case I do. Remember, though, I can only show up if I'm not already there. Let's say the shop. If I disappear, I'll try to get back there but only at night, or on a Sunday when my family is at church."

"What if it's daytime and not Sunday?" Sitka asked, fear clenching her stomach.

"Hide out until you see me leave the shop."

"Wait, how will I know which you is you?"

Davis chuckled. "Good question. If I call you honeybee, it's me. This me. If I don't recognize you, it's that me. Now, go get us some food before my stomach draws attention to us."

Davis went and ducked behind the corner as Sitka raised her hand to knock. She waited a moment and a small, older, caramel-skinned woman came to the door. The woman didn't seem surprised to see Sitka and gave a friendly smile. Sitka cleared her throat and ordered just as Davis told her to, handing the woman the money.

"Keep the change," she whispered.

The woman took the money and disappeared back into the doorway, closing it behind her. A little while later, the woman came back and handed Sitka a package wrapped in paper. She glanced around the alley, then met Sitka's eyes.

"Hurry on now, dear. You shouldn't be out alone."

Sitka bobbed her head and waited for the woman to close the door before she made her way to where Davis was hiding. When she got there, he was gone. Panic filled her and she glanced around, ready to scream his name. She clutched the package and ran out to the sidewalk, seeing him up ahead on the street. She dashed after him, as he wound his way through the people on the sidewalk.

Where was he going?

She saw him arrive at the front of the shop and fish in his pockets for his keys. All of a sudden, a wave of nausea came over her and she felt faint. He slipped into the shop and she tried to catch up to him when a hand grabbed her and yanked her into a nearby alley. The world around her began to spin and she almost dropped the package on the ground.

"Whoa, there, honeybee. Don't spill our breakfast."

She looked up to see Davis staring down at her as he caught the food before it hit the ground. "I don't understand. I saw you go into the shop."

"That you did. I was hiding when I realized the time and knew I'd cross paths with myself, so I needed to move. I saw you leave and thought you might be following me. I circled through the alleys to get you before you ended up with the other me," Davis explained.

The other him. The current time Davis. That's why he went to the shop. It wasn't her Davis. Something in her set off alarm bells again. She *was* in danger. Seeing the other Davis made her realize something she hadn't known until then.

She'd been there before.

Chapter Seventeen

∞

*S*itka kept that secret to herself. Now, she knew it to be true. Just like her mother. She'd lived in this time, or close to it, as well. Maybe not there in Wilmington, maybe not as herself. However, seeing Davis who lived in the current time brought back a feeling. A memory without pictures. Something about that Davis was too familiar, part of her wanted to run to him, the other part made her afraid for her life. None of it made sense, yet the feelings were there.

"What's going on in the little head of yours?" Her Davis's voice snapped her back to the moment and she shook her head.

"Nothing. It was just strange to see you, not being you... or I guess, being you at the shop," Sitka murmured, knowing that wasn't all. It was like déjà vu, but in a past she wasn't part of.

Davis chuckled, then nodded. "Tell me about it. I spend my time here ducking in alleys and avoiding myself."

Sitka tipped her head, trying to imagine that. "So, can you see them and not get sent back? Or does it happen both ways? Like, if they see you or you see them?"

"Both ways, I reckon. I can't say for sure. The times it's happened, I was shot out of there so fast, I'm not sure if they were aware of me or not. I just knew we crossed paths and I ended up elsewhere."

"Oh."

David rubbed his head with his hand. "Well, now, I guess we have to connect on some level, otherwise I'd be getting sent all over the place all the time. I mean, I lived here my whole life, so I must've crossed paths with a lot of these folks. As I said before, I don't know the rules of it. I only know when I've been around people here who I knew, I ended up being sent out of the timeline. Are you worried about something? Did seeing me in the timeline here make you scared about it?"

Sitka was scared but she couldn't explain why. She knew seeing the Davis here made her feel unsafe, vulnerable. She shook her head. "Not anything for sure, I just don't want you to disappear."

"We'll do everything we can to make sure that doesn't happen, then."

After they ate, Davis suggested they find a private place to go, to try and figure out how to open doorways to get Sitka back to her time. It was summer, so they headed for the elementary school and sat on the swings in the deserted playground. Sitka lifted her feet and swung gently back and forth, thinking about the day she and Tommy were on the swings. She wished she could go back to that day and start over. Never go to the shack or down the tunnel.

"Why did we come through that first door? Why did it open there?" she asked.

Davis shook his head. "I don't have a clue. I sensed you were in trouble the day with the hunters, and the tunnel led me to the hatch in the floor. I knew you needed to come with me, but I didn't know where the tunnel led. Maybe it has something to do with where it was at that particular time. Like, who was on the street when we came out. I've never come out to anyone I knew, so maybe it adjusts based on that."

That didn't help. "How have you gotten back, or to different times?"

"Hmm... let's see. Outside of just getting spit out at different times, I think I was called to your time. A door appeared to me and I just knew to open it. It was probably a normal door any other time, but that time I sensed to turn the handle. Then, I was in the cabin the first night you saw me. I didn't know why I was there, but I was."

"So, you were meant to find me," Sitka whispered. For some reason that made sense. "What other times have you been sent to?"

Davis stared at the sky, thinking. "Never before I was alive in this lifetime, I can say that. Doesn't mean I can't, but I haven't. I suppose nothing has called me to that time. I've been to when I was a boy, this time, and a few other random times in my life. Then, of course, when you were at the cabin, which was the first time since after I died."

Sitka thought about the different times. "Each was a different time in your life. Does that matter?"

Davis shrugged. "Your guess is as good as mine. The times I end up when I was a boy, I'm sent there when I'm grieving for Letty and Ruth. My emotion does seem to dictate when it happens unexpectedly."

"Before you had a wife and daughter. Maybe that means something?"

"Maybe. Maybe just a breather from all the pain. Sometimes I'm the age I was then. Most times, I'm an old man, like when I lived alone. Never after, 'til I came to you. There's rhyme or reason for it as far as I can tell."

A breather from the pain. Sitka could understand. Seeing her mother there, reminded her of how much it hurt to no longer be with her. "When you're an old man, what then?"

"I think that's just 'cause I can't be here with myself, so it sends me as far away as possible where I'm still alive. I don't honestly know."

"Why can't it let you be? Why do you keep bouncing around timelines like a pinball?" Sitka asked, frustrated.

"There has to be a purpose, I reckon," Davis agreed. "Work to be done."

Work to be done. What work? Sitka closed her eyes and let the sun warm her face. She wasn't supposed to be there. Davis couldn't control getting home. Doors weren't just anywhere, they had to appear for a reason. Sitka started to really miss Aunt Leigh and Tommy. Tears rolled down her cheeks as she pushed higher and higher, wishing to go back home. First, she lost her mother, now she was decades away from her only family left. All because of Glenn. Because he'd gone to pick her up at the skating rink.

This caused a feeling of dread in her stomach and she slowed the swing to a stop, wiping the tears off her cheeks. She opened her eyes as a brief memory flashed across her mind.

Glenn standing at her bedroom door. As quickly as it came, it went away, however, Sitka broke out in cold sweat. She glanced at Davis, but he was staring off to the edge of the playground. Her eyes followed his but nothing was there.

"You see something, Davis?"

His eyes shifted over and he smiled at her. "No, ma'am. Just letting my mind wander back to when I was a boy."

"Did you have a good childhood? Were your parents nice to you?"

"My mother was. She worked hard. Too hard. My father died when I was young. Heart attack while working at the shop. Left my mother to raise me and my siblings. We were poor, but I made sure when I got older to take care of her until she died. Luckily we had the shop."

"Did she ever remarry?" Sitka asked.

Davis's eyes darkened, then he looked away. His mouth was set in a grim line and he shook his head. "Don't want to talk about that. We deserved better."

Sitka pushed the swing back and forth with her foot. "Sorry, didn't mean to be nosy."

"No, little one. You were fine to ask. Let's just say there were a couple of tough years in there. My mother thought we needed a father and made a bad choice with a bad man. Ended up with us running in the middle of the night, never looking back. Water under the bridge."

"Did he hurt you?"

Davis stared at her, suddenly seeming like the boy he once was. "He did. A lot. He whooped us boys something fierce. However, it's what he did to my older sister, Anna, that put us on the run."

"Your sister? What did he do?" Sitka asked her heart starting to beat hard in her chest.

Davis didn't speak at first and when he did, he wiped a tear from his eye. "A little girl like you doesn't need to hear about such things. Mama got us all away from him. Made sure he never had rights to the business. My sister was never the same but Mama took care of her. Eventually, my sister married, but she died young. All the joy had been drained out of her."

Sitka imagined his sister, a lonely, young woman sitting at a kitchen table, crying. This hurt her heart and she wished whatever had happened to her never did. How could a grown man hurt a child? She leaned over and touched Davis's hand. "I'm sorry."

He nodded and rubbed his nose. "Me too, honeybee. There are some cruel people in the world. You need to keep your eyes open and watch for them. They usually come like the most charismatic. They will find out what you love and use it against you. My mother was just trying to get by and give us a family and a snake slithered in. He pretended to want to take care of her and us, but as soon as she let her guard down and he was in, he turned into something different altogether."

Like Glenn.

"When you go back and you're a boy, is it before or after that time?" Sitka wondered aloud.

"Well, now, that's a thought. It's always before."

"Do you think you can change things?"

"I haven't tried to change that. The idea of time travel is that you can't go back and change things, at least on that same timeline. Not sure I could change it on any others, seeing as I'm being sent without a choice on where I land," Davis said.

"Who says? Maybe those years didn't do anything but break your sister's heart. Who says that was meant to happen? Maybe that man wasn't supposed to do what he did."

Davis watched Sitka with an intensity she'd never seen before. His eyes wandered back to the memory of being a boy and a flash went through them. "I'd love nothing more than to stop the breath in that man. To save my sister."

They didn't speak for some time when Sitka turned to Davis. "Maybe in each time you're in, you're meant to change things. To set something right, that wasn't supposed to happen. Maybe that's why you keep bouncing around."

"I'd like to think that's true. So, why you? Why was I sent to you?" Davis asked

Sitka shrugged. "I don't know. I needed help."

"Maybe so, maybe so," Davis said.

Sitka did need help, but now she was stuck in this time. No doors were appearing and they didn't know the key to make it happen. Sitka thought about what happened to Davis's sister, then what happened to his wife and daughter. He'd been through so much in his life and now was trapped between planes of time, reliving it over and over, helpless. Pain squeezed her heart at his suffering and a thought popped in her head. One that made more sense than her getting randomly trapped in this timeline without a way back home. Even Dorothy had a purpose in Oz.

She pondered the thought, then turned to face Davis. "Maybe you weren't coming to help me. Or, at least, not only."

Davis cocked his head and frowned. "Why else would I have come, then?"

"Maybe you need *me* to help *you*."

Chapter Eighteen

For the next couple of weeks, Davis and Sitka slept in the clock shop at night and wandered around Wilmington during the day, trying to find a doorway back to her time. Davis seemed to be getting more anxious by the day, however, wouldn't tell Sitka why. She also had moments where her ears would ring or her head would start to hurt, but as they moved on it subsided. Sort of like a headache, but more like being exposed to a strange pressure or frequency. She mentioned it to Davis who eyed her, concerned.

"You aren't supposed to be here. That could mess with your head, I reckon. Physically, I mean. I'm not really here physically, but you are which is unnatural," he suggested.

"Could that hurt me?" Sitka asked.

Davis shrugged. "I imagine it could. I don't know but I'd think even time wants you to go back to where you belong."

"What if I can't? Go back. Do you think being here could kill me?"

"Now, we're going to get you home, don't worry about that. We'll figure it out, one way or another," Davis responded vehemently. "I think we're just missing something important."

"What if we never find the door?"

Davis watched her without responding. He rubbed his chin and sighed. Sitka thought he'd say more but he didn't. That scared her. Davis was always making sure she knew she was safe with him. It seemed he was at a loss.

After a bit, he glanced over, then away. "We will. As you said, we're here to help each other. Maybe there's just something more we need to do before the door comes to us."

They headed back to the clock shop, knowing the Davis there would've gone home by then. The sun was beginning to set and Sitka wished she was being called in by Aunt Leigh. Or being wrangled home by Tommy. Oh, how she missed Tommy. She hoped Glenn wasn't being mean to him. Thinking about Glenn made her stomach hurt and she sent a prayer out to protect Tommy. She'd give almost anything to see Tommy and Aunt Leigh again.

Davis jiggled the back door and pushed it open slowly, listening to make sure they were alone. Testing the waters, he stepped inside, then turned back with a smile.

"Coast is clear. Let's make dinner and get some rest while we can."

Sitka stepped in, liking the silence of the shop. Only the ticking of clocks. Davis cut on a small light and began making dinner. Sitka curled up in a chair, hugging her knees to her chest. She gazed at the photo on the wall.

"Davis, can you tell me about your daughter? About Letty? What was she like?"

Davis paused, his shoulders dropping slightly. "Letty is the best thing that ever happened to me. Before we had that girl, I hadn't a clue what it was like to be willing to die for another person. I love my wife, but loving a child of your own is something like nothing else in this world. The first time I held her, I knew I'd go to the ends of the Earth for her. When she died..."

He didn't say anything else, just got back to cooking. Sitka stood up and went over to his side. "Can I help?"

He smiled down at her and handed her an onion. "You want to cut this up?"

Sitka took the onion and got to chopping. Davis hummed a tune and for a moment, Sitka remembered what it was like to be with her mother. The two of them cooking dinner as her mother sang along with the radio. She slid the onions over to Davis, rubbing the sting from her eyes. He grinned and tipped his head.

"Why thank you, honeybee. You know, I used to call my daughter that. Honeybee. You remind me of her, with your curiosity. Letty was louder, though. Everything she did was loud. Laughter, crying, running through the house. It was like her body was simply a tool to express her mind." Davis shook his head. "I miss that. The sound of noise. Everyday things like a slamming door, dishes being washed, food frying in the pan. There is something beautiful about common noise."

Sitka listened, thinking about what it was like for Davis where he was. Before she was around. Was he floating in darkness, or observing from the outskirts? She placed her hand on his and peered up at him. "I guess you've been lonely a really long time, huh?"

Davis chuckled and stirred the pot. "Lonely doesn't even begin to cover it. I've been hollow. Empty. Longing. Until you came along, it was only me. I could see people and hear them, but it was like shouting out to the hills. No one knew I was there. Not even an echo came back to me. It's like being ignored forever."

Sitka thought back to when she walked through the cemetery. Sometimes it was peaceful but if she stayed too long, she felt like the only person left on Earth. Davis must feel like that all the time. "I thought that when people died, they went to a better place to be with their loved ones. This doesn't sound like that. It sounds like a punishment."

Davis finished cooking and scooped her a bowl of stew. They sat and ate in silence, each in their own thoughts. After dinner, Sitka could barely keep her eyes open and went to the couch. Davis sat in a nearby chair and began to sing. Sitka didn't know the song but it spoke to her heart. She let her eyes close and drifted off to sleep.

When she woke later, she saw Davis was still sitting in the chair, except now he was holding the photograph of his wife and daughter. Tears were streaming down his face as he clutched the picture close to his chest. Sitka watched, holding her breath. She didn't want to disturb him but felt maybe she'd done something wrong by asking about his daughter. Made him sad. Shame heated her ears and she sat up.

"Davis, I'm sorry. For asking about Letty. I didn't mean to bring it up and make you feel bad."

Davis loosened his grip on the photo and shook his head. "You can't bring up something that is always in my heart. Not a moment goes by, I don't think about my family. I'm sure you feel the same about your mother. Sometimes it's good to let it out. It's not just that, though. In this time, everything is about to change for me here."

"I don't understand. What's about to change?" Sitka asked, confused.

Davis set the photo down and stared off. "According to the newspaper, we are less than a week away from when Letty got sick."

Sitka wrapped her arms tightly around her body and shivered. "From when she died?"

"Well, from when we took her to the hospital and they turned us away. She held on a bit after we got to the other hospital, but it was too late."

"Can we do anything?" Sitka whispered, knowing the answer but needing to ask anyway.

"No, honeybee. We can't. The here now won't let me anywhere near her. What will happen will happen. I've tried, but I can't get close."

"What about me? Maybe I can do something," Sitka offered.

David chuckled, not unkindly but also without humor. "Unless you can make us not black, there's nothing that will change. This is the way this world is. We were turned away for not being white. It's as simple as that."

As simple as that.

Davis's daughter died because of the color of her skin. Not so different from Sitka's own. She lay back down and stared at the ceiling. Davis was going to have to watch his daughter die all over again. Or know it was happening. Why was time making him relive it over and over again?

The next morning, Sitka woke up before Davis again and peered out the window. The woman who looked like her mother was making her way down the street as she had the other morning. Sitka remembered how upset Davis was when she left without telling him and tried to think of a way to follow the woman without creating an issue. She scribbled a note on a piece of paper, hoping Davis wouldn't be mad.

Davis,

I went for a walk around the block. I will be right back. Don't worry, I know how to behave. I'll be back before the other Davis comes back.

Sitka

She left the note where she knew he'd see it and slipped out the door. She kept her eyes down, except to keep track of the woman, and made sure she knew where she was to find her way back to the shop.

The woman was dressed in a green, skirted suit and had her hair pinned up under a matching felt hat. She didn't notice Sitka and walked with her head up, greeting people she passed. Sitka reminded herself this wasn't her mother here, but found it hard to believe. The woman even had her mother's mannerisms, moving without a care in the world.

As they rounded another corner, Sitka held back as she observed the woman come up to a pair of large iron gates. The woman paused as the man behind the bars greeted her and opened the gates to let her pass through. The man tipped his hat and gave the woman a slight bow. As he lifted his head, he spied Sitka, who froze in place. The man's face changed to a grimace as he looked like he might step out of the gate toward her. The woman, noticing the change in his demeanor, moved her head to see what he was looking at.

The woman's eyes locked on Sitka's and for a moment Sitka felt as if she left her body. It *was* her mother, no one could ever convince her otherwise. The woman smiled and raised her hand in a small wave, as the man gaped at the gesture. He grasped the woman's arm, shaking his head. She frowned, glancing at him. She peeked back at Sitka, then turned and disappeared down a path.

Sitka fell to her knees, the world around her vibrating as if she'd stepped off a tilt-a-whirl. The sound of buzzing filled her ears and she had the sensation she was no longer fully within herself. The man behind the gate was yelling something at her and waving his hand angrily. Sitka couldn't move, pressing her hands against the ground as if to hold on to something solid.

At that moment, two strong hands lifted her off the ground, carrying her away from the gate and the man. She peered up into Davis's worried face as the world began to solidify around her. He wasn't angry, he was terrified as he clutched her tightly against his chest.

"You almost disappeared right out of here, honeybee."

Chapter Nineteen

∞

*D*avis ran with Sitka in his arms all the way back to the clock shop, attracting the stares of passersby. When he rounded the corner to the shop, he stopped dead in his tracks and spun around in the other direction. It was too late to go back. He could hear current-day Davis coming down the street, jingling his keys and whistling.

Davis glanced around and bolted down an alleyway. Once he was sure they were alone, he set Sitka down and put his fingers on her chin, tipping her head back. "Girl, can you hear me? Are you alright?"

Sitka mumbled incoherently and tried to nod but her head felt like it was detached from her shoulders. "Dizzy... shaking. Mama."

Davis peered into her eyes, then gently patted her cheeks. Sitka tried to sit up but fell back, her arms and legs feeling like they were made of rubber.

Davis sat down beside her and scanned the area.

"I gotta get you somewhere, we can't stay here and attract more attention. Me carrying you through the streets will definitely turn eyes on us, and draw unwanted stares. Can you move your legs at all?"

Sitka tried and wiggled her legs slightly. "Tommy," was all she said.

Davis frowned at her. "Tommy?"

Sitka nodded and tried sitting up again. This time she was able to stay upright as the world around her began to stabilize. She spoke clearly. "I saw Tommy."

"Your cousin?"

"Yes, when I saw the lady and she met my eyes, I went somewhere else. Home."

Davis gazed around, then sighed. "You can tell me later. Let's go to my home. I think Letty and Ruth would've left by now. Come on, let's get you up."

Davis helped Sitka to her feet, which buckled almost immediately. He put his arm under hers and helped her along. By the time they made it out to the main road, she was able to bear weight and walk a little. She staggered like a drunk and Davis did everything to keep her moving forward. They attracted some glances from those around them, so Davis talked loudly to Sitka with the intent of others hearing.

"Bad case of food poisoning. Let's get you home and into bed, dear. We'll never eat there again!"

People seemed to take this at face value or didn't care and hurried on by. The road Davis's house was on was quiet and they quickly made their way to the back of the house. Davis cracked the door open and waited to see if he heard anything inside. The house sat dark and unattended.

Once he had Sitka settled on the couch, he checked through the house and came back. He eyed her and cleared his throat. "Why don't you tell me what happened?"

Sitka proceeded to tell him how she saw her mother, then left a note to go follow her. How the lady lived in a big house and when she turned to see what the gatekeeper was looking at, she and Sitka locked eyes. From there, Sitka explained, everything became less clear. Her head began to hurt and a steady sound pulsed in her ears. She got dizzy and felt like everything near her was vibrating. At that moment, the world around her shifted. For a moment, she was between places where everything and nothing was happening.

Then she was standing in her Aunt's house. She could see pictures of herself on the dining room table. Hundreds of them. They were all the same, on a paper that read, "Have you seen this child?"

Missing posters... for her.

Sitka could feel she was in the home but not completely. Almost as if she was invisible. She heard yelling from the back rooms and made her way toward the sound. Male voices. It was coming from Tommy's room. She came to the partially closed door and could see Tommy, a mixture of fear and rage crossing his face. Glenn's voice bellowed out.

"Your mother is a stupid bitch and should know that girl is long gone by now. She's probably dead. Stop feeding into her delusions, just to get what you want!" he yelled.

Sitka moved inside the doorway and could see Glenn in Tommy's room, facing Tommy. The room had been destroyed and Tommy had a bright red welt on his face where Glenn struck him. Tommy clenched his fists and dug his heels in.

"Don't speak about my mother that way! She believes Sitty is okay and just needs to be found. This is *my* family and you can't stop us from finding her."

Glenn made a move toward Tommy. "You such a piece of shit, boy. You need to be taken down a notch or two. Like it or not, I'm here to stay and you *will* do as I say. Or maybe you'll disappear, as well."

Tommy stood straight up, meeting Glenn's stare. "Fuck you, Glenn."

Glenn took a swing at Tommy, landing his fist squarely against Tommy's cheek. Tommy fell back and scrambled to his feet. "What are you going to do now, Glenn? My mother's going to wonder where I got these bruises from. Then she'll kick you out."

Glenn wavered, knowing it was true. Leigh would never tolerate him hitting her boy. He grimaced and peered around the room, his eyes landing on a large trophy Tommy won for track. He made a move toward it, snatching it in his meaty hand. "I'll get rid of the evidence, then, won't I?"

He raised the trophy above his head, ready to bring it down on Tommy's head. Tommy's eyes darted to the door, but he knew he wouldn't make it in time. He was trapped. Glenn swung the trophy down at Tommy.

"Tommy!" Sitka screamed at that moment.

Glenn turned toward the sound, the trophy grazing Tommy on the shoulder, then knocking books onto the floor from the shelf. Tommy bolted for the door, passing right through Sitka, who was unseen by either of them. When he passed through her, she found herself kneeling on the ground in front of the gate, as Davis scooped her up and began to run.

Glenn hadn't seen her, but he'd heard her. Or he heard something because he was distracted and missed Tommy's head. Tommy had the chance to run. Sitka prayed he got away. She stopped the story and met Davis's eyes.

"I need to go back. He was going to kill Tommy. If he didn't catch him, he'll be after him."

"Did Tommy hear you?"

"I don't know. It all happened so fast. I saw Glenn swinging the trophy and I yelled, then Tommy was passing through me out the door," Sitka answered.

Davis shook his head. "I can't explain it. It's like you went back to your time but not in physical form. I guess because I died, I always go back unseen. Well... until *you* saw me. Also, now in this time with you. However, you returned to your time without your body."

"Davis, meeting that woman, my mother, is what did it. Maybe like you, I can't be in the presence of someone who knows me."

"But she doesn't know you. Even if it is your mother from your time, she isn't your actual mother in this time, so shouldn't have any effect on you."

"I'm not a ghost. I'm a person. Maybe it's different for me. Maybe she is my mother and since I'm flesh and blood, the timeline doesn't want us to cross paths because we will later. Is there a way seeing her could get me home?"

Davis shook his head. "The rules of this, I don't know. You saw her and didn't get all the way home. Just part of you. It doesn't seem strong enough. Perhaps the connection isn't enough to send you completely back. I was here in this timeline, that is my actual family, so I can't cross paths with them or I get spit out, so to say. If that is your mother in the future, it isn't your mother in this timeline. You shouldn't meet again, but the force isn't enough to send you back. You'd need to know who you were in this timeline and cross their path directly, I think."

"I could've been anyone, lived anywhere. How would I find that person?" Sitka asked.

"I'm not sure. Just rest for now and we'll come back to it later. Let me make us something to eat, then we best get on our way. Close your eyes, and I'll bring you a bite to eat." Davis got up and rubbed her head. "You scared me back there. It was like you were fading away out of sight."

"That's how I felt," Sitka agreed. Davis only knew the rules for himself, but clearly, she was affected by this timeline, as well. She closed her eyes and heard him cooking in the kitchen.

Maybe if seeing her mother there started to send her back, she could figure out how to make the force strong enough to create a door. The lady wasn't her mother in this time but *would* become her mother in another lifetime. So, perhaps Sitka was here as someone else. Were there clues? It seemed odd she'd see her mother there but not herself. Weren't they all connected?

Or was it random?

She thought back to when she was small and would climb in her mother's lap. Her mother would always sing this song with the line, "Always my baby you'll be." She was always her mother's baby.

Did the woman here have a child? Could that be her? She knew Davis was against it, but she needed to see the woman again, to find out if she had any children. She dozed off until Davis came in with sandwiches and soup.

"Eat up, honeybee. We need to head out soon. I already cleaned and ate, so once you're done we can go. Are you feeling better?"

Sitka bobbed her head. The sensation of being not within herself had passed. She ate the food and waited while Davis washed the dishes and made sure the house appeared untouched. She stood up and looked at a picture on the mantle. It was of Davis, Ruth, and Letty. She ran her fingers over the photograph, swearing she felt a slight vibration coming from the image. She peered in at Letty and had the sensation they'd met before. Maybe in this time, they'd crossed paths. Had even been friends.

Davis cleared his throat, glancing around the living room. "You ready to go?"

Sitka nodded and followed him out. In a few days, Letty was going to get very sick, then die. There was nothing they could do about it. Times were different then and Davis had done everything in his power to save his daughter. Sitka didn't want him to go through it again, but finding the way home was becoming increasingly difficult.

She thought back to the scene of Glenn and Tommy, willing Tommy to have escaped. Glenn would've killed Tommy had she not interceded. An image of Glenn standing outside her door popped into her mind again, but this time he was closer. She could make out the lines of his face. And his eyes. They were set with such an intensity, she felt powerless. He was coming toward her when the image evaporated. However, it left her with something else. A string to a memory. It was important but she couldn't think of why. She knew she'd been sent back for the moment to save Tommy, but was it enough?

In her mind, she saw Tommy running through the cemetery, hiding beyond headstones. He ran out past the skating rink to the main road. He stood there when he saw something coming down the road. He began waving his arms above his head frantically, casting glances behind him to see if Glenn was coming. He stepped out into the road, sweat pouring off his face. He jumped up and down, as vehicles whizzed by him. Finally, one came to a stop and he climbed in.

Sitka sat frozen in fear at the image, as she watched the blue van that had dumped the body in the woods, drive away with her cousin inside.

∞

Chapter Twenty

∞

The first time Davis disappeared, neither of them saw it coming. They were doing what they did every day. Walking the streets, looking for a doorway back. They rounded a corner as they tried every door along the sidewalk. Davis had his head down, peering at a map of the streets. They'd tried just about every door there was, even the alley ones. Nothing had come of their tireless searching and he was trying to see if there was anywhere they may have missed. At that moment, a tall, cocoa-skinned woman came whipping around the corner, carrying a basket of laundry and ran straight into him.

That was it, then he was gone.

Sitka stood astonished at how he was there and then wasn't. Nothing else happened. No shower of light, no sounds. Simply there, then not. The woman spilled her clothes in the collision and gazed around, confused. She set the basket down and rubbed her forehead.

"I swear I just saw Davis Butler come around this corner. Smacked right into him," she said as she gathered the piles of fabric. She stared at Sitka and shook her head. "You seen a man walking here?"

Sitka nodded and helped the lady gather her things. "You know Davis?"

The woman tipped her head back and laughed. "Everyone knows Davis. He's a staple of this community. Where'd he go?"

Sitka shrugged. How could she answer that? "Dunno."

"How do you know Davis? You a friend of his little girl, Letty's?"

That seemed like a logical choice, so Sitka cocked her head. "We go to school together."

"That right? Well, tell him I said hello if you see him. Name's Bertha. We've known each other our whole lives. I better get on and get this washing done."

Bertha hurried down the sidewalk, leaving Sitka scared and alone. Davis was gone. He said he couldn't control coming back, so he might never. Sitka could be stuck in that time forever. Tears stung her eyes and she glanced around. She needed to get somewhere safe.

Ducking into alleys, Sitka waited until she knew the clock shop would be empty and headed in that direction, careful to not attract any attention. She slipped around back and found the key she'd seen Davis hide. Shaking the door handle, she felt the lock give and turned the handle.

She was in.

The clock shop felt more ominous without Davis there and Sitka curled up on the couch, wondering where he was sent to. How could she bring him back? She got up and held the picture of his family in her hands, willing him to walk through the door.

"Davis, please come back. I'm scared and can't do this without you," she whispered.

She peered at the picture as tears fell onto the glass. Letty seemed to be staring right at her. The same vibration she'd experienced earlier in his home when she touched a picture there, crossed her hands as she held the photo. A buzzing started in her ears and she quickly set the photo down. Was Davis trying to communicate with her? No, that couldn't be it. He was in the house with her the first time she felt it. She stared back at Letty, realizing the clock was ticking on the girl's life. Only days before she got sick.

Sitka went back to the couch and chewed her fingernails. If Davis didn't come back, she'd need to find her own way home. Everything they'd tried up to that point had failed and the closest she got was seeing the lady who'd later become her mother.

That was it then, she'd need to look for the lady in the morning and follow her. Maybe try talking to her and see if she had any children. Setting her mind to the plan, Sitka ate a piece of bread and rested on the couch. If the lady had children, maybe one of them could be Sitka, and meeting them would send her back home. She could only hope.

The following morning, Sitka sat by the window, waiting for a glimpse of the woman. She wanted to talk to her before she got to the gate and the man stopped her. A few times she thought she saw the woman coming, but it wasn't her. What if she didn't come by this morning, or took a different way? Sitka began to panic, realizing she was running out of time before the current time Davis showed up for work.

That's when she saw her. The lady was strolling down the sidewalk in a yellow dress, with her hair pinned back. Sitka bolted out of the door to catch up with the woman. People blocked her way, so she ducked under and around their legs to get to the lady. They rounded the street to where she lived and the woman was almost to the gate.

"Miss!" Sitka yelled, trying to get her attention.

The woman turned with a slight frown, as a smile began curving the edges of her mouth. Sitka held her breath for a second. Her mother made the exact same expression when she was confused. The buzzing came back and Sitka knew she was running out of time.

"Ma'am, I think I know your daughter?" she sputtered, hoping the woman would stop to talk to her.

The woman tipped her head, her golden curls, cascading over one shoulder. "You must be mistaken, dear. I don't have any children. Oh, aren't you the girl from the gate the other day? Do I know you?"

Unfortunately, Sitka was unable to respond as she was being pulled out of the timeline. The man at the gate came up to speak to the lady, diverting her attention while Sitka faded from that time. The woman turned back, but Sitka was nowhere to be seen. The man began speaking to her again, so the woman glanced over her shoulder as she slipped through the gate, rubbing her head in confusion.

Sitka, on the other hand, was being cast into a stream of timelines. She didn't go home like the first time when she saw Glenn and Tommy. She had the sensation of slipping down a long slide, flashes of fragmented memories whizzing by her. She reached out but nothing was solid to grab onto and she attempted to lock her mind on one set image. Davis. As soon as she set her mind on Davis's face, she saw him. She stretched her arms out toward his image and was shocked when she felt the solidness of his hand grabbing hers. They tumbled for a bit when they came to a screeching halt, slamming down on a grassy hill.

They rested there, trying to catch their breath when Sitka looked over at Davis. "How?"

Davis sat up, rubbing his shoulder. "Ow. I don't know. I was in another time, not knowing how to get back to where you were. All of a sudden, I was snatched out of it and saw you falling, so I grasped onto you. That way, no matter where you went, I'd go, too."

"Where are we? Or when are we?" Sitka asked.

Davis shrugged. "Only one way to find out."

They got up and looked around. The hill seemed familiar and Sitka realized they were in the park they'd often visit during the day after leaving the clock shop. A newspaper was folded on one of the benches, so she wandered over and opened it. It was the same day. They came back to two days before Davis's daughter got sick.

Sitka sat on the bench with her head in her hands. She was never going to leave. Davis sat beside her, peering at the paper. He rubbed her back.

"I guess we're meant to be here for now. I don't want to be. The worst time of my life, but here we are," he muttered.

"Why, Davis? Why did it bring us back here? I just want to go home," Sitka said, tears springing to her eyes.

"I suppose we still have work to finish here."

Sitka stared out across the park. This wasn't her time or her people, but somehow she wasn't going to leave it until whatever she was there for happened. "I talked to the lady, that's how I ended up... not here."

"You did? Talking to her sent you away again?"

"Yeah. I asked her about her children and she said she didn't have any. So, I guess she's not my mother... here at least. I thought maybe if she had kids, I'd be one of them and get sent home. But, I'm not and I may be stuck here forever."

Davis shook his head. "Something is happening. Something wants us here. We need to figure out what it is."

Sitka wiped her face. "How many times have you had to watch Letty die?"

"Now, that seems like a pretty heavy question. I've been here countless times, but I haven't seen her die other than the time I was actually there. I can never get close. I try. I have racked my brain thinking about how I can save her, but as soon as I get close enough to anyone who could help, I get shot out of here."

Sitka thought about that. Everyone he dealt with that day when he was alive would be the same people he would have to deal with to try and save her. It couldn't be done. He was forever trapped on the outside, knowing she was dying over and over.

"Could I?" she asked.

"Could you what?"

"Could I get close enough to change things?" Sitka replied. She didn't know Davis's family, so maybe she could warn them. Not that it would help, considering the situation.

Davis eyed her. "I don't know. What could you do, being a black child? Besides, we don't know who you are connected to here and it could send you back into the loop."

That was true. Sitka had already been sent out of the timeline with the lady and more than once had the buzzing in her head, which warned her she was getting too close.

"Have you ever tried a letter?"

Davis laughed. "Oh, yes. A letter. Writing in the dirt in front of the house. Yelling from far off. Nothing gets through. There's always something that prevents what I'm doing from making it to who I need it to go to."

Sitka considered this. Davis couldn't exist when he existed, so nothing he did could leave a mark. She wasn't supposed to be there, but if she did exist there, it was as a previous version of herself. Her thoughts drifted back to her mother and a secret game they'd play. One only the two of them knew about. She drummed her fingers on the bench and thought about how she could use the game to help Davis. A scavenger hunt of sorts. A smile twitched at the sides of her mouth and she stared at Davis.

"I have an idea."

Chapter Twenty-One

*S*itka told Davis how when she was a little girl, she and her mother would leave each other obscure clues around the house for the other to find. They weren't allowed to speak about the game face-to-face and the clues would lead each other to a meetup point where they'd each bring something to share with each other. Since she couldn't get close to the lady, maybe she could leave her clues to help Davis and his family. Leading her to a place where she could perhaps intervene on Letty's behalf.

Davis seemed unconvinced. "Even if we tricked her into meeting my family, why would she want to help a family she doesn't even know?"

"She seems nice. Like she would *want* to help," Sitka countered.

"Nice or not, no white lady is going to help a black family get care at a white hospital."

"Why not?"

Davis sighed. "It's just not the way it's done here, in this time. Not that anyone would listen even if she did. There are rules which they won't change."

Sitka frowned. Who wouldn't want to help a child? The lady had a nice face, or maybe Sitka was confusing the lady with her mother again. Her mother would never let a child hurt or go without. She remembered one time when they were taking a road trip and came across a family living in their car, her mother practically gave them everything she had on her, including their extra clothes. Sitka remembered the dirty faces of the children staring out from the grimy half-rolled-down window. How they grinned with delight when Sitka's mother handed them apples and candy.

The lady here had to have some of that compassion in her, Sitka reasoned. She stuck her chin up. "I want to try."

Davis watched her and shrugged. "So, how do you plan to play the game, if the lady doesn't know you are playing it?"

Sitka tugged at the hem of her dress. "I don't know. I was thinking I could leave her secret messages. Like a treasure map to your family."

"How are you going to do that? You can't get close to her and that man guards the gate," Davis replied, pointing out the challenge of getting close.

Sitka thought about it. The woman walked back home most mornings. However, she had to be going somewhere first to go back home. "I'll follow her. In the morning. When she leaves her house, I'll see where she goes."

Davis shifted uncomfortably. "We're running out of time. Day after tomorrow, Letty gets sick. We don't have time to be playing no games, honeybee."

He was right, of course. She could follow the woman in the morning to see where she went, but that would leave only the day Letty got sick to try and reach her. "What time of day does Letty go to the hospital?"

"Well, she was sick overnight and we thought it was the flu, but by that afternoon she was hunched over, crying in pain. We got to the hospital around dinner time and they sent us across town to the other hospital. She was slipping in and out of it by the time we got there and they rushed her into surgery. She came out of surgery but never recovered. Her blood was tainted. She died the next day."

"So, we have until that afternoon to try and get the lady to help?" Sitka asked, more to herself than anything.

Davis didn't respond, feeling the conversation and plan was futile. Up until that point, the only thing the lady knew about any of them was that Sitka showed up at the gate. She had no idea who any of them were and had no reason to care about what was happening in their lives.

Sensing Davis's frustration, Sitka put her hand on his arm. "How can it hurt if I try?"

Davis nodded. "I suppose it can't. Or maybe getting another person involved will mess everything up more. Like, say she does step in and help, will that prevent you from ever going home?"

Sitka chewed her lip. "I'm not going home it seems, anyway. We can't find a door. If we're here, we should try to save Letty."

Davis wiped his face and Sitka realized he was crying. He cleared his throat and gazed out over the park field. "See, every time I've had to go through the loss another time. I don't want to get my hopes up, only to know she suffered and died all over again."

"But she will, anyhow. How many times have you come back here? How many times have you known she's died? At least if we try to do something, there's a chance to change it. If we do nothing, then what happened before will happen again," Sitka responded.

"I suppose you're right. It's gonna hurt either way, so let's try," Davis replied, still sounding defeated.

Sitka gave him a quick hug and jumped up. "Is it safe to go to the shop?"

"I reckon it is now. Stay by me and don't stray. We can't afford to get separated at this point." Davis stood up and took her hand. "Let's get something to eat and you tell me about your plan."

As they walked back to the shop, Sitka told Davis all about how she and her mother would leave each other notes or clues around the house, eventually leading up to a meetup point. Sometimes it was just for ice cream. Sometimes they'd get dolled up to go out to the movies. Because they each took part, neither knew until the end exactly how it would unfold. That was part of the game.

Davis chuckled as they walked. "Your mother sounds lovely. You must've been the apple of her eye."

His saying it made her heart hurt. That was just what mothers were to Sitka. She thought everyone had a mother like that. Silly, thoughtful, beautiful, and kind. Even though the lady looked sort of like her mother, she didn't look at Sitka the way her mother had.

No one ever would again.

After a light dinner, Sitka laid down and thought about her plan. She needed to be able to leave the lady a clue she'd come back to find. A clue that would lead her to current-day Davis and his family. One which didn't require Sitka to be present. Something intriguing enough, the woman wouldn't be able to resist. Sitka glanced around the shop and grinned as an idea began to form. On the far wall was a large, wall-mounted grandfather clock. One with all the golden gears visible and adorned chains hanging from the front. The hands were made out of ornately carved brass.

It was a lure and there was no way she could actually make it happen, but the lady didn't need to know that. They just needed to get her there. Sitka got up and dug around the counter until she found an advertisement for the shop.

"Davis, can I use this?"

Davis peered up from the newspaper he was reading and nodded. "Sure? This for your idea?"

"Can you write a letter to the lady? Like a 'you won a prize' letter?"

Davis frowned and cocked his head. "I can. To go with the flier? What's the prize?"

"Yeah... um, that clock?" Sitka pointed to the clock on the wall. "We need the lady's name though, to make it seem authentic. Tomorrow, when I follow the lady, do you think it would be safe for you to go talk to the gateman? To find out her name?"

"Well, not sure he'll be too keen on giving out her information to a stranger, but I can try," Davis replied.

The plan was beginning to come together. They had very little time and any one thing could prevent it from happening, but Sitka was determined to do her best to help Davis's family. He drafted up a prize announcement letter which Sitka stuck under the couch with the flier. The letter told the lady she'd won the grandfather clock from the shop in a random drawing, but she needed to sign for it to be delivered.

To not arouse suspicion, they told her she needed to come on the day they knew Davis would be home with Letty sick. From there, they'd leave a note on the door saying due to a family emergency, she'd need to come to Davis's home to sign the paperwork. So she wouldn't send anyone else, they told her she'd need to bring proof of identity with her.

Many things could go wrong. She could not get the letter. She could not care. She could show up at the clock shop and decide going to their house was too much work. However, one thing Sitka knew about her mother was she liked to win things, even if it was just a trinket or piece of junk. She also liked unique items and that clock was something special.

The next morning, Sitka was up early watching from the shop window. She'd never seen the lady leaving in the morning, only returning from whatever errand she was running. Sitka hoped she passed the same way on the way out and kept her eyes peeled on the sidewalk. Davis tidied up the shop and made sure to bring the letter with the advertisement with him. They'd have to go separately to each do their part of the plan, but agreed to meet back at the park as soon as they were finished with their tasks.

Sitka yawned and rested her head on her hands while she waited. As the sun rose, the woman came walking around the corner in a powder blue suit, her hair styled in an upsweep perfectly. She strolled with a little spring in her step. Knowing she couldn't get too close, Sitka held back and paused until the woman passed by the window on the other side of the street. Sitka nodded at Davis and dashed out to follow.

The woman walked through the city streets until she came to a nondescript door. She pulled out a key, unlocked the door, and went in. Sitka noticed there was a mail slot on the door and it sat between a shoe shop and a newspaper office. The woman was inside for over an hour when she came back out, relocking the door, then headed back down the street.

Sitka waited a few minutes, then wandered to the door. In gold letters on the door was written, "A. Danielson, Attorney at Law." The woman was going to a lawyer's office every day? Or just that day? Sitka chewed her fingernails. Now, she wasn't so sure the plan would work. What if the lady was just dropping something off? What if she didn't come back to the place the next day? They *needed* her to come there.

Sitka headed for the park, trying to think of a backup plan when she saw Davis sitting on the bench. She plopped down and told Davis everything. Expecting him to be disappointed, she was surprised when he began to grin.

"What is it, Davis?"

"Well, I spoke to the man at the gate. Told him I was interested in landscaping the property. He told me I'd need to come back later and speak to the owner. A *Ms. Abigail Danielson*."

Chapter Twenty-Two

*L*ater that day, Sitka and Davis headed back to Abigail's office. Davis put the flyer and award notification in an official-looking envelope and slipped it into the slot. They only had the next morning for the lady to find the prize announcement and respond to it. They needed her to get the letter, go to the shop Davis knew would be closed, then go to his house. From there, they'd hide out and watch, hoping to redirect her to help his family. How? They hadn't figured that part out yet. Davis could approach Abigail, however, Sitka couldn't for more than a minute without getting sent out of her body. They needed her to see what was happening and intercede without much prodding on their end.

They went back to the clock shop and waited. Once Abigail walked by, they trailed behind, keeping a distance. Not too close, but close enough that if she didn't go to the office, they wouldn't lose track of her.

Luckily for them, she did.

Abigail unlocked the door and slipped it, securing it behind her. Unlike the previous morning, she was inside for hours. Too long. Davis and Sitka began to panic, realizing if she didn't get to his house in time, she might miss the family leaving with Letty for the hospital. As the morning wore on, they began to think all hope was lost.

Finally, Abigail emerged, clutching the letter in her hand. She locked the door and paused to look at the flyer. Sitka held her breath, afraid Abigail would go in the direction of her house instead of the clock shop. Abigail tucked the flyer in her bag and strolled down the avenue. She crossed the street when she got close and headed to the shop, instead of home. They followed and watched her try to open the door, finding it locked. She peered in the window, using her hands to block out any outside light.

A sign on the door said there was a family emergency and asked her to come to their home location to sign for the clock. She bit her lip and frowned, trying to decide if it was worth the trip. Pulling the letter out again, she glanced at it and stared down the street, indecision on her face. She wasn't someone who needed money from the size of her home and appearance, so she needed to want the clock for other reasons. That was where Sitka hoped the similarities to her mother would come into play. Abigail went toward her home and their hearts sank. It was a long shot, however, they'd hoped she'd be intrigued enough to go to Davis's house. A check of the time and they'd be rushing Letty to the hospital shortly.

Now, every minute mattered.

Just about the time they gave up all hope, Abigail paused, then turned on her heel and began striding in the other direction in a hurry. Toward Davis's home. Davis grasped Sitka by the hand with a nod.

"Come on, let's go. She's moving quick!"

Sitka had to run to keep up with Davis's long strides and they hustled after Abigail as she deftly moved through the crowded sidewalk. Whatever had popped into her mind, she was determined to get there. It was as if she'd received a higher calling.

Maybe she had.

As Abigail took the turn for the street Davis's house was on, they realized the timing had to be just right. If she got there too soon, current-day Davis or his wife would be confused and send Abigail away, saying the letter wasn't authentic. They certainly didn't have the money to just give away the beautiful, antique clock hanging in the shop. She needed to arrive as they were leaving with Letty, so her attention would be distracted by their plight. Then the clock would, at least momentarily, be forgotten.

As Abigail raised her hand to knock, the front door flew open and she was suddenly face-to-face with Davis, his expression contorted with anxiety and stress. He stared at her, shocked by her sudden presence. She spoke to him quietly. Although Sitka and Davis couldn't hear what she was saying, she stuck the letter out to Davis and he took it, thoroughly confused. He read the letter, rubbing his hand across his face, as Sitka had seen many times before with her Davis. He shook his head as something happening in the house drew his attention away and he rushed back inside, leaving the door open. Abigail paused, clearly thrown off by the interaction.

She stepped off the stoop and turned to leave.

As Abigail's foot hit the last step, Davis shifted beside Sitka and she heard him whisper hoarsely, "No! Don't leave. Please don't leave."

Abigail walked down the sidewalk as Sitka felt Davis leave her side and saw him running toward Abigail. There was no way Sitka couldn't stop him in time. She froze in place, seeing him dash toward the very confused woman. He almost made it to her.

Almost.

"Ma'am! Wait! They need your help. I need your help. Please don't go!" His voice was desperate and Sitka could hear all the times he experienced losing his daughter caught up in the syllables.

At the moment Abigail turned to see where the voice was coming from, current-day Davis came back to the door with keys in his hand. He barely registered she was still on the path, but Sitka saw what his presence did in the timeline. Her Davis was running toward them and just disappeared. It wasn't like on television where it was a popping visual as if the film cut. It was like he was there, then hadn't ever been. His words disappeared as if they'd never been said.

Abigail spun back to current-day Davis, an apology on her lips. He shook his head and hurried past her to the car, yanking the back seat door open. Sitka moved toward them, then paused as Ruth hurried out with a limp Letty in her arms. Sitka's ears began to ring and the world around her distorted. She crouched down as the ringing got louder. Ruth either didn't see Abigail or didn't care as she rushed past, crawling in the back seat with Letty. Davis climbed in the front seat and fired up the car. He started to reverse out of the driveway when Sitka realized everything they did would be for nothing if he drove off, leaving Abigail clueless how to help.

She stood up and shook off the disorientation. She had to do what Davis couldn't and began to run toward the confounded woman. "Abigail! Stop them!"

Abigail shook her head, watching the lanky girl coming at her full speed. She took a step back. "What? I'm sorry, stop who?"

"The people in the car," Sitka yelled as she drew near. She couldn't get too close, so she had to get Abigail to understand before Sitka was also kicked out of the timeline. "Their daughter is dying. They're going to the hospital nearby but will be turned away because they're black. It's her only chance. Please hurry!"

Abigail shook her head, then glanced between Sitka and the family in the car backing out. Sitka felt herself fading fast and prayed Abigail would believe her. Abigail watched and her eyes widened as she saw what Sitka knew was happening. Sitka was passing between worlds. She was physically fading from that time.

Sitka took everything in her and yelled. "She will die without your help! Please go help her, Mama!"

At those words, Sitka knew her power to intervene was over, she was being pushed out of the timeline. The last thing she saw was Abigail running toward the car, waving her hands frantically at Davis.

Whatever happened next was a blur and Sitka found herself reliving the moments of her life as she was suspended through time planes. Wonderful moments, heartbreaking ones. She saw her mother in all their times together and tried to reach her, but they were just snapshots. She saw Aunt Leigh and Tommy.

She thought she saw her Davis but it was a flash moving past her, too fast to be sure. She saw nothing of Abigail, past Davis, or his family again. She didn't know if they'd changed anything. She was unaware if they'd saved Letty's life.

As if the time suspension realized Sitka was there, she was vomited out, cast into another time. Solid this time, not like when she saw Glenn and Tommy. She groaned and lay on the ground, reaching out to feel the surface beneath her. Dirt. Leaves. She cracked her eyes open and stared up. Trees. Wherever, or whenever she'd been sent, she was in the woods. Rolling on her back, she peered up, watching the sunlight filter through the tree canopy above. She listened to see if anything sounded familiar, but all she heard was the wind blowing through the tops of the trees.

She sat up and glanced around, the area seeming somewhat familiar. Familiar. Her stomach did flips as she realized where she was. The woods. The dirt road. She knew *where* she was. She stood up and tried to determine *when* she was. Just then, she heard the rumble of an engine and looked for where it was coming from. Dread filled her as she saw what she hoped she wouldn't. The blue van was coming down the road. She scuttled farther into the woods as it drew to a stop in the same place it had before. She was in a loop.

Again, she witnessed whoever was in the van drag a body into the woods and dump it. Once again she ran, hearing them coming after her. Again, she thought her name was being called. She stumbled and tried to understand what was happening. Had she been put back in time? She ran for the shack, hoping she could find Davis and make sense of it all. She followed the path she knew to go toward the shack and breathed with relief as she heard the woods fall silent again. Like before, they'd lost track of her.

She slowed her pace as she drew close, knowing Davis would know what to do if she could connect with him through the shack. He might be able to explain everything that was happening. Hopefully, he was sent somewhere he could come back there from. Maybe he could let her know if Letty survived. She thought about seeing Abigail running toward the car as it was almost out of the driveway, waving her hands. Seeing Davis staring at her as if she was crazy.

Did he stop?

Sitka paused and listened, thinking she heard the van again, but there were no nearby roads. They couldn't get close to the shack without driving. The hunters she'd seen before had probably come in by the old cemetery. The one where Davis was buried. That was the only other clear way into the woods. Even then, it was far enough away from the shack, she'd hear anyone coming in on foot. She just needed to get there and see if she could contact Davis.

She saw a deer dart away in front of her and paused. Something wasn't right. The deer was running from what should've been a clearing. The spot near the creek where the shack was built. Sitka turned around, her head spinning. There was no clearing and looked as if there'd never been one. She rotated on her heel, surveying the area. She was at the correct place but it wasn't right. It was off.

There was no shack.

Chapter Twenty-Three

here was it? Sitka ran to the spot she knew the shack should be and searched for any sign of it. The vegetation appeared completely undisturbed. She scoured the ground for broken glass or anything showing a building had once been there. Still, there was nothing. She even tried backtracking from the creek to see if she'd misjudged the location. However, when she came back to the area, everything looked like it had when she'd been there prior. Only, no shack. She sat down on a nearby rock and stared around. Davis had never been there. Something they did changed the timeline and the shack never existed.

Sitka got up and wondered what to do. If there was no shack, there was no Davis and she didn't have anyone to lean on. To figure things out with. She thought about the old cemetery and Davis's headstone there. That would prove he'd been there and she wasn't losing her mind. She must've come back to the day she went missing because she saw the body get dumped again. From that day until she went into the tunnel hadn't happened yet.

Heading to the cemetery, she saw the deer and it seemed to be watching her. She paused and met its eyes. There was something almost human about them, the way they peered at her so intently. She almost changed direction and followed it when it walked in the other way, but she had questions she needed answered.

The cemetery looked about the same, making her feel a little more sure about what she'd experienced. She wandered to the area where Davis's grave was and stopped. The weeds were high, but even so, she didn't see it anywhere. She shoved the tall grass down and gazed around. His grave was gone. Or had never been there, to begin with. Did this mean they'd managed to save Letty?

Did it mean anything?

To make sure, she meandered through the rows of dilapidated gravestones, searching for the name Butler. While she found a few, none had Davis's name on them. She did a mental calculation and assumed he would've still passed away by now, most likely. He simply wasn't buried in this cemetery anymore. There were small, community graveyards all over the south, so he could be anywhere.

Sitka sat down and leaned against a headstone, calculating her next move. If she was back to the day she went missing, she got there before Glenn tried to hit Tommy with the trophy. She could stop that from happening. However, she needed something on Glenn. If he was willing to hurt or kill Tommy, it meant he might try again. She closed her eyes and the image of Glenn at her bedroom door popped into her mind and she mentally shut it down. Whatever was there, she wasn't ready to face it. Not now.

The body. Who was it? Twice she'd seen it dumped, so maybe it meant something. Perhaps if she saw who it was, she could go to the police about it. She wasn't technically missing yet, and it might bring their family enough into the light to make Glenn lie low. In that time, she could think of a way to get rid of Glenn so he couldn't hurt Tommy. Or her.

The deer appeared at the edge of the cemetery, beckoning Sitka with its eyes. Sitka got up and brushed dirt off her shorts. This time she made her way over and followed it as it turned and wandered through the woods. It seemed to be making sure Sitka didn't lose sight of it as it went down the thin trail. Before they got to where it was leading, Sitka understood. Like her, the deer seemed to understand she needed to go back to the body. To see who it was. That was the only way she could go to the police and go home.

As they neared the site, the deer stopped, glanced back at Sitka, then loped off into the woods, leaving her alone with the one thing she didn't want to go near. Too afraid to approach the body, she crouched under the fallen tree roots and waited. And waited. For what, she didn't know.

"Just do it, girl," she whispered to herself, trying to summon the courage to pull back the tarp.

What if it was bloody, or parts of the body were missing? What if it wasn't dead and grabbed her, dragging her in with it? What if she was so scared, she passed out next to it? The more she thought about it, the more she knew she needed to get it over with as quickly as possible before she chickened out altogether. She stood up and took a deep breath.

∞

She peered around, not sure what she was looking for when she spied it. A long, skinny, but sturdy branch. She could use that to peel back the tarp from farther away, so she wouldn't have to get close to the body. She went over and picked up the stick, grasping it firmly in her hands. She could do this. She'd be able to go home.

She'd save Tommy.

"Davis, where are you? I need you right now."

She was answered only with birds chirping far off somewhere in the trees. She was alone. If she came back before the body was dumped, it meant she'd never met Davis. At least not here, in this time. None of it made sense and hurt her head to try and figure out. What she did know was she needed to look at the body, make sure it was what she was telling the police. She'd thought it was a man from the arm but wanted to make sure. What if she went to tell the police, then they came and the body was gone? Moved? She needed to at least have a description, so they believed her.

Summoning courage, she inched closer to the body, half-expecting it to pop up and chase her. No, it was laying like it had the first time she saw it, with one arm splayed out in the leaves. She poked the tarp with the end of the branch and waited. Nothing moved. Sighing heavily, she jabbed it harder.

Still nothing.

She slipped the tip of the branch under the edge of the tarp and tried easing it back, but the branch bent like rubber. She'd need to break off the thin tip, then get closer. She pulled the branch back and snapped off about six inches, leaving a thicker stub to work with. She stepped a little closer and closed one eye while she shoved the tip of the branch back under the tarp, praying it wasn't too gory under there. She lifted the tarp slightly, but she still couldn't see in.

It was starting to get dark and she needed to move quicker. She knew the woods better now, so as soon as she saw the body, she could run to the Zip Mart and tell them what she found. Then, they could call the police. She'd tell the police where she found the body and ask them to contact Aunt Leigh. Glenn wouldn't do anything once Sitka gave her statement. It would raise suspicion that she found a body, then her cousin went missing or was killed.

Sitka used both arms to lift the plastic sheet as much as she could and moved it aside, uncovering the top half of the body. The body was face down, so she could only make out the back half. It was definitely a man. She'd still need to see the face to describe the man to the police. That would require her to turn the body at least partially over. She wasn't strong enough to flip a full-grown man, though.

She went around the side the man's face was slightly facing, realizing she'd at least need to move the head enough to get a general idea of what he looked like. The sun was starting to drop behind the tree line, causing it to become harder to see. Sitka crouched down and peered at the head of the body, now becoming covered in shadows from the tree. Something made the hair rise on the back of her neck and she moved closer.

As she knelt in and used the thick end of the branch to turn the head slightly, a small scream escaped her throat. She scrambled back and pressed herself against the trunk of the tree. It couldn't be. She leaned over and wretched beside the tree as her head began to pound. There was no way she was seeing what she thought she was seeing.

The eyes of the man gazed at her, empty but open. She knew those eyes. She'd seen them staring at her in life. She lept to her feet, terrified at not only what she discovered, but at the impossibility of it.

In a moment, Sitka found herself running through the trees, ignoring as the brush ripped at her legs. She fell so many times, she lost count but didn't care. She wanted to get as far away from the body as she could. She tripped again, this time over something that felt manmade. She reached back and ran her hands against what the object was, feeling something very familiar. It was her roller skates she'd dropped the first time she saw the body get dumped. She picked them up, cradling them in her arms. It was something that felt like home. She got up and ran on, clutching the skates like a baby to her chest.

She found herself back at the cemetery and she scurried to the shadows, hiding behind a gravestone. She drew her legs up to her chest, pinning the roller skates against her body. Her mind reeling, she didn't fight it when she began to pass out, falling... her head pressed to the soil.

When she came to, it was dark and she sat up, determining if she saw what she thought she did. It wasn't possible, but now she was unsure of everything. The shack was gone as if it never existed. Davis's grave was missing, like the shack. He didn't die there. He wasn't buried there. Maybe they did save Letty, so he didn't live out his days in the woods. That would explain the missing shack and the headstone.

However, if Sitka was back to the day she went missing and saw the body as she had before, shortly after leaving the skating rink, there was no way the man she saw could be who she thought it was. The Zip Mart would now be closed, so she'd have to wait until morning to go there. Until daylight to piece everything together. She rested back against the ground, using her skates as a pillow, and closed her eyes.

"Davis, wherever you are, please find me. I need your help. I don't understand anything and am really scared. Where did you go?"

Sitka dozed off, picturing Davis sitting right next to her. She imagined him humming like he always did, a soothing low song. Somewhere out there, Davis still existed and she hoped he could see her now wherever he was. To keep a watchful eye on her.

When morning came, Sitka sat up and pulled her skates to her, knowing she needed to go back to the body to make sure. If it was who she thought she saw, it would turn everything she thought upside down. She ran her fingers over the skate wheels and frowned. She peered at them in the light and shook her head. The wheel bearings were rusty. As if they'd sat out in the weather for weeks. She'd only dropped them the day before.

Well, the time before the day before.

She stood up, setting her resolve. The skates confirmed something wasn't right about the timeline. She practically marched through the woods back to the body. When she got close, she took the edge of the tarp and tugged with all her might, forcing the body to shift onto its side. As she stared back down at the face of the man, she knew they'd messed up the timeline when they tried to save Letty.

At least now, she wouldn't have to figure out what to do about Glenn anymore. His lifeless eyes stared out at the trees with a bullet hole placed neatly between them.

Chapter Twenty-Four

Who murdered Glenn? Sitka left the body and headed through the woods toward Zip Mart. The blue van brought the body and dumped it, reminding Sitka about the image of Tommy waving it down and climbing in. Could Tommy be in danger? Did whoever killed Glenn have some sort of vendetta against Glenn? Against their family? Fear gripped Sitka's stomach as she picked up the pace to the convenience store. What if Tommy was somewhere hurt?

Once she got to the backside of the Zip Mart, she paused to think of a plan. Finding Glenn dead was definitely not part of her original plan of calling the police. Seeing the deterioration of her roller skates, let her know it wouldn't work, anyway. She needed to find out what day it was and go from there. The newspaper rack was outside the door, so she might be able to get a look at it without being seen. She waited until she saw a car leave the parking lot and paused a moment before heading to the front.

All was quiet as Sitka crept along the brick side of the building and peeked around the corner to the front of the store. The newspaper rack was right outside the door, on the side where the man at the register could see it. There was no way she wouldn't be seen standing there. Considering her options, she picked up a rock and headed back behind the store. She lifted the rock and banged as hard as she could against the steel door, then scooted around the side. Once she heard the man open the door, she dashed to the front of the store to look, before he could make it back to the register.

She stared at the date on the paper, not believing what she saw printed there when she saw the man lumbering back to the front of the store. She ran as fast as she could to the woodline and collapsed on the ground, digging her fingers into her legs. Five weeks. She'd been gone five weeks. The time she'd been in the shack and the time she'd been with Davis in 1929. How was that possible? She saw the body get dumped the day she got lost. How did she see it get dumped again yesterday? How was it Glenn? Nothing was adding up.

Watching from the woodline, she saw cars come and go all day. What could she tell the police? What would she tell Aunt Leigh? None of it made sense. If she'd been gone five weeks, she could see how it was Glenn, but she knew she'd already observed the body get dumped the day she left the skating rink. However, that couldn't have been Glenn because he was outside the skating rink, waiting to pick her up. He couldn't have been there, then been killed and dumped in that short span of time realistically. Could there have been two bodies dumped?

No, it was the same body.

Sitka remembered the van, the arm, the tarp. It was in the exact location both times. Each time, she saw the van slow down and yell at her. Both times, she ran. The first time, she dropped her skates. The second time, she tripped over them. It was impossible. Also, they'd clearly been outside for all those weeks, getting exposed to the weather.

Not brave enough to go into the store, Sitka slept outside of it that night. She dug in the trash once they were closed for any food. She found a half-eaten bag of chips and was relieved to find the spigot around back had running water. She went back into the woodline and curled up at the base of a large pine, the needles acting as bedding.

As she slept, Sitka dreamed she was home with her mother. The apartment in New York. Her mother had her back to Sitka and was staring out an open window, standing on the sill. She turned to Sitka and waved her over. As Sitka came close, her mother grasped her hand and pulled her up to the open window, then out onto the ledge. Sitka resisted, afraid they'd fall when her mother smiled down at her.

"Trust me."

Sitka nodded and climbed up next to her mother. It was so good to feel her close again. To smell the patchouli perfume she liked to wear. Her mother let one foot dangle off the ledge, tugging on Sitka's hand.

"Let's go."

"I'm scared," Sitka replied.

"I'd never let you fall. You'll see." Her mother guided them both out and Sitka gasped as she felt her feet hit the air.

They didn't fall. Her mother took her above the building and it was as if they crossed miles in the blink of an eye. Sitka saw a black man riding a train, his head resting against the glass. She could feel his sorrow, his loneliness. She saw Aunt Leigh crying in the shower, pounding her fist against the glass door. She saw Tommy inside the blue van, his hand pressed against the glass, worry encasing him.

Sitka's mother held her hand tightly and then let go, allowing Sitka to fly on her own. Sitka reached out for her but her mother shook her head. "It's time, Sitty. You have to go back and fix things. They can't do this without you. You carry the key to everything. Remember?"

Sitka watched as her mother smiled and faded away into the clouds, leaving Sitka suspended in the air. She turned back to the man, to Aunt Leigh, to Tommy. They needed her to come back. They needed her to set things right. She felt the weight of their suffering pulling her down, back to the tree she was sleeping under outside the store.

Returning to time.

Sitka sat up and cried out, the pain of losing her mother fresh in her mind. In coming back, she felt the grief she did when her mother first left. It wasn't fair. She rested her head on her knees and thought about the dream. She didn't know the man but he seemed so familiar. Like family. Family. Her father. He looked different... worn down, broken. Not like the picture of him her mother had, laughing without a care in the world. Something happened to him. Something only she held the power to fix. Tommy was alive but he was in the van and worried. Was he trapped?

Aunt Leigh had lost so much, Sitka could feel the unending sorrow in her. Her sister, her husband, now Sitka. She might lose Tommy, too, if Sitka didn't get back. Sitka knew it was time to reach out to Aunt Leigh. No matter what came of it. It was better to let her know she was alive and suffer the consequences. At least Glenn couldn't hurt them anymore.

Glenn couldn't hurt *her* anymore. At that moment, the memory of Glenn in her doorway formed, but this time she didn't turn away from it. Of Glenn coming in and shutting the door behind him. Of Glenn crossing the floor to her bed. Of her crying and pleading with him to leave her alone. Of him pressing his weight on top of her, hurting her.

Sitka dropped her skates and screamed. She couldn't hide from it anymore. She couldn't allow her fear to deny that Glenn abused her. All of a sudden, the memories of climbing the fence surfaced in her mind and she knew why. She was running from him. From the secret he forced her to share. From her fragile state, that he used against her after her mother died. Glenn deserved to die. It was the only way she'd be free of the torment he'd burdened her with. Now that the memory came back, she could no longer run from it. Glenn was dead, but what he did to her was marked on her soul.

Sitka picked up her skates and bashed them against the tree, over and over until the wheels began to break off. Once her arms were too tired to move, she threw them down and sobbed into the bark of the tree. She wanted her mother. She wanted Aunt Leigh. She wanted Tommy. She wanted to be an innocent child again, without these horrible weights around her neck. It was too much to carry, too much to remember.

Sitka stumbled toward the store, not caring if anyone saw her, now. Nothing could be worse than the reality of what she'd been through. The pain she'd endured. No one could injure her more than she'd been hurt at a time when she was most vulnerable. Glenn was dead but he'd left his existence on her. One she could no longer run from. One that haunted her waking and sleeping moments.

When the blue van pulled into the parking lot, she didn't even see it. Not that she would've cared. She heard it slam on its brakes and doors fling open. She fell, skinning her knees, and got back up, heading for the doors of the store. She'd call Aunt Leigh, she'd know what to do. She'd hold Sitka and tell her it would be alright. It wouldn't, but Sitka would listen and let the words soothe her. She couldn't tell Aunt Leigh what happened. She couldn't give it power outside of her own mind.

The world around her wavered as she heard voices yelling in front of her. Desperate voices. Were they calling her name? She stared up and saw figures rushing toward her. From the van. She didn't care. They could take her. Kill her. Put an end to the misery she had consuming her brain. She fell again, this time not even trying to get up. She lay on the pavement, feeling the heat sear into her skin. None of it mattered anymore. She was destroyed.

Sitka felt hands grabbing at her, dragging her up off the ground, and clinging to her. Her head lolled back and she tried to comprehend the faces but her eyes were out of focus. Water was being put to her lips but she turned her head away, refusing any sort of comfort. Of sustenance. She could hear her name being called and saw she was being moved to the blue van. They had her now. They knew she'd seen them dump the body. She'd be next.

"Davis," she whispered and closed her eyes. Maybe she'd find him on the other side.

"Honeybee, don't be going on like that, hear?" a voice told her.

She looked up into Davis's face with relief. "I knew I'd find you again."

"Not like this, you won't. You need to go back. Your Mama told you so. You need to find your daddy."

"Davis, Glenn did bad things to me. He hurt me."

"I know, honeybee. You can't let that define you. You can't let him continue to control you," Davis murmured, stroking her cheek.

"I don't know how not to," Sitka cried.

"You have to speak your pain, you understand? You take away its power when you let it out. Don't carry his secrets, it only keeps you locked away. I'll always be with you, but you have to go and set things right."

Davis was gone.

Set things right. Speak her pain. There was no way to go but back which was forward. She allowed the light to draw her up and she opened her sore eyes. They came into focus and she cried out.

"Tommy!"

He held her tightly to his chest as tears streamed down his cheeks. She reached up and touched his face. It was Tommy, he was alive. They were in the blue van with another boy about his age. Tommy rocked back and forth, clutching Sitka close, his heart pounding in his chest.

"I thought he killed you, Sitty. I thought you were gone for good."

Chapter Twenty-Five

S itka rested her head against Tommy's chest, so many questions swimming around her mind. Who was the other boy? Why were they in the blue van? She closed her eyes and let the questions rest while she pushed the other memories away. All of a sudden, she sat upright as the last couple of days came rushing back and stared at Tommy.

"Glenn is dead," she whispered.

A look passed between Tommy and the other boy sitting in the driver's seat. Tommy shook his head. "What do you mean, Sitty?"

"I saw his body in the woods. I saw..." She glanced around the inside of the van and swallowed. "I saw this van on the dirt road, and I saw his body get dumped in the woods off the road."

Tommy's face turned red and he dropped his chin, his voice tight. "When? Are you sure you think it was this van? There are a lot of blue vans around."

Sitka nodded and pointed at the triangle sticker in the back window. "It had that sticker. It was the same. I saw it happen the day I went missing, too."

"What do you mean? You couldn't have. We... uh, shit. Sitty, I need to tell you something, but you have to promise to never tell anyone," Tommy said in hushed tones. "Ever."

Sitka eyed the other boy, who was staring out the front window. She could see his Adam's apple going up and down as he nervously swallowed. She tipped her head at Tommy. "I know Glenn tried to hurt you. To hit you with the trophy in your room."

Tommy jerked back, his eyes wide with shock. He stared at Sitka wordless, then ran his hands through his long hair. "What the hell? I don't understand. Sitty, did you go home at some point? You were in the house?"

She shook her head. "No. I can't explain it but I saw it, like in my mind."

Tommy glanced at the kid in the front seat. "This is Jerry. He's my friend from school."

"Did Jerry kill Glenn?" Sitka asked.

"No. I did. I had to, Sitty. He was going to murder me. I thought he'd killed you. He came home from the skating rink the day he took the car, so I couldn't go pick you up. He said he was getting you and left in a huff. When he came back, you weren't with him. We searched everywhere but couldn't find you, so I thought he'd done something to you when he picked you up that day. He was being weird about it and refused to help the police with information. I think they also suspected him, but without a body, they couldn't do more than list you as a missing child. He said you weren't there when he went to get you. That you weren't inside, either. But he was acting strange, like almost relieved."

"He didn't pick me up. I saw him waiting and went around the other side of the building. Something about him being there scared me and I didn't want to go with him. I tried to walk home a different way, so he wouldn't see me but got lost in the woods," Sitka explained.

"For five weeks? We scoured the area for you. Everyone came out and looked. The whole neighborhood. Your pictures are all over town," Tommy told her.

How could she answer that? Tell him she hid in a shack, then went through a tunnel under the floorboards to 1929? Even she knew that sounded crazy. Tell him the ghost of a man who died decades ago was her friend and that she saw her mother in another time? He wouldn't believe her. Even if he did, no one else would.

She frowned. "I saw you dump the body the day I went missing. Off the dirt road."

Tommy cocked his head. "You couldn't have, Sitty. I... uh... I shot Glenn *yesterday*. I'd gone home to get my things to leave for good. I brought a gun I bought from a friend of Jerry's with me in case. Glenn caught me in the house and came at me, saying he was going to kill me. I knew he'd murder me if I didn't shoot him. I didn't want to. It was horrible, even if he deserved it. Jerry helped me move his body in the van and we dumped it in the woods in the afternoon. Yesterday."

"I saw that, too, but I saw it happen the day I got lost, Tommy. It happened twice."

Jerry turned toward them and watched her. "Did you eat anything in the woods?"

Sitka bobbed her head. "Yeah. Berries, leaves, some mushrooms."

"What kind of mushrooms?" Tommy asked.

"I don't know. I was so hungry and they tasted awful, but I needed to eat."

Jerry and Tommy looked at each other and nodded. Tommy took her hand, giving it a gentle squeeze. "It's possible you ate psychedelic mushrooms, they make you see and believe all kinds of things."

Sitka considered the possibility. While it would explain many things that happened, her gut told her it wasn't true. Then there were her skates. "The day I got lost, I dropped my skates fleeing from the van. Yesterday, I tripped over them running again. They were rusted like they'd been there for a long time. Like five weeks."

Tommy rubbed his chin. "Maybe you did run the first day and drop your skates, then tripped over them yesterday. Perhaps the mushrooms messed with your memory of the timeline when things occurred. When did you last have any?"

Weeks. It'd been weeks. The first time she saw Davis, but not after that. So, they couldn't have affected her perception of reality, seeing Davis after that, then going back in time. She shrugged. Tommy wouldn't understand.

He sighed. "Regardless, you're here and alive. We can figure everything else out later. I need to tell Mom. She's been freaking out, not sleeping, not eating. Where have you been all this time? Where did you get that dress?"

Sitka quickly formed a timeline in her head. She'd been staying at a shack that didn't exist, then in another plane of existence. How could she explain the dress? Letty's dress. The clothes she'd been wearing when she went back in time were still somewhere in 1929. She thought about the time she found the canned food. "I was hiding in a root cellar. There was a box of old clothes down there. Jars of food, too."

"Why, Sitty? Why didn't you just come home, have someone call us? I thought you were dead. Mom has been frantic, putting your picture up everywhere. She refused to give up on finding you. Even when everyone else said it was too long, too late."

Now, Sitka knew she needed to speak the truth about Glenn. The one she was only coming to grips with herself. To speak her pain. Tears began to burn her eyes as the memories ripped at her soul, and she buried her face in her hands. How could she do this? She took a deep breath and met Tommy's eyes, seeing nothing but love. It was time to stop keeping secrets. "Glenn hurt me. He did things to me, Tommy."

"That day? Did he do something to you that day?" Tommy's voice was hard and his eyes flashed in anger.

"Not that day."

Tommy furrowed his brow, trying to understand. "When? Where?"

"At night, in my room. I didn't remember at first. I kept waking up in the cemetery and wetting the bed, but I knew something wasn't right. I'd get this feeling in my stomach when he was around or he'd touch or look at me in any way. When I saw him in the parking lot of the skating rink, I knew I couldn't go with him. It's like part of my brain remembered but was protecting the other part not to."

As she spoke, she could see the horror of realization forming on Tommy's face. He leaned in close, his eyes filled with concern. "Sitty, did he touch you in bad ways? Like down there?"

She nodded as the tears fell. Tommy pounded his fist against the wall of the van in rage. "In our home? He hurt you when I was right next door?"

She didn't respond but didn't need to. The secret was no longer hers to bear alone. Tommy reached forward and pulled her to his chest, sobbing into her hair. "I'm so sorry, Sitty. I didn't know. I would've stopped him. I would've killed him for hurting you."

The truth was, he did. Not at the time, but Tommy stopped Glenn. Now, they needed to make sure it didn't come back to punish Tommy. They had each other's haunting secrets to protect. Sitka wrapped her arms around Tommy's waist, squeezing as hard as she could. "I won't tell anyone, Tommy. That I saw Glenn's body. I don't want you to get in trouble. He deserved it. He was a mean, cruel person. Don't tell anyone what I told you though, please."

Tommy nodded and sat back, wiping his nose. "Not even Mom?"

"Not Aunt Leigh. I'm so ashamed of it and don't want her to know. To think less of me." Even saying it made Sitka feel dirty. Her cheeks burned.

"Sitty, you did nothing wrong. If you don't tell her, she won't understand why you ran away for so long. Glenn was a horrible person and I'm glad he's dead. I'd kill him twice if I could," Tommy replied bitterly.

In Sitka's timeline, Tommy had. How she saw them dump Glenn's body the day she left the skating rink, then again yesterday didn't make sense, but she knew it occurred.

Seeing it the first time, drove her to the shack to find Davis, so it needed to happen. The timeline made sure she witnessed it before it happened in real time through a parallel timeline.

To get her back to the past to try and save Letty. She believed they'd saved Davis's little girl. Sitka had to go to the shack and through the tunnel. To fix things in that time. Now, she had to fix things in hers. First, she needed to get her story straight. She'd have to tell Aunt Leigh what Glenn did to her. It was the only explanation for why she didn't come home with Glenn that day after skating. Truth be told, had she remembered sooner, the outcome would've been the same. She would've run. She would've escaped Glenn. Since she didn't, the timeline made sure she escaped him that day. To save not only Letty but to save Sitka. Eventually, Glenn would've made sure she never came home. To become the missing child everyone thought she was.

Aunt Leigh would wonder where Glenn had gone. He never wasn't holding down his chair at the end of the dining room table, smoking cigarettes, and telling everyone what they should be doing. He wouldn't have come home the night before. That had to send up red flags.

Sitka turned to Tommy. "What did Aunt Leigh say about Glenn not coming home last night?"

Tommy shook his head. "Not much. She thought he went out drinking with friends."

"Why did she think that?" As far as Sitka remembered, Glenn didn't have any friends.

"'Cause I told her he did. After we disposed of that piece of shit's body, I went home and told her I saw him get picked up in a white truck. That Glenn said it was a buddy of his from a previous job or something. She was pissed but didn't seem surprised. Glenn hadn't been supportive with you missing. He made it about himself, berated her for holding on and not giving up hope. Then, I told her I was spending the night at a friend's house. I'd been staying there, anyway."

"Jerry's house?" She motioned to the quiet boy, who smiled shyly back at her. He reminded her of someone. Someone she liked.

Tommy shrugged. "I didn't get specific, just in case someone had seen us. I guess someone had." He glanced at Sitty and a small, sad smile twitched on his lips as he let his eyes rest on her face. "I'm so fucking glad you're here, sprout. I was lost without you. You're my little sister and I couldn't bear the thought of you never coming home."

Sitka took his hand and smiled. "I missed you, Tommy. You and Aunt Leigh so much. I just wanted to come home. To be safe. I didn't know how to make that happen, but I thought about home every day."

Home.

That was the next step. To let Aunt Leigh know she was safe and tell her story. To start putting the last five weeks behind her. As they drove toward her aunt's home, Sitka felt a lightness she hadn't felt since before he mother died. She felt the chains she'd been forced to carry slip away. She could never go back to before Glenn abused her, but she could let go of the fear which had been driving her for a long time. Tommy did the one thing she hadn't been able to. In saving himself, he unknowingly saved her from a present and future which was slowly killing her.

Like Davis's sister.

As they drove up to the house and she saw Aunt Leigh step outside with a frown on her face, Sitka knew she was home and could stop running. She opened the door and climbed out, watching as Aunt Leigh realized what she was seeing. Her aunt bolted across the yard and scooped Sitka into her arms, bawling with relief as she clutched the little girl she was unsure she'd ever see again to her chest.

Sitka buried her face in her aunt's hair and for a moment felt like she was back in her mother's arms. She could never have her mother back, but she could have the love of a mother in her life. The protection of a brother and the security of a family.

She could bury Glenn once and for all.

∞

Chapter Twenty-Six

∞

*B*y the time the police arrived, Sitka had repeated the story so many times, she had it down pat. Glenn was abusing her at night, so when she saw him outside the skating rink, she ran. She got lost and hid in a root cellar, eating the food there, scrounging what she could in the woods to survive. Finally, scared and not feeling well, she went to the Zip Mart to get help, where she collapsed from exhaustion and malnutrition. That's when Tommy spied her in the parking lot while he and Jerry were out searching for her again. He got her to the van, then brought her home to Aunt Leigh.

The police asked the same questions, then requested to speak to Glenn. Aunt Leigh told them he'd gone out drinking with friends the night before and hadn't come home yet. It was unlike him but he'd been acting strange as of late. Hiding things and being very aggressive with them. The police explained if he showed up at the house, to call them immediately, not to engage with him.

Before they left, a woman arrived and asked to speak to Sitka alone. She was a small, redheaded woman with sharp blue eyes and thin lips. She seemed nice, but Sitka was still nervous about talking to her. The lady pulled out a notepad and smiled genuinely at Sitka.

"Sitka, right? My name is Ms. Byers. I'm with Social Services and need to ask you a few questions about what your aunt's boyfriend did to you. Are you alright if we sit in the backyard and talk?"

Sitka nodded and followed the woman outside. They sat on a bench in the shade, facing the back fence. The woman drew out a doll from her bag and showed it to Sitka.

"We can use this doll if it makes you feel more comfortable. Or you can point to areas on your body, okay?"

"Okay."

"You told your aunt and the police that Glenn touched you inappropriately. Can you point to areas he touched you and tell me exactly what he did?"

Sitka bit her lip, not wanting to bring up the memories. Her cheeks flamed as embarrassment flushed over her. She shook her head. "I don't want to."

"That's alright. We can take our time. You need to know, no one is mad at you and you didn't do anything wrong. You are the victim. We're just trying to gather information on what he did, so Glenn can never abuse you again."

Glenn would never hurt her again, regardless. He was rotting in the woods where he deserved to be. Sitka raised her hand and pointed at the doll. "He touched me there... and there. He held me down and tried to stick his thing in me. It hurt and I tried to get away. I begged him to stop. He did when

I got loud enough for Aunt Leigh to hear. He didn't want her to know, so he left."

The woman nodded, not seeming surprised. "Alright, honey. I know this is hard to talk about. Did he put any part of himself, or anything else, inside of you? Did he ejaculate?"

Sitka didn't know what that word meant but shook her head. "He tried, but it hurt and I cried, so he stopped. He kept coming back to try... until I started waking up in the cemetery."

"The cemetery? Where's that?"

"Behind the fence in the backyard. I started waking up there. I guess to get away." Sitka pointed at the fenceline separating the neighborhood from the cemetery.

The woman stopped and wrote notes, setting the doll down next to her. "How many times did he try before you found yourself waking up in the cemetery?"

Sitka shook her head. "I don't know. A lot. I don't remember exactly. I also started wetting the bed at that time. I didn't know why, until now. It all just came back to me when..."

"When what, dear?"

"When I saw him in the parking lot of the skating rink to pick me up. It came back to me that he was in my room at night, hurting me. I was scared of Glenn, of going in the car with him. So, I ran. Bits and pieces keep coming back to me after that. I remember him coming into my room and to my bed. He first touched me with his hands. Stuck his fingers down there." Sitka remembered the roughness of his hands and how she froze in fear.

"Then he tried putting his penis in you?"

Sitka nodded. She didn't like that word. Penis. "He held me down and... I don't want to talk about it anymore."

"We don't have to. I'm going to ask your aunt to have you speak to someone, though. What he did was wrong, Sitka. He was a sick man and should never have abused you like that. I want you to know we all are doing our best to protect you. You'll need to see a doctor and I'd like to recommend a therapist. They are nice and can assist you in dealing with what happened and the memories that are surfacing. You're a special little girl and we're going to get you help."

Sitka watched her, seeing the compassion in the woman's eyes. A dedication to protection. She knew Ms. Byers was on her side. "Thank you."

They went back in and the lady pulled Aunt Leigh aside. Aunt Leigh cried as the woman shared what Sitka had told her. Tommy overheard them talking about what Glenn did to Sitka and his face became bright red. He clenched his fists and stared at the wall, his eyes fixed on a specific spot. If he hadn't already killed Glenn, he certainly would now.

Once the police and social worker left, Tommy came over to Sitka. He tousled her hair and smiled. "Come on, let's go for a ride. I think I've had enough of this place and these people today."

"Where are we going?" Sitka asked, seeing Tommy was doing his best to keep a positive attitude around her.

"To Wrightsville Beach. To the amusement park. We need to remember we're still kids."

Sitka looked to Aunt Leigh for approval and her aunt smiled wobbly. "Go on, Sitka, enjoy yourself. Tommy's right, you two deserve to go have some fun."

Aunt Leigh looked like she'd aged ten years since the day Sitka disappeared. She gathered up fliers and photos off the table, shaping them into a neat stack. Her shoulders dropped and she appeared defeated.

Sitka paused at the door. "Aunt Leigh, do you want to come with us?"

Her aunt met her eyes, then sighed. "Aw, no, honey. That's sweet of you, though. You go on. I'm going to tidy up here and see if I can figure out where Glenn went. I don't want him just showing up here randomly. Like nothing happened."

He won't, Sitka thought to herself. She wanted to tell Aunt Leigh, Glenn was *never* coming back. That her aunt had nothing to worry about, but she couldn't. Hopefully, no one would ever find Glenn's body. He could disappear without a second thought as far as they were concerned. Sitka walked over and hugged her aunt as hard as she could. Aunt Leigh rubbed Sitka's head and smiled down at her.

"I never gave up hope you were coming home, Sitty. I could see you in my mind's eye alive. Lost and alone... but alive. I knew you were out there."

Sitka nodded but didn't speak. Aunt Leigh knew what it was like to lose someone, however, she still held out hope for Sitka to come home. Like a mother would for her own child.

Tommy cleared his throat by the door. "I'll keep a good eye on her, Mom."

Aunt Leigh smiled at Tommy. "I know you will, hon. You're a good kid, you know that? I'm lucky to have you. To have the both of you."

Tommy grinned and touched two of his fingers to his brow in a small wave as he and Sitka left. They went to the car and he sat for a moment, letting it idle after starting it up. He turned to Sitka, watching her. He shook his head and reached out to squeeze her hand.

"Things will be different, now. Just the three of us. Mom will be okay. Once Glenn is obviously not coming back, she'll relax. She feels guilty about what happened. I do, too. I hate that he hurt you, Sitty. Had I known..." his voice trailed off as he stared out the front window. "Anyway, let's go ride some rides and play some games. It's summer, damnit."

Once they got to Wrightsville Beach, they parked and Sitka practically ran down the boardwalk to the rides. Tommy laughed, attempting to keep up with her. They stopped and played a game where they tried to get a coin into a fishbowl, however, failed horribly at it. They bought cotton candy and stood in line for the roller coaster. In times like these, Sitka could forget about what happened. About Glenn. Even about Davis. It seemed like a story she made up in her head. She knew it wasn't and it was important to remember all Davis had taught her, but sometimes she needed to simply be a kid.

After the roller coaster, they played a few more games. Tommy won her a small, multicolored bear which she swore she'd cherish forever. She meant it, tucking it under her arm. They headed for her favorite ride, the Ferris Wheel, when she saw Dean, the boy from her neighborhood. His eyes grew wide when he saw her and he ran over, clutching a hotdog in his hand. He tried to hug her and balance the hotdog at the same time, dripping mustard and onions on the ground.

"Sitka! You're back!" he exclaimed.

They stood awkwardly for a moment, staring at each other when Sitka smiled shyly. "Sorry to worry everyone."

"We *were* worried! It made national news. Did you know that?" Dean asked.

She didn't. She was on television all across the country? She turned, staring at Tommy with her mouth open.

Tommy shrugged. "I guess 'cause you were from New York, people thought maybe you'd ended up back there. All kinds of stories were going around. Some people thought maybe your father kidnapped you from us and took you with him up north."

"I don't even know my father," Sitka whispered. Why would a man who'd never been in her life come all the way to North Carolina to snatch her when he didn't even want her in the first place?

"Yeah, I know. But you know how people are, they like to talk. It doesn't matter. You're home, now. People will move on to other gossip," Tommy assured her.

Dean reached out and touched her hand. "I'm glad you're back. Those tadpoles turned into frogs. I'd brought a couple of them home a few days after we went, to chart their progress, and was going to release them at the pond in a few days if you want to come along. They're jumping out of the container I put them in and my mother is pissed. Said I'd better get them out of the house or she'll fry them up."

Sitka nodded. "I'd like that. To set them free, not fry them. Come by my house when you're ready to let them go. Maybe my aunt will let me use the Polaroid camera to take pictures of the release."

Dean grinned and turned back to a group of friends he was with. "I'd better go before they leave without me! I'll come by soon, okay? I'm really glad you're home."

He ran off, still clinging to the hotdog in his hand, then gave her a quick wave as he disappeared into the crowd. As she watched him go, Sitka hoped once school started back, he'd be as outwardly nice to her. She turned to Tommy and grasped his hand, grateful for him standing by her.

By the time their turn on the Ferris Wheel came, the sun was beginning to set over the water. Sitka secretly hoped they could get stuck at the top of the ride because she loved it when she could see the world from the top. They climbed in and used their bodies to make the chair rock slightly back and forth. As the wheel began to turn, Sitka held her breath, reveling in the way the chair pulled away from gravity effortlessly. She felt like she was flying and tipped her head back, laughing. Up there, no one could touch her.

Up there, she ruled the world.

The Ferris Wheel went around and around, giving them a bird's eye view of the amusement park, beach, and ocean. Sitka never wanted it to end. As if her thoughts controlled the mechanics, the wheel came to the top and stopped. She could see the workers below, pointing at various aspects of the mechanics as they discussed what was going on.

Other riders were getting impatient, rocking their chairs back and forth and yelling down at the staff. Sitka and Tommy's chair was right at the top, so Sitka peered around, taking in the world around them. This world where she lived, where her mother once lived with her. Where Davis and his family once lived.

As she watched seagulls fly past them in synchronicity, she appreciated how it all fit together. One gull flying next to another veered off on its own path.

∞

It made Sitka realize, maybe Davis and his family were still there. Existing on another plane out of her sight, as he said. Maybe her mother was, too. The layers of realities existing parallel to one another, yet not crossing. Usually.

The thought made Sitka smile as she considered perhaps those she loved were still with her, vibrating on another level. Out of sight, but not out of reach. She could still send mental messages and talk to them. Even if she didn't hear back, she believed somehow they'd receive them. If only as a sensation or imagery. As the Ferris Wheel creaked to a start, Sitka understood what she never had before.

There was no end to any of them.

Chapter Twenty-Seven

∞

*D*evelopers found Glenn's body about two weeks later. As was the case around Wilmington at the time, growth was booming, and empty land was at a premium. It was right before school started and word spread like wildfire around town. It made it to Aunt Leigh before the police did, so she wasn't surprised when they knocked on the door. They spoke in hushed tones and she invited them in out of the summer heat. Over glasses of sweet tea, they discussed Glenn.

"So, he never came home from that night he went drinking with friends?" One of the officers, a thin, young guy asked, pulling out a small notepad.

Aunt Leigh shook her head. "No, and he wouldn't have been welcome here if he had, after what he did to my niece. Don't take this the wrong way, but I wanted to kill him. I'm not sad someone got to him first."

The police officer nodded, jotting down notes. "I don't blame you. I have a sister that age and if anyone-"

The older, chubbier police officer stopped him short, placing his hand on the young fellow's shoulder. "Understood, ma'am. Do you have reason to suspect anyone would want harm to come to Mr. er, what was his last name? Hold on, let me check my notes."

"Collis. Glenn Collis," Aunt Leigh replied with a bite to her words.

"Right. Mr. Collis. The friend or friends he went out drinking with? Good friends?"

"Honestly, I don't know. My son said his friend drove up in a white truck. An old friend from work Glenn told him. Glenn has been out of work for some time, so I have no idea who it was. He preferred sitting here at home, smoking cigarette after cigarette," Aunt Leigh answered wryly.

"Is your son here? We'd like him to give a description of the person in the truck."

Aunt Leigh chewed her lip. She didn't want the kids any more involved in this than they had to be. "Yeah, he is. Let me get him."

She got up and left the room, glancing back at the officers. She was hoping to leave Tommy out of it, once and for all. The cops peered around the living room, taking alternating sips of their tea.

The younger one whispered, "Sorry about that thing about my sister. I just feel for this family. I can't even imagine what they must be going through."

The older one nodded. "I know, me too. It sounds like the trash took itself out on this one, but we need to follow procedure. Let's get the statement from the kid, and chalk this up to bad ties. We can put the description out and see if anything comes back on the truck. Did this guy have any family?"

The younger police officer shook his head. "Uh, I think a brother out of state was notified. He didn't seem all that surprised. Said his brother latched onto whoever he could. Parents deceased. I think that was it. Never married, no children known of."

"Ah, so he saw this poor lady coming a mile away. Free meal ticket."

At that time, Aunt Leigh came back in with Tommy trailing behind. Both appeared unhappy with the situation. Sitka stood at the doorway and watched them quietly, picking at the wood molding.

"Hey, son, come take a seat. We have a couple of questions for you. You aren't in any trouble, we just need you to tell us what you saw the day Mr. Collis left. Can you give us a description of the truck and the person driving it?"

Tommy looked nervous and glanced at Sitka, who smiled at him for encouragement. "It was like, uh... a white pickup truck. Older. Had a dented bumper."

"On which side?" The younger officer asked, scribbling down whatever Tommy said.

"The left, or I guess, the truck's right."

"So, the passenger side?" The older cop suggested.

"Yeah, the passenger side," Tommy agreed.

"Did you notice the make and model?"

Tommy shook his head. "Maybe a Chevy. I didn't really notice but I feel like it was built like a Chevy."

"What about the guy? Age? Race? Did you happen to see what he was wearing?"

Tommy squinted like he was trying to remember. "I only glanced out the window for a second, so I don't remember. I know he was white, wearing a ball cap. Brown hair maybe. I don't know his age. Like Glenn's age."

The younger cop flipped back through his notes. "So like mid to late thirties?"

Tommy shrugged. "Sure?"

The older officer laughed. "To you kids, we probably all look the same age."

Tommy chuckled and turned a little red. "Sorry, I didn't think any of it was important at the time. I was just glad he was leaving for a while."

Aunt Leigh rested her hand on his shoulder and squeezed. "You did good, hon. Do you officers need anything else from my son? I'd like it if my kids didn't get dragged into this nightmare anymore than possible. It's been a hard summer on our family."

The officer's eyes flitted to Sitka in the doorway, then back to Aunt Leigh. "No, that should be all. If anything else comes to mind, please let us know. Oh, Tommy, right? Do you remember if it was an in-state plate?"

Tommy furrowed his brow, acting like he was picturing the vehicle. "I think so. Maybe."

"Good enough," the older officer said and stood up, his knees cracking loudly as he did. He grinned and rubbed them vigorously. "Old age, you know? Gets the best of us, or the worst of us in my case, ha. We appreciate your time. Oh, and the iced tea. It's hot out there and that was a welcome treat. We'll be in touch if we find out any more information on the case. Y'all have a nice day."

Aunt Leigh walked them to the door, making small talk about the weather and the new mall. Once they left, she came back and sighed. "You kids okay? I know it's a lot."

Sitka nodded and Tommy went to hug his mother. He stepped back and muttered, "I'm glad he's dead."

Aunt Leigh smiled, tipping her head. "Me too. I'm sorry I ever let him into this house. Into our lives. It looks like someone did our dirty work for us. I hope he suffered."

Sitka was taken aback by her aunt's words but couldn't disagree. She knew more than her aunt did and knew he would've made Tommy suffer. Glenn had no soul and would've made sure Tommy died slowly. The memory of Glenn with the trophy in his hand flashed in her eyes and she knew it was no mistake she was sent back at just the right time. Nothing was random and the timeline made sure she stopped Glenn from hurting Tommy.

From killing Tommy.

A theory about time popped in her head and she bit her lip with the realization. Time was not insentient. It was living with objective. It knew she needed to see Glenn's body get dumped the day she left the skating rink, so that she would run to the shack and find Davis. It knew she needed to be sent back to stop Glenn from murdering Tommy. She'd always been taught that time only moved forward, an insensate march into the future. Now she knew differently. It was like her. A conscious, living, entity with a purpose and intent. People always said, "Father Time", but to her time was more like a mother. Watching out, trying to protect.

Once Aunt Leigh left the room, Stka met Tommy's eyes. "Can we take a ride? Go to the library?"

Tommy cocked his head. "Sure, I wouldn't mind. What's up?"

"I want to look up some things on time travel."

"Like stories about time travel?"

"No. Well, maybe. Like people writing about it, but not made up. Books about time travel," Sitka answered.

"Oh, hmmm. Yeah, okay. Not sure what they'll have, but we can check it out. I think the college has a library, too. They may have some stuff. You wanna grab lunch and go? Maybe I can see if Jerry is around. Do you mind if he tags along? We've gotten pretty close since... well, you know."

"Sure. I like Jerry. He's really nice." Sitka meant it. Jerry had become part of the family in the strangest of ways, but family he was.

"He saved my ass that day. Actually, both days. The day Glenn came at me in my room, I saw him on the road and flagged him down. I stayed with his family until I came back to get my things. Jerry was down the road, waiting on me. When... anyway he helped me transport the *thing* in his van."

The thing. Glenn's body.

Nothing was random. Jerry was meant to help Tommy on both days. Sitka nodded, glad Jerry was at the right place, at the right time. Tommy left to call Jerry and Sitka went to find Aunt Leigh, who was staring out the kitchen window with tears streaming down her face. Sitka went over and hugged her.

"I'm sorry if you're sad about Glenn."

Aunt Leigh stroked Sitka's hair. "Oh, honey. I'm not sad about Glenn. He deserved what he got. I was thinking about Tommy's father. Thomas was the best man I ever knew. I guess my loneliness drove me to Glenn, but I ignored all the red flags. I'm sad because I miss Thomas. Glenn was a monster and it's my fault he hurt you. My fault I let him into this house and trusted him around you kids. If I hadn't met him, none of this would've happened. I'm so sorry, Sitty."

"It wasn't your fault. Monsters have a way of telling people they aren't monsters. That's what my therapist told me. She said bad people are sometimes the most charming, convincing people to trust and like them. Like the big, bad wolf in Little Red Riding Hood."

Aunt Leigh wiped her face and gave a pained smile. "Your therapist is a smart woman."

"Maybe you should talk to her, too, Aunt Leigh?" Sitka suggested.

"Maybe I should. I love you, Sitty. I hope you know you're a daughter to me. A true gift."

Sitka smiled at her aunt. "I know. You are my second mama."

A little bit later, Sitka heard a horn honk in the driveway and peered out the window. Jerry was in the driveway in the blue van, however, he also had someone else in the passenger seat. Tommy called to her from the front hall, so she grabbed a bag with a notebook and pencils and ran out to meet him. Aunt Leigh gave Tommy money to pay for lunch before she headed out to work.

Tommy turned to Sitka as he snagged his bag by the front door. "I hope you don't mind, but Jerry asked if his little brother could come along to the library. He's about your age, I think. I guess he's really into time travel stuff and was interested in going to get some books, too. If you don't want him to though, I can let Jerry know. I should've asked first."

∞

"I don't mind," Sitka replied as they headed out the door. As they got close to the van, she broke into a huge grin. Dean was waving to her from the passenger side. Jerry's little brother was the kid Dean from the pond and the amusement park. Her friend.

Nothing was random.

Chapter Twenty-Eight

O n the ride to the library, Dean and Sitka talked nonstop. About frogs, the pond, the amusement park, school... and time travel. Tommy wasn't kidding when he said Dean was also interested in time travel. He knew way more than Sitka and quickly lost her in the conversation, mostly talking about sci-fi books and theories. Jerry and Tommy were in the front seats, having a talk of their own. About much more serious issues.

Tommy told Jerry construction workers found Glenn's body and the police were searching for a middle-aged, white man in a white, possibly Chevy, truck. They hadn't suspected Tommy at all as far as he knew. Jerry and Tommy had discarded the gun that day, dumping it in the river. They'd also worn gloves, so they didn't think any fingerprints would be tied back to them. Not that the police seemed to be digging all that hard.

Deaths of child molesters weren't high on their list.

"So, what makes you interested in time travel all of a sudden?" Dean asked Sitka as he tapped his watch.

"I don't know. Just interesting, is all," Sitka replied, not sure how to answer the question.

"It really is!" Dean exclaimed. "Not just like in books and television, either. There is so much more to it than that."

"Yeah, there was actually a lady from Wilmington who wrote theories on time being a conscious thing. Like living," Jerry chimed in from the front seat.

"Really? Like a spirit or something?" Sitka asked.

Jerry shrugged. "Something like that. Interactive, so it could adjust to events and people. Sounds crazy, I know."

It didn't sound crazy at all to Sitka. That's exactly what she'd been sensing. Like time was a being, guiding her to where she needed to go. "What was the lady's name? Did she write any books about it?"

"I don't know. I just remember in high school, I was writing a paper on famous Wilmingtonians and came across an article on her from the college newspaper. She died in the sixties but made some waves in the scientific community. Unfortunately, she was pretty ostracized in the academic world because she was a woman and black. Other than that article, I never heard anything else about her."

A black woman? Something about that made Sitka proud and she wanted to learn more about this woman. "Do you remember anything else about her? Or how you found the article?"

Jerry laughed and nodded. "I was no A student, so likely I did the most basic search on the microfiche. I can help you look for the article if you want when we get to the library."

Jerry had never spoken so much to Sitka and she smiled. She nodded enthusiastically. "That would be awesome. Thanks, Jerry."

They parked at the library and headed in. Dean immediately went to find books on time travel. Tommy perused the car repair section and Jerry guided Sitka to the microfiche machines. They searched through the cards, trying to find any info on famous people from Wilmington. Sitka also searched black famous people, hoping it might narrow it down quicker.

Jerry took one machine and she took the other, scanning through the slides they'd gathered. Sitka came across the Wilmington Ten. This stopped her in her tracks as she gazed at the faces of the kids, who didn't look much older than Tommy. She read the articles, some of which were slanted against the students and others taking a more neutral standpoint. She realized those students would likely still be in Wilmington and not too old. She wanted to speak to them, to hear their stories.

She'd almost forgotten she was searching for the article on the woman who wrote about time travel when she heard Jerry exclaim.

"Got it! Come here, Sitty."

She'd never heard anyone outside of her family or Davis call her that and didn't mind so much. Jerry was grinning, pointing at the screen. He pushed his shaggy, blond hair out of his face with his other hand and made room for her to see. "I can't find the article but here she is in this photo."

Sitka came around and peered in at the grainy image. The woman was seated at a table with a group of younger people, who were smiling in her direction. She wasn't smiling and had a stern look on her face. It was dated September 14, 1962. The woman appeared to be in her forties and was staring out from behind a pair of thick glasses. Something about her struck a chord with Sitka, but she couldn't put her finger on it.

Under the picture was a description that read, "Meeting of Scientific Theory Organization." Sitka had never heard of it and furrowed her brow.

"What is that? The Scientific Theory Organization."

"That was a group that formed here because they weren't allowed anywhere else. Woman, minorities, high school dropouts," Dean answered behind her.

"How do you know that?" Sitka asked.

"'Cause I'm a nerd," Dean joked. "But seriously, they wrote some papers on time travel. One of the books I read mentioned them. They questioned a lot of existing scientific theories of the time."

"Does it say anything else about them?"

"Nah, but maybe the college library has more info on the group. They met there back in the day. There's even a small plaque for the group in the garden."

Sitka peered closer at the photo and saw the people in the group were just that. Young, long-haired guys, women, people of different races. They were all looking at the lady like she was the leader. No names or other information were listed.

Tommy came around the corner with a couple of books in his arms and leaned down to see what they were all looking at. "Any luck?"

"Sort of. Can we go to the college library?" Sitka asked, jotting down the name of the group.

"Sure. You cool with that, Jerry?"

Jerry grinned. "I'm always down to solve a mystery and am in no rush to go home and do chores or deal with my father. I'm at your service."

As he'd been when they needed him the most. Sitka resisted the urge to hug Jerry and turned to Dean, who was fumbling with a stack of books in his arm. "Did you get some books on time travel?"

"A few. We can take a look when we get back to your house if your aunt is okay with that."

"She is," Sitka replied, knowing they couldn't go back to Jerry and Dean's house. Their father didn't like *black* people as she remembered Dean telling her.

Too many adults had angry, inflexible beliefs, Sitka realized. She wanted to change that. They checked out and loaded back in the van, stopping for ice cream along the way. As the wind blew through the window and she ate the ice cream cone, she glanced around the inside of the van at the other passengers. Jerry and Tommy were cracking up about something in the front seat. Dean was rattling off facts from the book he was holding. Since her mother passed, she hadn't felt so accepted and part of something until now. This felt like connection, like family.

The college library was smaller but focused more on academic books. Dean showed them the plaque for the Scientific Theory Organization in the garden as they made their way to the library doors. It had only been placed there a few years before but honored the group's challenge to long-held beliefs on time and space. The college library had an educational air and for a moment Sitka felt like she shouldn't be there. Tommy grabbed her hand, smiling, and pulled her through the door.

"It's for everyone. This is a public school. We have every right to be here. Come on, let's go ask at the desk."

They made their way to the front desk and a girl in her late teens behind the counter made eyes at Tommy. They at least had that on their side. Tommy drew attention from just about any girl he met. Tommy leaned in, flashing his grin.

"Hey, lovely day, isn't it? And you're all cooped up inside. You should be outside enjoying the sun," he said, a hint of flirting in his voice.

The girl blushed and fiddled with her hair. "I wish. Can I help you find anything?"

"You sure can. We're trying to track down information on a group who used to meet here back in the early to mid-sixties. Maybe still do. They have a plaque in the garden?" Tommy said, running his finger along the desk.

The girl cocked her head. "Oh, which group?"

"The Scientific Theory Organization?"

The girl frowned as she thought about it. "Hmmm, I don't think they meet here anymore. I haven't seen any fliers or announcements for them. Do you know any of the members?"

They didn't. The most they had was the name of the group. Dean stepped forward, fixing his bespectacled eyes on the girl. "Do you have a section on time travel theory?"

The girl shook her head. "I don't thi-"

Dean cut her off. "Okay, how about the space-time continuum or quantum physics?"

They all stood with their mouths hanging open. Leave it to Dean to know what to ask for. He didn't blink and waited for her to respond. The girl turned red, then pointed to a back corner of the library.

"Maybe over there. That's the uh... like, the science section. You might find what you are looking for in that area."

Tommy winked at her and they went to where she'd pointed. Sitka wasn't even sure what Dean asked the girl, but he rapidly went down the line of books with his finger out, trailing along as he walked. He knew exactly what he was searching for. He disappeared around a corner and Sitka stared at the books in front of her. She wouldn't even know where to begin. Everything had titles well above anything she was familiar with.

Dean peeked his head back around the corner and smiled. "Hey, Sitty. Over here."

Sitka followed and Dean already had books pulled out. She glanced at each one, not sure what she should be looking for. One appeared like it had been hand bound and Dean waved it in the air.

Sitka cocked her head. "What is that?"

"These are papers written by the Scientific Theory Organization and cataloged here. I can't believe that girl didn't know they had this. We can't check them out, but we can read them here," Dean explained.

They sat down and Sitka began to read an article theorizing time wasn't linear, but rather layers of the same timeline, where events played out differently. In each timeline, a person, or a version of themselves, could exist but how things unfolded could be different. Davis had said something to that effect with the leaves in the park and it's what Sitka felt when she was on the Ferris Wheel. Much of the language was above

Sitka's comprehension, but she understand the general idea. She flipped to another article written by someone with the same initials. L.B.

That article explained how because of the layers, time travel was possible, but the grandfather paradox, where someone could travel back and kill their own grandfather when he was young, effectively preventing themselves from being born, was moot. Because it would only kill the grandfather on one plane, stopping that timeline, but not the others. The article explained how linear time travel was impossible, but rather a person would go back, or forward, *and* over, landing on the timeline on another plane. They could never change their actual timeline directly.

If an event took place that changed the theoretical future on the plane they traveled to, that timeline would cast them to another, and that first one would cease to exist. They could change certain factors, but nothing which would change their original timeline as a catastrophic result. It would always adjust to get the same unaffected result. The article said a person could change an event that didn't change the overall outcome of the future, but only the timeline knew if that was the case. Whatever plane needed to move forward to keep the outcome intact, would.

The article also explained a person could go back and fix an event that unfolded incorrectly, without affecting the future timeline, as it would become fluid to fill in the gaps. So, in essence, the timeline could change but only how it was supposed to be, however, people couldn't go back and save Martin Luther King Jr.

Unless he wasn't supposed to die in the first place.

Sitka sat back and tried to understand what she was reading. On some level, it made total sense to what she'd experienced. On another level, it went against everything she'd ever been taught about time and their purpose on Earth. According to the article, they couldn't break time, but could actually fix it. If it was *meant* to be fixed. Some events were intended to happen, others not necessarily. It made her wonder about her mother, about Tommy's father.

Sitka went to the desk and asked the girl if she could make copies. The girl was watching Tommy across the library and nodded, waving her hand mindlessly to a copier beside the desk. Sitka set to making copies of the pages, glad Tommy was distracting the girl with his presence. She pretty much copied the whole booklet when a name printed at the back of the book caught her eye and she gasped. The girl glanced over, then back at Tommy, not bothered to be distracted by whatever Sitka was making noise about.

Sitka peeled back the page again and stared at the name. Now, she knew why the lady in the picture struck a chord with her. The woman looked like a male version of Davis in glasses. She ran her fingers over the name as a smile formed on her lips. The author of the articles was Leticia Butler.

Letty.

Chapter Twenty-Nine

∞

They'd saved Letty... and she'd gone on to write about time travel. Or something like it. Sitka clutched the papers to her chest as she saw the library girl give Tommy her phone number. Letty had lived, maybe still was alive. Sitka would check the phone book as soon as she got home. Leticia Butler. So, either she'd never married or kept her name for professional purposes. Did she have children? Grandchildren? Could Sitka be in school with one of Davis's great-grandchildren? The possibilities were endless.

As she was pondering the different scenarios, Dean nudged her playfully. "A penny for your thoughts."

Sitka smiled and shrugged. "Just daydreaming. I can't believe we found her."

"Yeah, that's neat. I don't get it, though. Why is she so important to you?" Dean asked.

Sitka stared out the van window. Why was she important? Because Letty living to write those articles meant it all happened. They changed the outcome, saved Letty, and life was the same. More or less.

The shack and Davis's grave were gone, but everything else was the same. As far as Sitka could tell. They proved Letty's theory by using Letty as the test subject. It was all too wonderful to consider.

"Tommy, I need to tell you something," Sitka blurted out, needing to share what she'd been holding inside.

Tommy turned back from the front seat with a grin. "What's up, munchkin?"

Sitka thought of how to form it all into words. Either he'd believe her, or he wouldn't. It didn't change that it happened. "I wasn't hiding in a root cellar."

Tommy's grin faltered and he looked confused. "Where were you, then?"

"If I tell you, you have to believe me. Promise?"

"Of course. Whatever you tell me, I will believe you. So, where were you?"

"I... uh. When I saw what I saw..." Her eyes darted to Dean, realizing he didn't know about Glenn's body. "When I got scared and ran, I found a shack. I hid there."

Tommy shrugged. "Why didn't you just say so? No one would've been angry."

"It's not that. The shack doesn't exist anymore. It's gone," Sitka explained. "Or maybe it never existed."

Tommy chuckled, shaking his head. "Sitty, what the hell are you talking about? Did you dream it?"

Sitka stared at the papers in her hand. "Not like that. It was there when I was there. I stayed in it for a couple of weeks. Then, I met a man named Davis. He used to live there.

He was a ghost. He took me through the floor to another time. To 1929."

Jerry glanced at Tommy, his eyes wide. Tommy climbed into the back and sat next to Sitka, listening intently. "Okay, so what happened next?"

Sitka let the story pour out about Davis and his family. About Letty. About seeing her mother, who wasn't her mother. How Abigail helped save Letty. How she saw Glenn try to hit Tommy with the trophy and that she saw Tommy get in the van with Jerry. Tommy listened, never acting as if what she was saying wasn't the honest truth. When she got back to the part of being sent home, she again omitted seeing them dump Glenn's body and said how she went back and the shack was gone, had never been there. That Davis's grave had also disappeared.

The silence in the van was palpable. Dean watched from the back, tapping his chin as if he was considering the possibility. Jerry kept driving, his face looking straight out the windshield. No one spoke at first when Dean sat up straight in his seat, his eyes bright.

"Oh! Letty is Leticia Butler. Davis Butler. Letty Butler. That's her!" he said as if a light went off in his brain.

"I think so," Sitka replied, holding out the papers. "She wrote about all this. I need to find her, to ask her if she remembers me or Abigail from that day. If that's why she went on to research this."

Tommy took the papers, flipping through them. Sitka watched, expecting him to scoff at what she said. To tell her it was all in her head. He got to the end and peered at Letty's name, focused on the letters typed on the sheet. His face was like stone, showing no expression, either way. He nodded and handed the papers back to Sitka. "Well, then, let's find her."

They pulled over and looked in the phone book at a phone booth. While there were a lot of Butlers, none were Letty. Tommy began calling the numbers before he ran out of change. They headed back home to continue the quest. Aunt Leigh was at work, so Tommy got to calling the rest of the Butlers in the phone book. Dean and Sitka read through the books he checked out from the public library. Sitka rubbed her eyes from taking notes and watched Dean. He was in his element, drawing lines and charts connecting what he thought the timelines were. How they fit within each other.

"Dean, I think time is living. Like a tree, or us," Sitka whispered.

"It could be. We don't know anything, really. Why do you think that?" Dean asked, peering up from his work.

Sitka ran her fingers across the lines he drew and looked at him. "When I was there in the past and lost here, I felt like time was watching over me, helping me make the right choices. Guiding me to certain places and things. Like a ghost. No, not a ghost. A spirit or something. Time is a being."

Dean nodded, chewing the end of his pencil. "What time is, *is* religion or spirituality. You know, like God but not the make-believe god they talk about. Not some guy sitting on a cloud. What if time is everything we can and can't see around us, so it's the Supreme Being."

Sitka liked that thought. Instead of manipulating time, they needed to open up to it and allow it to take them where it needed them to go. She wasn't sure how to do that, but she knew she needed to keep trying. It was no accident she ended up at the shack. She wondered how many other opportunities to go to other planes of time were existing right around them. Doors that weren't doors.

Tommy burst into the room, with a pad of paper in his hands. "I got something. I talked to a woman who was a distant relative of Letty. A second or third cousin twice removed or something like that. She remembered Davis and Ruth. Anyway, I'm sorry, Sitty, but Letty died years ago. She had a heart issue and died around a decade ago. The person I spoke to confirmed her parents had passed, as well."

"Oh." Sitka felt tears spring to her eyes. They'd hit a dead end. None of them were still alive, so it didn't matter, anyway.

"Wait, there was something. Letty never married or had children, but she did have another lady she lived with, who is still alive. Here in Wilmington. I got her number and on a whim called her. She'd love to talk to us about Letty. She said she thought she still had boxes of Letty's papers in the attic she could give us."

It was something. Sitka would never get to talk to Letty, but she could at least read her papers. Maybe the woman would be able to tell her about Letty. About Davis and Ruth. It was a start. At this point, she'd take anything to understand what happened after she left 1929.

"Can we visit her?"

"She's busy today but said we could come have lunch at her house tomorrow. She seemed excited to meet you and talk about Letty," Tommy assured her.

"Did you tell her anything? Anything I told you about what happened?" Sitka asked.

"I told her you were trying to find out more information about the family and you were very interested in Letty's theories on time travel. The woman, Josie, was ecstatic to hear that. She said Letty died trying to get people to listen to her. After Letty died, no one carried on her research. It's been on dusty shelves and boxes until now. Josie admired Letty's work but said she didn't comprehend it completely, so hoped someone would eventually pick up where Letty left off."

Sitka felt an ember burning in her chest. Maybe *she* could be that someone. Dean and Jerry said it was dinner time and their parents would be mad if they weren't home in time. Dean left the books for Sitka to continue reading and said he'd be back in the morning. Jerry offered to drive out to Josie's house, curious to see where it would all lead.

That night over dinner, Sitka wanted to tell Aunt Leigh everything but could see the stress on her aunt's face. Her aunt wouldn't be as open as Tommy was. For now, she just needed to assure Aunt Leigh she was home and okay. Sitka touched her aunt's hand.

"Thank you for dinner. I missed this."

"Aw, Sitty, I'm so glad you came home. It wasn't the same without you. Maybe on my next day off, we can go shopping and spend some time together," Aunt Leigh said, a genuine smile crossing her lips.

"I need school clothes," Sitka offered.

"It's a date. Let's go to the mall and pick out a few new outfits. Grab a little lunch. Tommy, you can join us if you'd like? I know shopping isn't your thing but we can go by the arcade, too."

Tommy chuckled. "Maybe."

That was a first. Tommy never went shopping with them without pulling teeth or making jokes. He leaned back in his chair and winked at Sitka. Tommy was making an effort to help his mother move forward. Without Glenn there, all the strife in the house melted away. Sitka kicked him under the table and grinned.

"I need new skates since I lost mine," Sitka teased. "You want to help me pick out some, Tommy?"

"I think you need to take your speedy little legs back to the skating rink and win another pair," Tommy replied.

"Will you go with me?" Sitka wasn't sure why, but the idea of going back to the skating rink made her nervous.

"How about this weekend? I haven't roller skated in years, but there *are* some legs in shiny short-shorts I wouldn't mind checking out."

"Tommy!" Aunt Leigh chided.

He laughed, shaking his head. "Just kidding, Mom. Sort of. I'd love to go skating with you, Sitty. Maybe we can invite Dean?"

He knew he was pushing a button and Sitka blushed. Dean was a friend she liked being around. He was smart and listened to her. She focused on her plate and kicked Tommy again under the table. Maybe there was a chance to go back, to find the simple joys. To just be a kid.

When she woke up in the cemetery again, Sitty knew there was still work to be done.

Chapter Thirty

*L*ate the next morning, Jerry showed up at the house to pick them up. Sitka was disappointed to see Dean wasn't with him. Maybe she'd freaked him out the day before with her story. Jerry assured her Dean had robotics camp and was bummed he couldn't come, as well. Sitka hoped that was true. School started in a little over a week and she didn't want to burn any bridges. She was hoping to have a friend she could count on when she went back to class.

Josie lived outside of town on a farm. Goats greeted them in the driveway and Sitka giggled when a chicken landed on the hood and pecked at the windshield. Josie waved at them from the front door. She was older but sturdy. They unloaded from the van and skirted around the plethora of animals that had gathered around them. Josie shooed ducks away that were attempting to sneak past her into the house.

"Come on in. Don't let the cats out or the ducks in," she instructed in a gravelly voice.

Following her lead, they made sure the door was secured shut with cats in and ducks out. She led them back to a sunroom off the kitchen. There was a round table with plates of food and glasses on it. Josie pointed at the food.

"I made duck egg salad sandwiches and lemonade. Please have a seat and introduce yourselves. Clearly, as the only human here, I'm Josie. Letty was my partner."

They sat and went around the table introducing themselves. When it came to Sitka's turn, Josie eyed her like a hawk. She reached out and placed her hand over Sitka's. She left it there until it felt like a vibration was caught between their hands and she let go. Sitka smiled nervously. Josie leaned back in her seat, never taking her eyes off Sitka.

"You've seen things, haven't you? Been places?" she asked, not as a question. By places, it was clear she meant not in this time.

Sitka felt her cheeks get hot and nodded. "Yes... I went somewhere."

"When was it?"

Sitka noticed she didn't say *where* she said *when*. "When Letty was a little girl and died. Or, I guess now, almost died. 1929. Davis took me with him to there."

"Davis? Letty's daddy? Well, ain't that something? Fine man. How'd you get back to this time?" Josie asked, her eyes intent and curious.

"It kinda spit me back," Sitka answered. "After we saved Letty."

"Lucky for you, then. The time gods sometimes like to stick people wherever they damn well please. You must have work here to do. Y'all go ahead and dig in. Don't wait for me,

I'll talk all afternoon. There's plenty. I have something to show you when you're done. Letty was quite the artist and she did a piece you may find interesting. Especially you, little one."

They ate and made small talk around the table. Occasionally a cat would jump up, wander across, then jump back down. Sitka liked the ease at which Josie existed. She didn't seem to stress about anything. A question tickled the back of Sitka's mind and she set her sandwich down.

"Josie, how did you know Letty? Were you friends?"

Josie chuckled and waved her hand beside her. "You could say that. We lived together. I sought Letty out because of her writings on time travel. I was pretty young back then. Maybe late twenties. Letty was a few years younger than me, but worlds ahead. She was so brave and brash, I immediately fell for her."

Fell for her? What did she mean? Sitka tipped her head and frowned. "I don't understand. You wanted to be Letty's friend?"

"Honey, I wanted to be everywhere and anything Letty was. I worked as her assistant for years, so we could live together without people making an issue of it. People aren't too keen on two women being together and certainly not a black woman and a white woman."

"Oh. You were a couple?" Sitka asked, remembering her mother's friends Diane and Carol who were a couple.

"Indeed we were. I adored that woman. Does that make you uncomfortable?" Josie inquired.

"No, I just didn't know. You loved her?"

"Like the ocean loves the sand. Most people didn't know and we couldn't outwardly do anything about it. That's how the world works, especially back then. We lived together for over two decades before she passed. Bad heart valve. Probably from being so sick when she was a child."

They fell back into silent eating as Sitka ran her mind over what Josie told her. Letty never had children, but she had Josie and that was something. She'd found love. She wondered about Ruth and Davis. They'd passed but she wondered if they'd been happy and lived out their years together.

"Did you ever meet Letty's parents?" she asked.

"Her mother had passed by the time we met. Young, too. Letty said she was always sad and ended up drinking too much over the years. She obviously suffered from depression but didn't know how, or wasn't willing, to get help. Letty suffered depression, as well, but understood it better because of her mother. She threw herself into her work and her art, instead of the bottle. Never saw her drink a drop."

"And her father Davis? You met him?"

"Oh, yes! Davis lived with us his last few years of life. He was quick with a story or a joke. I loved having him around. He died the year before Letty, so I lost them both in a short amount of time. They were my family."

"When did Letty die?"

"January 17, 1968, just as the sun rose into the sky."

Sitka almost dropped the glass she was holding and stared at Josie. "That's my birthday. My mama said I was born at home. She was making breakfast when her water broke. I was born a couple of hours later in her bed."

Josie nodded and smiled. "Now, that doesn't surprise me at all. Remember, I said I had something to show you? Why don't you finish up and I'll take you out to the shed. You boys are welcome, as well. Or if you want to explore the farm, I have a mini bike behind the garage I use to check fences. You're welcome to take it for a ride."

Tommy and Jerry's eyes lit up at the word minibike and they were out the door before Josie had a chance to tell them anything else. Sitka and Josie cleared the table and wandered out through the garden. Josie paused to pick a tomato and peered at Sitka. Her eyes were knowing and she smiled in a way that made Sitka feel seen.

"I want you to know, I believe you. Not just because this was Letty's life work, but how I came to find Letty in the first place. I was married to a man I didn't love. He was very heavy-handed with me if you know what that means. One night, I told him I didn't want to be with him anymore and he chased me, threatening to kill me. I ran to hide in a tool shed when he cornered me. I could see it in his eyes, he would bury me. I grabbed a shovel and swung it as hard as I could, hearing it crack against his skull. The next thing I knew, I was standing in front of a door. I opened it and was on a random street. Nothing seemed familiar. Cars were flying by me and let me tell you, cars were not something I was familiar with. I hid and watched people going by, eventually ducking into a dress shop. The lady there took one look at me and shook her head. I was bruised and barefoot, wearing a shabby dress. She took pity on me, thinking I was homeless, which I guess I was. She was elderly and offered me a job to help her sew the dresses."

"Was that here?" Sitka asked, thinking she understood what happened to Josie.

"No, I was from Oklahoma. I left my time in 1889 when I was twenty-two years old. Ended up in 1937. The dress shop was in Tulsa, about thirty miles from my hometown. I lived there for seven years before I came east."

"How did you get there? To that time?" Sitka asked. With Davis, she was in danger and the path opened. Josie was also in danger.

"Not exactly sure, but when I heard the shovel hit the side of his head, I felt myself falling, like through the floor. I was disoriented and when I stood up, there I was with the door. I just needed to open it."

"Did he die?" Sitka responded, thinking about Glenn's body in the woods. Did someone have to die for them to pass through?

Josie shook her head. "No. I searched up his obituary and he lived many more years and had many more wives. Some of which were never found."

"So, you weren't sent away because you killed him. He didn't die. Why do you think you were sent somewhere else, then?"

"Because if I hadn't, he would've killed me and I had work to do," Josie answered without a doubt.

Work to do. A purpose. Again, the timeline sending someone somewhere they needed to be. Except, Josie stayed in the new time and wasn't sent back to her old one. She was stuck on the time plane she was transported to.

"Why were you never sent back to your time? I was."

"If I'd stayed in Tulsa, maybe I would've been. Or maybe because I went forward in time and you went back in time. I'd never been here before. The dress shop closed and the woman moved in with her children when she got too old to sew anymore. After selling everything off, she gave me some money and I set out. Something told me to come here, so I did. I found Letty and the rest is history. I believe that was why I never went back to my time. Why was I sent to this time? Letty needed me. I needed her. I was meant to be in this time."

The rest was history. By now, they'd made it to the door of the shed and Josie pulled it open. It wasn't a dirty shed with tools like Sitka was expecting, but rather an artist's studio with paintings and sculptures set just perfectly around the space. There were paintings of Josie. Paintings of Ruth and Davis. Sculptures of cats. Letty had been very talented and showed her expression in the things she loved most.

However, the painting that caught Sitka's attention was the centerpiece on the back wall. It took her breath away and she wandered to it, running her fingers along the textured colors. The bottom was signed Letty B and it ran from floor to ceiling. It was the answer to the question she'd never get to ask Letty in person.

Sitka stared at the piece as tears welled up in her eyes. If she'd ever doubted everything that occurred, the painting proved it had. She stepped back in awe and crouched down, staring up at the piece. She went back in time, except without leaving her own time. The painting transported her mentally to that day in 1929.

She stared up into her own face. The painting was of her running as she disappeared into the colors behind her. Abigail was moving past her, her arms out-stretched, waving as her mouth curved in a yell. The painting was of the last time she saw Abigail or Letty. The day she and Davis lured Abigail to Davis's home. Of them trying to save Letty's life one last time. And succeeding.

Sitka stood up and turned to Josie, tears streaming down her cheeks. "How?"

"Honey, Letty painted that piece right before she died. She told me it was from the day her parents had to rush her to the hospital and a white lady, a lawyer, showed up from nowhere to make sure the hospital took her in. However, it wasn't the lady she was most determined to share the story about. There was something else which lead to her life's work about time travel."

"What was it?" Sitka asked, starting to feel like the world around her was spinning. She knew, but she needed to hear it. To confirm everything she believed to be true.

"You. Letty said it was the day she came back from the future to save herself. She said she looked different but as soon as she saw the little girl outside her house as her parents rushed her to the car, she knew she was seeing herself. You were going back to save yourself, child. You weren't born the day she died by chance. Her soul was moving into a new body."

Sitka fell to the floor as the room around her spun and everything began to make sense in the chaos. She was sent back to save herself. In both timelines. Save herself from Glenn and save herself in 1929. She saw Glenn's body to make sure she met Davis and that happened. She wasn't helping Davis, she was helping herself.

She *was* Letty.

Chapter Thirty-One

No one spoke on the ride home, each in their own thoughts. Josie ran to find Tommy when Sitka hit the floor. He came as fast as he could. By the time he got to the shed, with Jerry on his heels, Sitka was sitting with her head in her hands. The giant painting with Sitka in it didn't escape his attention and he helped her up to leave. He stared at the painting while he spoke to Josie.

"I need to get her home. This has been a lot and she's still recovering from being missing. Thank you so much for lunch," he muttered as he guided Sitka out the door. She stumbled in the yard and he pulled her up, bracing her under the arms. Sitka tried to steady the spinning as they traversed the yard toward the van. Even though she knew she wasn't going anywhere else, it felt like the time she first met Abigail.

"You are welcome here anytime you want. I can show you Letty's other papers," Josie offered as they moved toward the van. Her face was worried and she followed close behind.

Tommy raised his hand in a wave as Jerry yanked the van door open, both of them lifting Sitka inside. She collapsed on the seat and stared at the back of the van. Glenn's body had been back there. The image forming in her mind, she shoved past Tommy and vomited outside before he had the chance to shut the door. Josie had gone inside, so they waited a minute to make sure Sitka was done. She nodded and climbed back in.

Jerry cranked the engine, which took a couple of tries, then backed out of the driveway. They avoided the stubborn goats who refused to move. They got out to the main road and Jerry clicked on the radio. Pink Floyd's "Comfortably Numb" filled the space. He rolled down his window for fresh air.

Tommy turned to face Sitka. "What was that all about? Why is there a painting of you on the wall in there?"

Sitka placed her hand in the window and shook her head. "Letty painted it. Of me the day we saved her life. The other lady in the picture was Abigail. My mother, well kinda, from that time."

"I thought she looked familiar, but I remember your mom being way more flower child."

"Tommy, Josie told me she's from another time and was never sent back. She found Letty and they lived together until Letty died. She doesn't know why she wasn't sent back to her time. Davis told me I couldn't stay in that time because it could eventually hurt, or even kill, me because I wasn't supposed to be there. Josie's been here for over forty years."

Tommy nodded, staring out the window in thought. "Maybe she's meant to be here? What if people are born in the wrong time and are sent to where they are supposed to be? Perhaps Josie was meant to come here to change things."

"Cosmic destiny," Jerry murmured from the driver's seat. "Instead of reincarnation, the timeline finds a back door to get them there quicker."

Sitka wished she'd been able to see Letty's papers but it was all too much. Seeing herself painted on the wall and discovering she was likely Letty in another lifetime pained her head. She thought about Davis and how he always called her *honeybee*, as he did with Letty. She chalked it up as his particular term of endearment, but maybe it was more. Maybe on some level, he knew she was Letty. Even if he didn't know it at the time.

It explained why she couldn't get close to them that day. As soon as she got too close, she was sent back home. Like Davis, she couldn't exist as herself in the same space. If she was indeed Letty, it meant she still had to complete Letty's purpose. A purpose cut short by a bad heart. She was aware she wasn't near as smart as Letty, as she struggled with the concepts and theories Letty wrote about in her papers. Then again, Letty had years to define those. Sitka needed to give it time to understand how to continue Letty's work.

Jerry dropped them off at home and promised to get Dean over to hang out with Sitka before school started. Tommy helped her out and they headed inside. Aunt Leigh was still at work, so they had the house to themselves and Sitka rested on the couch, her eyes feeling suddenly heavy. Tommy clicked on the radio and grabbed one of the time travel books Dean left. He plopped in the recliner, kicking his feet up.

"Take a nap, Sitty. I'll be right here reading. Now, I'm totally invested in learning more about all of this."

"Okay. Thanks, Tommy, for believing me."

"Well, regardless, the signs are there. You can't deny it when a dead lady painted you on a wall, right?" Tommy joked.

That was true. There was no way that could've been planned. Letty painted it before Sitka was born. "I want to go back and see Josie. Spend some time with her."

"We can do that. I have a feeling she has a lot more answers than could be uncovered in an afternoon. Close your eyes, you look beat."

Sitka closed her eyes and the image of herself from the painting popped in her head. She was scared in the painting. Desperate. She recalled seeing Davis just disappear, not knowing if he'd come back and if she could get Abigail to help Letty. To help *her*. They weren't alone though, and time had given them the power to break through.

When she woke up later, Tommy had dozed off in the chair and she heard Aunt Leigh's car pulling in the driveway. It was dinner time and Sitka felt like she'd slept for days. Her aunt's key turned the lock and the door swung open, as she tried to balance the bags she held in her hands. Tommy jumped up and grabbed them for her, peering in.

"Should I put these away?"

"No, it's ingredients for dinner. It's stuff for one of Marie's favorite meals. I thought I could make it for dinner. Eggplant Parmesan," Aunt Leigh explained.

Sitka remembered the dish well. Her mother made it at least once a week and Sitka hadn't had it since her mother died. She grinned and helped pull the ingredients out. Tommy grabbed a load of French bread and set to making garlic bread while Aunt Leigh and Sitka sliced the eggplant. Tommy boiled water for noodles and turned up the radio to Sister Sledge belting out, "We Are Family." By the time dinner was ready, they were all out of breath from dancing and were starving. Sitka felt her mother in the room with them.

As they ate dinner, a knock came at the door, causing Aunt Leigh to frown. "I'm not expecting anyone. Ignore it."

"It might be Jerry, I told him he could borrow my skateboard," Tommy replied as he jumped up and went to the door to answer it.

He was gone for some time and Sitka could hear him talking to a man. Not Jerry, a man. The man's voice was deep but soft. Tommy came back to the dining room, meeting his mother's eyes, his own concerned. "Hey, Mom, can you come here for a minute?"

"Is everything okay?" she asked, setting her napkin down as she pushed her chair back.

"Yeah, just come for a moment."

Aunt Leigh stood and followed Tommy, making Sitka wonder what was going on. She got up and peered out the front window but couldn't see who was at the door. A small, rust-colored car sat in the driveway and Sitka could see it had New York plates. New York plates. Maybe someone who knew her mother. She was about to go check when Aunt Leigh and Tommy came back in the room.

"Who was that?" Sitka asked.

A glance passed between her aunt and her cousin but Tommy shook his head. "Just a guy looking for someone. He's gone. Let's finish dinner."

The mood shifted and Sitka worried something bad was going on. She set her fork down, watching their faces. "Please tell me. Did something happen?"

Aunt Leigh smiled. "Nothing happened. Everything's okay. Tommy was thinking about taking you roller skating after dinner. You haven't been in quite a while. Does that sound like fun?"

"Yes!" Sitka practically bolted out of her seat.

"Well, finish your dinner first, sprite," Tommy responded, laughing.

Sitka ate at record speed and tapped her fingers on the table, eyeing Tommy. He made a dramatic effect to eat the last few bites painfully slow as she bounced up and down impatiently in her seat. When he finally couldn't drag it out any longer, he grabbed their plates and set them in the sink.

"Alright. Are you ready or what?" he asked Sitka. She squealed and ran to the front door.

Tommy snagged the keys and kissed his mother on the cheek. "Eight-thirty?"

She nodded, chewing her bottom lip. She started to clear the rest of the table as they left. Tommy was quiet on the drive and Sitka could see he was thinking about something. They drove into the skating rink lot and Sitka clasped her hands together. She hadn't been there since the day Glenn came to pick her up.

"I have a surprise for you," Tommy said, his attention back in the moment.

"What?"

"You'll see soon enough."

They went in and Tommy went to the skate counter. He came back with a box, handing it to Sitka. She opened the box and peered in. Her skates! Or new ones just like them. Her mouth dropped open and she stared at Tommy in disbelief.

"How did you do this?"

"I called and told them what happened to your other pair. They remembered you and wanted to replace your skates free of charge."

Sitka jumped up and hugged Tommy around the neck. He laughed, pushing back. "So, you want to skate or what?"

Sitka couldn't get the skates on fast enough and was on the floor before Tommy even had the chance to get a rental pair on. He followed her out, not as adept as she was. She circled the floor twice to his every one time and teased him about being a slowpoke. He took it, grinning the whole time.

At one point, she saw him watching the clock with a concerned look on his face. She skated over, poking him in the ribs. "Hey, are you gonna skate or just stand there, staring at the clock?"

He turned and smiled, but she could see he didn't mean it. He shook his head. "I'm going to go over and play some arcade games for a bit. My feet hurt already. You okay out here alone?"

"Yeah, I'm having the best time," Sitka assured him.

"Alright, we need to leave about eight-twenty-five to make it home on time. That gives you about an hour. Go have fun. I'll be playing pinball if you need me. Okay?"

Sitka didn't have to be asked twice and darted out onto the floor, deftly moving around a middle-aged man falling in front of her. Tommy went and took off his skates, pausing to chat with the girl at the counter.

Sitka went as fast as she could around the floor, enjoying the forced air on her face. She'd missed this so much. She weaved in and out of other skaters, feeling like she was flying. She thought about the dream with her mother where they were in the air and closed her eyes. It was like that. This was the most free she'd ever felt and she didn't think about Davis, Letty, Glenn, or any of that while she was on the floor.

The hour passed far too fast and she saw Tommy waiting for her near the door. She skated over his direction and hopped on the carpeted floor which slowed her down. She rolled up to him. "Can I wear my skates to the car?"

"Of course, maybe change in the car so you don't get clumps of grass in the wheels from the yard."

Sitka play-pouted and followed Tommy out. She put her sneakers on in the car, running her hands over her skates. "Thanks, Tommy. I love them. I love you."

Tommy ruffled her hair and grinned. "Anything for you, kiddo."

When they drove down their street, Sitka saw the rust-colored car in the driveway again and frowned at Tommy. "Who *is* that?"

Tommy grimaced and slid in behind the car. He cut the engine and looked at Sitka. "Mom and I love you, Sitty. You're our family. You're my little sister and Mom thinks of you as her daughter. You know that, right?"

Sitka nodded. She felt the same. Tommy got out of the car, so she followed him to the front door of the house. He paused and looked down at her. "Nothing has to change for us. Now, or ever."

"What do you mean, Tommy?"

He pushed the door open and walked into the living room. Aunt Leigh was sitting with a man, who had his back to the door. She stood up and bobbed her head at Tommy.

Tommy put his hand on Sitka's shoulder and squeezed gently. The man who'd been sitting stood up and turned around. Sitka recognized him immediately. The man from her dream on the train. The man from the picture her mother had. The black man with the big grin, wearing a poncho and smoking a joint.

Aunt Leigh cleared her throat. "Sitty, I'd like you to meet someone. This is Doug, he's-" she was cut off by Sitka, who stepped forward.

"My father."

Chapter Thirty-Two

*D*oug stepped forward and smiled, his mouth hiding the worry in his eyes. "I'm so glad to finally meet you, Sitka. Your mother used to send me pictures and letters about you. I kept all of them. I'm sorry about her..." He stopped there and frowned, not sure what else to say to her.

Sitka sighed, suddenly feeling much older than her age. "You can say it. She died. She had cancer."

Doug nodded, sadness flitting across his face, then resting in his eyes. He no longer looked like the carefree guy from the photo her mother had shown her. He looked like the man on the train she saw in her dream. Years of worry and stress making his face more gaunt, his eyes sunken.

"How did you find me?" Sitka asked. Why was he there now, standing in her aunt's living room? After all this time?

"Doug saw the news report of you missing and knew it was you from your name and the pictures Marie sent him. He called the station and they told him you'd been found safe, so he tracked you down from there," Aunt Leigh chimed in. "He came by earlier this evening, but I wanted to talk to him alone first. To find out what his intentions were in coming here."

What did that mean? His intentions. Sitka stared between them for an explanation. "So?"

"So, I just want to be part of your life," Doug explained. "I'm not here to take you away from your aunt and cousin. They're your family and I respect that. I'm glad you had them after Marie died. I regret all those years I missed and hope you'll let me be a part of your life."

"What, so you can just leave again? I don't even know you. You're just a story my mother told me. I don't need a part-time father," Sitka spat, with more anger than she knew she could feel toward him. Her heart ached.

"Honey, give him a chance to talk to you, at least. Okay?" Aunt Leigh said in a soothing voice. "We've been talking and Doug is looking to move here. To North Carolina. He wants to be closer to you. He has extended family in the area and he'd like to set roots down here."

"Why now?" Sitka was fishing for anything which might give her an argument. To keep the wall up.

"Sitka, when I met Marie, I was young and selfish. I guess we both were to a degree, but when she found out she was pregnant with you, she grew up and I didn't. She was thrilled, however, I was scared. Terrified. I could hardly take care of myself, much less a child. Or, that's what I told myself at the time. Your mother told me she was fine raising you alone and I stupidly took that offer. I ended up getting caught by the draft and did a couple of tours in Vietnam. That opened my eyes to a world outside my own. I came back all screwed up and didn't think coming into your life, then, was fair to you. I was a mess on so many levels."

"Why now?" Sitka asked again, knowing she was being petulant. She couldn't be let down again by him.

"Why now?" Doug repeated with a sigh. "Because it should've been years ago. I loved your mom. So much. I don't think we would've ever made it as a couple, but we were good friends. I don't know, maybe we could have. I really cared for her. I wanted to come back so many times, to work something out, but I was ashamed... and an alcoholic."

An alcoholic? "Did my mama know?"

"She did and told me unless I got my shit together, I couldn't be a part of your life. She was right, even though I didn't see it at the time. I've been sober for a couple of years. I heard what happened to your mother, however, I knew I wasn't in a place to be a good person in your life. I would like to believe I am now. If you'll let me."

Sitka moved to the couch and sat down. She wanted to tell him to leave. She wanted to hug him. She wanted to scream at him and cry. She wanted to let him in. She wanted to run away and never come back. How could he just show up and step into a role he'd never once filled? How would that work? Sitka looked to Tommy for guidance. Tommy came and sat down next to her, putting his arm over her shoulders for comfort and support.

Aunt Leigh, reading the room, put her hand on Doug's arm and motioned toward the door. "Let's take a walk around the neighborhood and give the kids some room. Tommy, why don't you cut the front light on when it's alright for us to come back inside?"

Tommy nodded and waited for them to leave. He turned to Sitka with a tired smile. "I know this is a lot to handle. When he said who he was earlier, I almost sent him away... but, Sitty, maybe hear him out."

"What if he just leaves? What if I'm not the child he was hoping for and decides to move away? I have you and Aunt Leigh. I don't need anyone else, now."

"True, but needing something and having it are different. He could end up being what you wanted in your life. You can never have too many people who love you," Tommy countered.

Sitka was afraid to get her hopes up. Part of her wanted her father in her life, part of her was used to being without one. She wasn't sure which was better. She rested her hand on her chin and thought. "What if I say no and don't want him in my life?"

Tommy watched her and shook his head. "It's your choice, but some of us don't get a second chance with our fathers. Some of us would do just about anything for that chance, you know?"

Sitka felt shame creep up as she realized Tommy's stance and put her hand on his. "Tommy, I'm sorry! I didn't think about that. About your dad. I know you'd do anything to have him back."

"I would. I think about it damn near every day. Imagine him showing up at the door, grabbing me in a hug. I know this is a shock to see him, but Doug seems like a nice guy. Like he wants what's best for you. You can make the rules. Decide how much you want him in your life, when, and where. You can say yes and still set your own boundaries."

That was true. Doug was coming with an open heart and said he wasn't trying to step into their family. Maybe she could simply get to know him. Find out more about his story and tell him some of hers. She nodded at Tommy. She was ready for them to come back in, so he went to cut on the porch light to let them know.

About fifteen minutes later, Aunt Leigh and Doug came in. Aunt Leigh was laughing and it was good to see her not so stressed again. Doug had a calm demeanor that put them all at ease. Like he was there to exist in his own space and not take up any of their's. He sat down across from Sitka, then smiled. More like the him from the picture her mother had when they met.

"So, am I in or out?" he joked.

"In. Sort of. I want to get to know you, but Aunt Leigh and Tommy are my family. I'll decide if you get to be part of it," Sitka replied firmly.

Doug bobbed his head with a chuckle. "Fair enough, I would expect nothing more. Tell me, what do you want to know about me?"

Sitka screwed up her face, considering the question. What did she want to know? "Where did you grow up?"

"I grew up in New Jersey. I have family there, in New York, and here."

"Where did you meet my mother?" She knew part of the story but wanted to hear it from him.

"I met your mother at a block party in New York City. I lived there at the time and went with my neighbors. Marie... your mother was the life of the party, making sure no one felt left out. She was singing along to a song playing and handing out beers. When she got to me, I teased her about being the 'welcome wagon'. She took a small bow, then took my hand to dance. I don't think we took our eyes off each other for months after that. She was something special."

"So, why didn't you stay together?"

Doug rubbed his chin, staring off. "We were on different planes of existence. Your mother lived to nurture. I lived to run. She never went past a stray animal or ignored someone in need. I admired that in her, but didn't see it in myself," Doug said honestly.

"Do you now?" Sitka whispered. She was like her mother and didn't want someone in her life who wasn't.

Doug turned his large, brown eyes on her and smiled, letting the question rest between them. For the first time, Sitka felt like she was looking at her father. He tipped his head. "So much so, it hurts. Going to war, seeing the suffering... it changed me. I want to stop people from hurting. I want to make things better."

Aunt Leigh came back in with cups of hot cocoa, handing them out. "Thought it might be nice to get to know each other over hot chocolate."

Doug smiled up at her as he took his. "Thank you, Leigh. For the hospitality, for giving me a chance to state my case. For the hot chocolate."

Aunt Leigh chuckled and sat next to him on the couch. "It's not me you have to convince here, Doug. It's that tough, little bird over there. She's the boss," she said, gesturing to Sitka.

"Don't I know it?" Doug replied, then glanced at Sitka. "If it takes the rest of my life, I'll try. I promise you that.

I come to you with my heart on my sleeve, hoping to eventually win yours."

Tommy sipped his cocoa and watched the repartee. He set his cup down. "The way to Sitka's heart is through roller skating. She's a speed skating queen. She was beating adults at the local rink. She's a legend over there."

Doug tipped his head back and laughed, a full, melodious sound. "Well, now, there's something we have in common. I've been known to dance on eight wheels myself. Mostly on the street, but a few times in a rink."

Her father liked to roller skate? That was something that surprised Sitka. She squinted her eyes at him, testing the waters. "You have skates?"

"Not anymore. I sold just about everything to come down here. If you'll let me, I'd love to take you roller skating. See what kind of moves you have," Doug teased.

Sitka didn't respond, not ready to let him in quite yet. She blew on her cocoa, considering her next question. "Why did you never write to me? I never heard from you. That was hard, knowing you were out there but didn't even write me. Not even on my birthday."

That was a tough one and Doug's face showed it. He waited a moment before replying and when he did, his voice was hoarse. "Sitka, I'm not going to lie and try to convince you I was misunderstood or was prevented from being the father you needed. I wasn't. Did I think about you? Yes. However, I couldn't get past my own garbage to do something about it. Your mother sent me letters and photos a couple of times a year. At first, I was angry at her for doing it, after we'd decided I wouldn't be involved. Then, I started looking forward to them, to watching you grow. Eventually, I regretted my decision but it was too late. I didn't write because you were better off without me in your life. I'm not looking for pity, I'm being honest. Not every man deserves to be a father. I didn't deserve to be. That's the god's honest truth."

His answer made Sitka pause. At no point was he asking for forgiveness or absolution. He was coming to her now to get to know her from this point forward. That was all. She didn't need to forgive him. She needed to hear him out, see if he was someone she wanted to have in her life. She thought about Davis and how much he grieved for Letty when she'd died. She didn't want to make Doug feel that way. She cocked her head, eyeing him carefully.

"I have my mother's last name. Ellison. What's your last name?" she inquired, knowing it was partly hers, as well.

"Butler. I am Douglas James Butler, the fourth."

∞

Chapter Thirty-Three

∞

Sitka got up and went to bed, not saying another word to any of them. Tommy followed her and paused outside her door, his eyes trying to read her face. She sat on the edge of her bed, staring at the floor.

Tommy came over and sat down, rubbing her back. "You want to tell me what that was all about?" he asked, confused.

"Butler? Remember, that was Letty's last name? Davis's last name?" Sitka replied flatly.

"Oh, yeah, right. That's a little strange. Maybe just a coincidence? I mean, Butler isn't all that unique of a name."

"Davis said his brother was DJ Butler. DJ? Like Douglas James?"

"Okay, getting a little weirder, I'll admit, and he did say he has family here. Still, what would it matter if he was related to them? It seems like you are tied in there anyway," Tommy said, shifting back on the bed.

"I guess... I don't know, Tommy. It just freaked me out to hear that, is all." Sitka threw herself back on the bed and stared up at the ceiling.

She *was* freaked out.

"Yeah, it's a lot to absorb. Do you want me to ask him to leave for now? To give you some time to process this? I'm sure he'd understand."

Sitka closed her eyes and thought about it. What if Doug was related to Davis and she was Letty? Were there some kind of family bonds that tied them all together over time? Did everyone have that? Was everyone on Earth simply recycling into the same family groups over and over? If so, why? What purpose would that serve? Sitka rolled over and looked at Tommy, who had his eyes closed and his head resting back in his hands as he lay on the bed.

"Do you think we were meant to be family? Like it was chosen?" Sitka asked.

Tommy opened his eyes and faced her. "Absolutely, one hundred percent."

"Why?"

"Hmmm, good question. So we can protect each other. So we can get stronger through our bonds. So we can look out for one another."

"What about people who are put in families who hurt them or don't want them? Why are they put in those families?" Sitka asked.

"Wow, getting all deep on me here, Sitty. I don't know. Maybe they grow stronger or develop skills to help others because of it. Or maybe the universe is just cruel. That's a question I can't answer, to be honest."

Children died at the hands of their parents, people abused their spouses, like Josie's husband. Not all family bonds were good ones. "Maybe time makes mistakes."

Tommy sat up. "It could. We tend to think of something divine as infallible, but nothing is infallible. Can I ask you something? Something hard?"

Sitka nodded. "Okay?"

"What Glenn did to you, do you feel like it made you stronger? The saying goes, 'That which doesn't kill you makes you stronger'. Do you feel that?" Tommy asked his voice low.

Sitka sat up next to him. "No, but I don't want it to happen to anyone else. It made me feel broken, not stronger. I want to stop it from happening ever to another person."

"Do you think maybe that's why people end up in bad families? To stop it?" Tommy suggested.

Sitka considered that, then shrugged. "It seems unfair for them to go through something to stop it for someone else."

"Do you think time is fair?" Tommy responded, nudging her to think further.

It certainly wasn't. Time had continually put people she knew and loved in harm's way. Whole races and genders of people had suffered over time. It was conscious but it wasn't pick and choosing, necessarily. What needed to happen, needed to happen to move time forward. Good or bad. Tommy's father was destined to die young. So was her mother. It changed both Tommy and Sitka as people.

Was that the point? Did it define them to move forward in an intentional way? To move time forward in an intentional way? Or was it random? There were more questions than answers, the more she thought about it.

Sitka hugged Tommy as hard as she could. "I'm sorry about your dad. I really am."

Tommy hugged her back. "I'm sorry about your mom. I'm sorry Glenn ever came into our lives. We have each other though, and I count myself lucky for that," Tommy whispered into her hair.

"Me too."

"So, do you want me to tell Doug to go away and never come back? Hit the road, Jack?"

Sitka giggled and shook her head. "No. I'm tired and don't want to talk anymore tonight, though. Tell him to take me skating tomorrow."

"I can do that. Do you want me to go, or do you want to go with just him?"

Sitka felt nervous at the idea of being alone with her father but knew she needed to do it. "It can be just him and me this time."

"Alrighty. Jerry wanted my help tomorrow working on the van. Hey, remember when we went to the park and saw the cicada shells?" Tommy asked, changing subjects.

Sitka nodded. "Yeah?"

"Did you know, they go underground and stay there for years, then come up just for a little bit? Like weeks. Then, they die. So, they spend most of their life cycle underground. That seems like a waste."

Sitka didn't know what he was getting at and met his eyes. "That's sad."

Tommy bobbed his head. "We can't be like that, Sitty. We have to enjoy the sun. Appreciate our lives above ground. We can't live as just shells. You know?"

This time she did. She leaned over and hugged Tommy again. "Thanks, Tommy. I want to be happy. To appreciate the good things, like you and Aunt Leigh. To get to know my father." She'd been down in the darkness for a long time and had come up from out of the ground. It was time to turn her face to the light and appreciate what she did have in her life.

To truly live.

Tommy got up to leave and Sitka thought about Dean and Jerry. "Tommy, do you think we're related to Jerry and Dean in another life?"

Tommy paused at the door and tipped his head. "I don't think so. I think sometimes we meet people who we connect to in this lifetime moving forward. Keeping the family pool growing. Jerry is like a brother to me but in this lifetime. Probably in the next. Our circle is continually expanding."

Sitka liked that thought. After he left, she brushed her teeth and climbed into bed. She heard Doug and Aunt Leigh talking as she drifted off to sleep and hoped their circle would continue to grow.

The next day, like clockwork at the designated time they set, Doug showed up to take Sitka roller skating. She climbed next to him in the car and eyed him from the side. "Was your grandfather named Douglas?"

"He was but went by DJ. I'm the fourth, so him, my father, my great grandfather, and me," Doug answered. "Douglas, DJ, Dougie, then me Doug. My friends used to call me Dug. Doug without the 'o'. Dug the Rug because of the poncho I always wore. You're mother thought that was funny."

"Do you know if your grandfather had a brother named Davis?" Sitka asked.

"Oh, I'm not sure. I think he had a few siblings. I don't know their names off the top of my head."

"Does the name Letty Butler mean anything to you?"

"Letty Butler? I think my father had a cousin named Leticia who died fairly young, like in her forties. I seem to remember him talking about her funeral. They called her Letty, I believe. Someone you know of?" Doug inquired as they drove out of the neighborhood.

"Kind of. I know her... uh, a friend of hers. She lives here. Letty lived with her."

"That right? Small world."

He had no idea how small it was.

They pulled up to the skating rink and he cut the engine. "I think my mother has an old bible with a family tree. Both sides. I can see if she can send make a copy of the family tree, so we can peek back and see your ancestors. Might be fun to take a look."

"Your mother is still alive?"

"She is. My father, too. They'd like to meet you if you're willing," Doug told her.

"They know about me?" Sitka asked, surprised.

"They do and were very mad at me for not having you in their lives all these years. I got an earful when I told them about you."

She had grandparents who wanted to know her? Sitka rubbed her nose, trying to hide the tears threatening to come out. "Do I have other family?"

Doug watched her and realized how much he'd taken away from her. "I have a sister and a brother. They each have children. You have cousins."

More cousins?

"Where do they live?"

"My parents live in New Jersey but are wanting to move down south now that they're older. My brother lives in Richmond, Virginia and my sister in Winston Salem, North Carolina. Not too far from here."

Sitka stared wide-mouthed. "I have other family in North Carolina?"

Doug chuckled and put his hand on her head. "You have more family than you can shake a stick at. They're all waiting to meet you. That's if you want to meet them."

"I do!" Sitka had spent so much of her life feeling alone, especially after her mother died, she couldn't imagine having so much family. "They need to meet Aunt Leigh and Tommy, too. We come all together."

Doug nodded and pushed the door open. "The more the merrier. We'd have it no other way."

They spend the rest of the day skating and Sitka let her father into her life in small increments. She let him buy her lunch and they sat in the booth across from one another. Doug was intent on eating his nachos when Sitka nudged his foot with her skate and smiled at him.

"I'm glad you came. I had a dream about you once. You were on a train and seemed so sad. I didn't know it was you until you showed up at our house that night. Then, I recognized you from the dream."

Her father met her eyes and tipped his head. "I used to take a train to work every day in the city. I like to think you were there with me in some reality. I thought of you all the time, wishing I could see you."

"Will you stay? Like forever?" Sitka asked, her voice suddenly seeming tiny and frail. She was out on the ledge now, needing to hear him say it.

Doug set down his chip and reached out for her hand. "Sitty, I'll never leave if you'll let me into your life. I'd live in a tent on your front lawn if you'd allow me to be your father. Even if you don't want me to be your father, I'd be happy just to see you grow up. To be present in your life. If I could magically wave a wand and get all those years back I wasn't in your life, I would. I wish I'd known where life would've taken me when I walked away from Marie, then I'd have realized she and you were the best things that ever happened to me. I can't go back, but I can be here, now. In whatever way you want me to be. It's all I have to give."

Sitka knew what she wanted but was too afraid to say it. Too afraid to let the words hit the air and become real. She slid out of the booth and stood awkwardly for a moment before skating off to the rink alone. Doug cleaned up the table and went out to the floor, giving her space. As Sitka flew around the rink, her wheels barely touching the smooth surface, she knew the only way she could make this time count was to let her soul hold on.

To hope.

She circled around the rink, seeing her father skating to the music blaring around them. His skates slid effortlessly in sync with the rhythm and he bopped his head along to the music. Sitka skated up beside him and liked how he squeezed her hand when she slipped it into his.

She'd been in different places and other times. She'd watched her mother die and found a family with Aunt Leigh

∞

and Tommy. She'd found Davis and saved herself. In both timelines. She learned to depend on herself and fight back against those who meant her harm.

What she hadn't done was learn to trust she wasn't alone in the world in her heart. That things she loved didn't always disappear. She had a family who loved and wanted her. Who needed her as much as she needed them. Who were determined to protect and keep her safe. As she skated around the rink with her father, hand in hand, she let the walls fall away and let him into her life.

She let the circle expand.

The beginning after the beginning...

No one was surprised when Doug and Aunt Leigh fell in love. It took a few years but the spark was lit the night they took a walk while Tommy and Sitka talked when Doug first showed up at the house. Sitka understood the family bonds were only growing stronger. Aunt Leigh and Doug got married in the backyard with so much family around, there was hardly room to move.

All Sitka's aunts, uncles, grandparents, and cousins from her father's side gathered to celebrate the occasion. No one from her mother's side, except her aunt and cousin, was there. They'd been forgotten a long time before and Aunt Leigh marrying a black man was the nail in the coffin. They all were absorbed into Doug's family like they'd always been there. Aunt Leigh adopted Sitka, explaining it in no way took away her mother or their bond, but simply gave her two mothers to love and watch over her. More family. Tommy was officially her brother and the best friend she ever had.

The copy of the bible pages from her grandmother's bible indeed proved Davis was Doug's great-uncle. Not that Sitka was surprised. That made Davis her great-great uncle in this timeline, and her father in another. Connected throughout time.

Somewhere along the way, Jerry's father kicked him out of the house when he gave Jerry the ultimatum to either not be friends with Tommy because of his mother and her black boyfriend and black child, or leave. Jerry chose Tommy and he, too, joined the family. By the time Dean was fifteen, he also came into the family for the same reasons, though he and Sitka had already found their own spark by then. Like her sister, Aunt Leigh never could walk away from a person in need and never questioned opening her heart and door.

Not wanting to live around such hate, they sold the house in town and moved out to Josie's farm with her blessing. She was getting old and more than happy to have extra hands to do the work. Not to mention, she saw Letty in Sitty and enjoyed sharing Letty's work with her. Josie became another grandmother to Sitty, Tommy, Jerry, and Dean, again increasing their family circle. She told them her name was Josefina Stanley, but took on Butler when she met Letty, the love of her life. She wanted to put her old life behind her. They didn't have family records that far back but part of Sitka told her if they did, they'd find Josie's name somewhere in there. Either way, she was family, now.

When Sitka turned thirteen, she and her father took a drive to a list of cemeteries outside of town. Doug had gone to county records and pulled up as many ancestors in the area as they could find. They took a tour using the sheet and found the gravestones of the family on the list. Sitka cried by Davis's grave, feeling like he'd finally been set free.

Next to his were Letty's and Ruth's on either side. He was with his family again. She didn't know if he was sent to them when he left 1929 with her, but later that day the question was answered. He wasn't immediately as he had one more time event to set right.

Her father pulled into a very old cemetery where some of the headstones were crumbling. They pulled down the side and parked, walking over to headstones marked with Butler. She saw Davis's father's and mother's stones. There were other family she didn't know but to the left of them was another name. Simmons. One of the headstones was a woman named Anna Butler Simmons. Her parents were Davis's parents. It was his sister, the one who was abused by the man his mother married. He said she'd died young and childless, but the headstone said otherwise. She'd lived into her seventies. A check of the record Doug had, said she had many children and grandchildren.

Davis had gone back and changed things. How? Sitka didn't know. Somehow though, he'd saved his sister. Records showed his mother never remarried. So, maybe he prevented his mother from ever meeting the man who abused them. Some secrets were left to be buried and she'd never know for sure.

What Sitka did know is not only did he save his sister, she went on to have a life and a family. A family which never existed before. He'd stopped one timeline, which allowed another parallel one to move forward, like in Letty's papers. Family wasn't set in concrete, in the existing timeline and others, it could change based on events.

Once the family moved in with Josie, Dean was ecstatic to dig into Letty's papers and began compiling them into a book. His love of knowledge drove him to study time travel in all scientific and theoretical realms. Sitka's drove her to want to study journalism and learn people's stories.

Fulfilling her childhood dream, she reached out to the members of Wilmington Ten she could find and documented their stories, wondering if somewhere along the timelines, they'd all crossed paths previously. Sometimes events made people family and not just blood.

The more she spoke to people, the more she found the threads. Their connections through time and space, how each was a link to another. Together, she and Dean found the missing piece, which was that time travel required the human element, the ties that bind. People were meant to find each other.

What Dean and Sitty didn't know at first, was that would eventually bring them together to expose the world to theories outside of human understanding. To shift the way time was viewed and understood. It would eventually lead them to a lifetime as a couple, inseparable until their last breaths. Then beyond. They published all of Letty's papers, her theories finally being embraced by the scientific community.

After their deaths, their children, Davis and Abigail Marie, continued their work around the globe. Explaining how by understanding time was part of the web of family and human relationships, not a linear motion, they were able to cross boundaries previously understood by science. Time had consciousness and adjusted to make sure events meant to happen, did. Time travel was possible, as long as they moved to different planes, as well.

Connection was the key as it created coordinates to follow across the planes of time.

One summer night, when Sitka was nearing adulthood, they all gathered around the table, eating and talking up a storm. She sat back and appreciated the journey she was on. In this lifetime and others. Every single person around the table had been sent to her life for a specific reason and each one connected through time to another... past, present, and future. She knew on other planes of existence, they were just as intertwined in each other's lives as they were in this one. In the many years to come, they'd continue to find one another and build this incredible family.

On another plane, she was growing up in New York with her mother by her side and never came to live with Aunt Leigh and Tommy. Never suffered at the hands of Glenn. On yet another, Tommy's father never died in Vietnam and Glenn never came into their lives. On this one, she was surrounded by this amazing family she wouldn't trade for the world. She had the sense of déjà vu she'd been at this exact moment with these exact people before, and perhaps she had. On each plane, she had a unique and perfect family who loved and supported her, despite their differences and circumstances. In each one, she was meant to be where she was and to discover the people that were supposed to be in her life in many different ways. Nothing was random, each person was there for a reason. There was no end to it all as they passed in and out of each other's lives, over and over.

Only beginnings.

Déjà vu is the time traveler's reminder...

Acknowledgments

Thank you to my beta reader, Chatika B, for the wonderful insight and suggestions! Also a big thank you to ZaBrina Houston for her keen eye and suggested edits.

To my son, Jack, who never tires of talking about time travel, physics, and science theories with me. Always thinking outside the box.

Thanks to Robert Kiser and Justin Sexton for humoring my last minute, late night discussions on time travel theory the day before publication.

To science—those who pursue and challenge it to discover new possibilities and realities.

Thank you to my readers. Without you, I am just sitting in a room talking to myself.

Author info

Available books:

Do Over
We Don't Matter
Prick of the Needle
Through the Surface
Trigger Point
Carrying the Dead
Catch the Earth

Please visit me at:

authorjulietrose.com

Thank you!

Made in the USA
Columbia, SC
12 August 2023

21510342R00171